BLUE MASQUERADE

T.K. Blackwood

Chromatic Aberration Publishing

Chromatic
Aberration

FOREWORD

As a child who grew up in the shadow of the Gulf War at the tail end of the Cold War and watched Red Dawn too many times, I wrote the book I wanted to read. My hope is that you'll enjoy reading it as much as I enjoyed writing it. If so, please leave a review and let me know your thoughts.

https://www.amazon.com/dp/B09QYXL65Y

Dedicated to my parents who gave me the tools to succeed and without whose support this book would not have been possible.

-T.K. Blackwood

Yugoslavia - August, 1992

1

The air in Moscow was unseasonably warm for August. Most of the city's citizens were out and about doing their daily errands, enjoying the warmth before the inevitable cold snap that would start late October and drive the city well below freezing until the thaws of spring the next year. Here, in the heart of the Soviet Union, the deep winter that many outsiders considered characteristic of Russia in particular had not yet come to grip the city.

Minister Andrei Gradenko marveled at the bustling streets as he was chauffeured from his nearby residence and into Red Square in the heart of the city. In the not so distant past Moscow's streets had been devoid of most vehicle traffic save for heavy trucks making deliveries and street trams carrying commuters and shoppers. Since the economic reforms under Andropov, vehicle ownership had risen dramatically, approaching Western-levels. To see the city come alive like this reminded Gradenko of the bustle of many urban centers in the West, the opulence and glitter of Paris, the metropolitan charm and press of London, the architectural marvels of New York City. Even without these things Moscow held charm all its own. The city had a quiet dignity to it, one that refused the decadent trappings of the West and instead commanded respect not through commercial glitz, but because of the vastness of its history and the untold misery it had endured and survived. Moscow had been burned to cinders and ash in 1812 to deny refuge to Napoleon, and it had been fortified at all costs against Hitler through the blood and sweat of its civilian population. Gradenko had no doubts it would be defended to the last should the time ever come.

The Soviet Union had faced its share of hardships but had managed to successfully evade the stagnation and degradation of its off-and-on communist rival, the People's Republic of China. Gradenko found it easy to imagine what might have happened should the Soviet Union have continued on its old course of stalwart bureaucracy and unwillingness to adapt. It had been practically written on the walls in 1968 when the Soviet Union swatted down its bloc state of Czechoslovakia. If a deranged assassin's bullet hadn't claimed General Secretary Brezhnev just a year later, then perhaps it would be the Soviets looking out from beneath a dilapidated economy with their people clamoring desperately for denim jeans, rock and roll, and washing machines—a position the Chinese now found themselves in.

The transformation to a socialist market economy under the command of Yuri Andropov had been a strange time. Gradenko had been a young man then, young enough to feel the exciting promise of the future as the once monolithic Soviet Union began a great campaign of Reform and Opening. Gradenko had once had the opportunity to meet with Andropov late in his life. *Bayonets and barbed wire cannot replace bread and butter,* he'd said then in passing. Despite how some in the West had tried to portray him, the former head of the KGB was no dove-holding, baby-kissing liberal. He had cold, calculated reasoning for his decisions and the reforms were kept closely in check. The bloodshed of the last decade in Warsaw was evidence enough of that. There were limits to the tolerance of the new Soviet Union, limits that the People's Republic of China would have done well to note.

Gradenko had seen sprawling, chanting mobs of student protests turn Beijing into a gridlock as they demanded all the freedom and chaos that democracy would bring, even as China's far-flung ethnic minorities began to speak about freedom of their own. While China's barbarian border peoples rattled their sabers and hinted at bloody dissolution of the state that had been a nation for only a handful of decades, the Soviets had instead welcomed the Ukrainian and the Georgian. They'd uplifted the Muslim and Cossack and shown them the benefits to be reaped from true socialism.

Or so it was said.

The engine of Gradenko's Lada purred as it crossed the Bolshoy Moskvoretsky Bridge over the cold, blue waters of the Moskva River. As they approached Gradenko got his first clear glimpse of the ancient buildings of the Kremlin. The blocky and gilded form of the Grand Kremlin Palace remained every bit as impressive as it was when it was first built one hundred and fifty ago. The minister of foreign affairs wondered to himself how the old Tsars who'd overseen its construction would have felt knowing that their palaces would one day house a revolutionary government, a government of the people whose power derived not from a self-proclaimed God-given mandate, but from the inevitability of history, power held by the common man, the working man.

The thought brought a glimmer of a smile to his face, one that he was careful to keep in check.

It was a government of the people to be sure, but it was hardly perfect. All he had to do was spare a glance at his driver to be reminded of that. Poor old Yuri must think he was in good standing with the Gradenko family and Andrei in particular. Yuri thought that he could hide his fresh income source from his boss, as if the golden flash of the Rolex on his wrist was not a dead giveaway that Gradenko's driver was in the employ of someone else.

The foreign minister suspected the old ghosts in the KGB—Karamazov and his ilk—though it was just as possible he was working for another faction in the government, the military, or perhaps even a rival in the Ministry of Foreign Affairs. Gradenko was certain enough that they existed, even though they were too afraid to openly reveal themselves. It was the Soviet way: act in the shadows and strike only when you were certain of victory. Risk nothing, gain everything.

It was all very traditional and all very off-putting.

The Lada's old tires rumbled as it cleared the bridge, drawing near to the towering walls of the Kremlin. The tires were in dire need of replacement, something that was easier now than it had been during the dark, early days of Andropov's government, but still a tall task, especially with the military expansion projects drawing in vast quantities of supplies. The economic liberalizations of the 1970s and 1980s had helped to relieve some—but not all—of the strain on the old economic system, one that had survived since the bleak days of Stalin. The powerful concept of a central "command economy" was unassailable on paper, much like the ideals of communism itself. It was found in practice that conceptualizing such heady ideas was often easier than carrying them out. The ideal outreached the real.

The Bolshoy Moskvoretsky Bridge was emblematic of Moscow as a whole to Gradenko. Not only was it a landmark of the city, it was functional and practical as well. As the first concrete bridge in the city it dated back to before the Great Patriotic War. Gradenko could not help but think of it as an edifice that spanned not only a river, but time itself. It connected the dim era of the Tsars, the turbulent darkness of the revolution and Stalinist era, and the glittering future of the Soviet Union as a global superpower and pioneer of outer space itself. But —and Gradenko could not help but reflect on this, no matter how anathematic it was to him—it was also aging. Major city infrastructure was wholly dependent on a bridge that was not getting any younger. It was a problem that existed across the nation.

During the "Socialist Spring" in the 1970s they had taken steps to fix this, moving younger men into power. Many felt that the Soviet Union had thawed, a fact that Western commentators never hesitated to point to as a glimpse into a bright future of co-operations between East and West.

Gradenko sometimes wondered if it was just an unseasonable warm spell before the winter.

The car passed through two separate checkpoints where stolid guards checked papers and inspected the car, once with dogs. The Kalashnikov carbines slung on their backs were prominent and very visible reminders of the stakes and tension of the cold war that had consumed the globe for the last half century. Any perceived lifting of restrictions certainly had not taken effect here at the Kremlin, where KGB and internal security troops conducted their jobs with the same ruthless efficiency that their grandfathers had. Eventually Gradenko was admitted and entered the Grand Palace itself.

The hushed murmur of a dozen separate private conversations echoed from the marbled walls. Gradenko's footfalls sounded as sharp as rifle cracks as he walked through its warm, gilded halls. It was as though he'd stepped back in time to another era, a time before the revolution wiped the stain of the Romanovs from the face of Russia. Some saw it as ironic that the world's first communist country centered its headquarters in a monument to the excesses of the very Tsar that spawned the revolution. Gradenko instead saw it as an opportunity to remind himself of their mistakes.

Do not take leisure in the few luxuries afforded to you by your position, Andrei Gradenko. The people can give and the people can take away.

It was a lesson the Tsar and his family had learned in a blood-spattered basement far from here. It was a lesson that Gradenko always kept in mind.

The meeting chambers of the Politburo were far different from the ostentatious grand entry hall of the palace. The walls were sparsely decorated; only a portrait of Lenin and a pair of red flags broke the otherwise plain white walls. A broad table filled the room, a solid oak construction that was ringed with stone-faced old men, all looking up at the late arrival.

"Apologies, comrades," Gradenko said, striding confidently to take a seat at the table. "I hope you will forgive my tardiness."

"All is forgiven, comrade minister," General Secretary Kavinski said, his tone betraying no resentment. The general secretary was fairly average for a member of the Politburo.

Sixty years of age, he was first brought into the Politburo as a non-voting candidate member while still a young man, back under Andropov's leadership. He'd risen the ranks in the intervening twenty years. His background was in industrial management and it was under his leadership that the Soviet Union once again consistently hit its steel production quotas and successfully deployed an array of Japanese-made precision manufacturing equipment. Once obtained, that same equipment had dramatically increased productivity at some of their most problematic production facilities. This included those responsible for manufacturing the specialized piping utilized in compact nuclear reactors like those deployed aboard their advanced submarine fleet.

Gradenko winced inwardly at the recollection of the cost of that particular acquisition. The price they paid had not been in hard currency; the Soviet treasury had no shortage of that now that natural gas exports to Western Europe were in full swing. No, it was the political cost. Overtures about the joint governance and ultimate return of the Sakhalin islands —occupied since the conclusion of the Second World War—to Japanese rule. This had merely been a cost to pride as no lasting changes had been implemented. There had been, however, a very real reduction in stocks of medium-range missiles deployed at Vladivostok, not to mention the decommissioning of three older coastal patrol submarines. It was a small price to pay all things considered, but it was the latest drop in the bucket for the battering of Soviet prestige.

"Comrade Minister Radomir was going over our petroleum production numbers," the general secretary explained.

"The outlook is good, comrades," the minister said, adjusting his round glasses in a way that caught the lighting of the room, making the rimless lenses flash. "Production in our far eastern wells is up—well above expectation—and our new offshore platforms are nearly reaching their established quotas." He looked up from his notes to his fellow politburo members. "Additionally, our aid agreements with Iraq, courtesy of Comrade Gradenko," the minister said with a bow of his head in Gradenko's direction, "has paid dividends."

"After their disastrous outing against the Iranians in the Persian Gulf War, the Iraqi regime has found itself short of friends. It seems the Americans have grown tired of propping them up. As it is, our Iraqi clients are in desperate need of military and economic aid. Without American help they're even more dependent on us now," Gradenko said.

The Defense Minister, Anton Tarasov, cleared his throat. He was the oldest among them which was impressive even given previous attempts to bring 'younger men' into the upper echelons of Soviet leadership. He was a crag-faced, mountain of a man, though he had a substantial paunch and walked with a cane now. Tarasov's voice was a gravely rumble, like a cliff face threatening to cave in. "The cost to our armed forces is negligible. Military advisors and second-hand military equipment, mostly monkey models—" he said, referencing the intentionally inferior versions of weapons marked for export.

"How much have they received so far?" Gradenko asked, meeting the defense minister's eyes.

Gradenko had seen photographs of Tarasov as a young combat engineer in the Red Army during the Great Patriotic War and found it hard to reconcile that image with the aged relic before him.

In his youth, Tarasov was pictured festooned with grenades, toting a drum-fed submachine gun and unreeling spools of telephone wire in ruined cities. While he looked soft now, Tarasov's background was as rugged as they came. He was a native of the wild Caucasus Mountains and his mannerisms were somewhat rough, off-putting to those who did not know what to expect. This, coupled with his violent, martial background made him something of a wildcard in the otherwise stoic and reserved Politburo.

"Enough weapons and equipment to outfit three motor rifle divisions and two tank divisions," Tarasov said, reciting the figures from memory. "Even now they clamor for advanced jet aircraft and more ballistic missiles," he snorted. "No doubt to waste on their neighbors the first chance they have."

"Iraq is a rabid dog," Gradenko agreed, "but we hold their leash now. So long as they are dependent on our weapons, they will not act without our approval. As long as the West maintains their sanctions, they will have to rely on us."

"Now that we have heard of the successes in the field of military exports and petroleum production," KGB Chairman Alexei Karamazov said, steepling his fingers on the cool wood surface of the conference table. "I would like to hear of the situation in Yugoslavia from Comrade Gradenko."

The twenty odd members of the Politburo turned their attention fully to Gradenko. Any goodwill given for his cool handling of arms deals to Iraq had gone from the room.

The minister grit his teeth invisibly.

Karamazov, you bastard, are you trying to pin this on me?

Gradenko inwardly debated the best way to handle the delicate situation before speaking. "The situation is largely unchanged. Yugoslav government forces hold the eastern stretches of the country." Gradenko decided that in this case, less was more. He would not lead himself to his own political grave.

"What of the splinter states?" the general secretary asked.

Another prickly topic. "While the late President Tito was a revisionist and an enemy of the revolution," Gradenko said, speaking carefully, "he was adept at keeping that nation's ethnic tensions in control."

"And dodging our assassins," Tarasov chortled.

"The current Yugoslavian president—Aleksic—has so far *not* lived up to his predecessor's reputation."

"You are saying that the situation is growing more unstable?" the general secretary pressed.

Gradenko knew the truth would have to be revealed sooner or later. In fact, the truth was clear to many in the Politburo, but Gradenko was being forced to be the one to give it voice. No doubt it was Karamazov's design. "The situation is that the nation of Yugoslavia has effectively ceased to be."

Those few remaining Politburo members unaware of the severity of the situation in the Balkans looked on gravely.

Gradenko glanced over his shoulder to make eye contact with a nearby aide, waiting silently in the corner—one of his people. He gestured and the aide distributed photocopied maps to the other members.

"As it stands, the 'nation of Yugoslavia' is nothing more than a 'Greater Serbia'. As the situation is—" Gradenko licked his dry lips, "I see no choice but to accept that Aleksic does not have control over the northwest of his country and will not regain it on his own."

Gradenko had seen the television reports of mobs of Croats, Slovenes, Bosnians, and the other marginalized ethnicities in the multi-ethnic state. They'd been marching in the streets bearing banners demanding rights and an end to the Yugoslav strain of socialism that had caged them for so long. They were not dissimilar to the protestors of the Eastern Bloc states or the Baltic region of the Soviet Union. In the Soviet case, a combination of liberal economic policies and judicious application of military force had kept their demands in line.

It seemed Aleksic either did not have the stomach or the military power to see a repeat of the Warsaw Massacre executed in Sarajevo or Zagreb.

"And what should it matter to us?" the agriculture deputy spoke up. "The Yugoslavs have made their own bed. They abandoned our treaty and refused our help. Comrade Gradenko is correct, they are revisionists. Let them fall."

Gradenko held in a sigh. If only it were so simple.

"Comrade," Tarasov said with an excess of patience. "The strategic defense of the Soviet Union is a simple arrangement. We carefully maintain our socialist brothers in Eastern Europe to act as a bulwark against expansionist Western ideals."

It was a nicer way of saying "human shield."

"As an independent, neutral nation," Tarasov continued, "Yugoslavia was agreeable to both NATO and ourselves."In effect it was a no-man's-land. With the breakup of the state ..."

"Croatia has already established diplomatic relations with the Western Powers," Karamazov revealed. "Their elections are looming and the Croatian Communist Party is expected to lose. I believe it will only be a matter of time before they are admitted to NATO. Would you agree, Comrade Gradenko?"

The gaunt old man was really dragging Gradenko through the mud on this one, but Gradenko could not cast blame elsewhere so easily without appearing to be simply avoiding the problem.

"We have not yet established formal relations with the Croatians ourselves," Gradenko said, a true statement, but a transparent dodge. Again Gradenko cursed the KGB chairman. What was he playing at?

"What choices are open to us then?" the general secretary asked. "We let them fall?"

"I have been drawing up a plan," Gradenko said, "of selective support of Aleksic's government. With a military and economic aid package we may bolster support for the government and perhaps induct them into the Treaty of Friendship, Cooperation, and Mutual Assistance." Gradenko used the formal term for what Westerners so crassly referred to as the Warsaw Pact. "It would be in effect a partition, as was done with Korea, Germany, and Vietnam."

"A rump state," Karamazov said, dismissing Gradenko's proposal out of hand. "You would leave almost the whole of the Adriatic coast open to NATO? And what if Aleksic's government sides with the West after all? Austrian and Yugoslav neutrality kept our Balkan brothers shielded from the West, but if you allow Yugoslavia to fall, then we will be exposed from Hungary to Bulgaria. I am sure that Comrade Tarasov would agree with me that it is a totally unacceptable situation strategically."

The old veteran did not disagree. His silence spoke for him.

"Comrade Karamazov," the general secretary said, "we are acquainted with the particular details of our predicament. I am interested in solutions."

"A mutual occupation perhaps," Gradenko began, "a UN peacekeeping force. I am certain the West would be agreeable with this." He was grasping at straws now.

"The United Nations—" Karamazov's tone was derisive, "will not manage to reach an agreement on this, not when so many of the enemy sit on the security council. The United States won't allow us a dedicated peacekeeping zone of our own and they will insist on free elections and self-determination. The result will be inevitable."

Gradenko couldn't help but notice that Karamazov was dictating so foreign affairs policies to him. He couldn't dwell on it though as the breakup of Yugoslavia risked the destruction of a vital piece in the "bulwark" against the West that the Soviets had so carefully cultivated. This was a situation which concerned more than just the foreign ministry.

"Already NATO peacekeepers are in Slovenia," Tarasov agreed.

"What then can be done?" another Politburo man asked, directing his question not at Gradenko or the general secretary, but at Karamazov. It was clear then: the KGB chairman's production of destroying Gradenko was not to simply sacrifice his colleague to the proverbial wolves, but to establish himself as the man in charge here by putting down any potential rivals.

Are you gunning for the general secretary next? Gradenko wondered.

"Comrade Tarasov," Karamazov asked, "what about Blue Masquerade?"

This time all eyes went to the aging defense minister.

The surprise that registered on his jowled face was impossible to miss. "Blue Mas— Comrade Karamazov, such plans are in the purview of the Defense Ministry, *not* the KGB."

"I had overheard the name during a defense briefing last summer," Karamazov replied, pressing on undaunted. "Forgive me."

General Secretary Kavinski cleared his throat, attempting to regain control of the meeting. It was no secret that he was a compromise candidate for the position, the safe choice to head the Politburo rather than the best one. It was a fact he'd tried to shake by approaching his job with confidence and optimism, but he had not yet managed to distinguish himself in any real way. "I think, comrades, for the sake of discussion we must assume that knowledge of this Blue Masquerade is an open secret."

"Very well." Tarasov inclined his head slightly toward the general secretary before looking back to address the others. "The Defense Ministry maintains a selection of war plans on file in case of unanticipated changes in political direction. Masquerade is the plan assigned to Yugoslavia. Red Masquerade was constructed during the split in our relations. Blue Masquerade is the modern variant, updated with our current capabilities in mind."

"It is a plan to subdue Yugoslavia then, yes?" Karamazov prompted.

"That is correct, comrade."

Gradenko took a certain sick satisfaction seeing the KGB chairman leading someone else around by the nose, though Tarasov was much worse about hiding his displeasure than others. Perhaps Karamazov had finally overstepped his bounds. It was true that Tarasov was not the most skilled schemer, but he was respected because of his age and experience. Not to mention the fact that he helmed the whole of the massive Soviet military. He would make a dangerous enemy and a powerful ally.

"May I ask, Comrade Tarasov, for the specifics of this plan?" Karamazov asked.

"The specifics would take a stack of paper up to your knee to detail," Tarasov said with no shortage of vitriol. A second after this rebuke he seemed to deflate slightly as if recognizing that hostility would get him nowhere. "The plan is essentially a three-pronged attack from Hungary, Romania, and Bulgaria, coupled with airborne deployments to seize vital infrastructure. We anticipated the Yugoslav government forces to capitulate within ten days. It involves one hundred and fifty thousand men. Nine hundred jet aircraft."

Karamazov nodded as if this was his first time hearing the info. "I propose, comrade general secretary, that we seek to implement such plan at once before the situation gets worse."

This statement was met only with stunned silence, with no one sure how exactly to counter such a plain admission. Even the general secretary was at a loss.

"Comrade," one of the other members spoke up, "you're speaking of an invasion. A military invasion."

"I am proposing an intervention," Karamazov countered. "I am proposing a protection of our nation against collapse. We cannot stand idly by as our bloc is chipped away."

"Comrade Karamazov," the general secretary said, mustering as much authority into his voice as he could, "this is a very serious request."

"One that should not come from the chairman of the KGB," Gradenko added. He ordinarily didn't take sides in power struggles that didn't involve him directly, but what Karamazov was attempting here was something that the Soviet Union had not done since intervening in Czechoslovakia in 1968.

"Does Foreign Affairs fear the application of 'politics by other means'?" Karamazov challenged, loosely quoting Clausewitz.

Gradenko swallowed, willing his hands to stop sweating and hoping he looked more composed than he felt. He'd heard rumors of Karamazov's plans, but did not anticipate that it would mean war. "I merely want what is best for the Party and the State," Gradenko said. "I feel that perhaps, Comrade Karamazov, you may not be best to make this suggestion alone."

The ghost of a grin slipped over Karamazov's features, the indication that perhaps Gradenko was not as in control of the situation as he thought.

"Perhaps not. Comrade Tarasov," the KGB chairman looked to the minister of defense. "What is your professional assessment?"

"Regarding?" The old soldier couched his answer carefully, his hooded eyes betraying nothing of the thoughts in his head.

Gradenko held no illusions that Tarasov would cooperate with Karamazov. If there was one certainty in Soviet politics, it was the ever-present rivalry between the military arm of the party and the internal security one. It was a rivalry that stretched back to the earliest power struggles in Soviet history.

"Regarding Blue Masquerade," Karamazov explained, "regarding the need for its employment."

"The plan will work," Tarasov said with no reservations. "There is no question there. Even our most pessimistic forecasts show total success within fifteen days." Here he paused, eyes fixed on the intricate woodwork of the table, unmoving.

The silence in the room was deep enough that Gradenko imagined he could almost make out the rumble of city traffic through the sound proof walls.

"If we are to safeguard Eastern Europe, Yugoslavia must be maintained," Tarasov said.

The words, as soft as they were, exploded in the conference room with as much effect as a literal bomb might have. The KGB and the military were cooperating on this plan. It was all but certain now, unless ...

Gradenko's eyes flicked to the general secretary, perhaps the only one who could put a stop to this madness. Yes, Tarasov was certainly correct that Yugoslavia could be swiftly conquered, but for what reason? This was the same "domino" reasoning the United States had employed when investing themselves in Vietnam, the same flawed logic that had nearly entangled the Soviet Union in Afghanistan, a potential disaster they had only barely avoided. It was easy to imagine the Russian bear getting embroiled in the same sort of humiliating and bitter brush conflict that had so neatly humbled the United States, a bullet skillfully dodged.

The general secretary's face betrayed no emotion, his jaw set with firm determination. It was a look not out of place for a party boss on a factory floor. This same sort of stubborn determination had ensured workplace quotas were met; perhaps here it could find reason.

"An invasion may draw retaliation from the West," Gradenko said, speaking before the secretary could. "They will be too timid to interfere directly of course, but it will mean economic sanctions."

The general secretary stiffened at the golden words.

"And at a time when our next five-year modernization plan is set to begin, it could mean trouble. Missed quotas. I know that a trade arrangement for Italian medical equipment to update Moscow Central Hospital is on the table currently. Likewise, a renewed military investment in the Balkans will mean less to be spared for our client states. Iraq, Libya, Syria, Korea, Vietnam. Are we to assume they will wait patiently as we sort out our own economic woes and not go crawling to the West or the Chinese?"

The threat of outside meddling in the Soviet sphere was a real one. It was no secret that nearly one million Soviet combat troops were stationed eternally on the Chinese border, most of them in the Far East, running from Vladivostok in a sickle-curve around Manchuria. These soldiers were not just for show and more than once the "Communist Brothers" had nearly come to blows.

The general secretary nodded, considering this insight and looked to Tarasov. "Has the Defense Ministry taken political ramifications into account for this 'Blue Masquerade'?"

Tarasov hesitated. "Such matters are the domain of the Ministry of Foreign Affairs. Blue Masquerade assumes a secure diplomatic front."

"Comrade chairman?"

Karamazov flinched visibly at being addressed and deliberately avoided looking at Gradenko. "The political factor has been considered," he allowed. "The risk is minimal."

Gradenko restrained an outburst. It was the greatest irony that the men who helmed the mighty Soviet Union were in truth, sheep. The British might call them "donkeys leading lions." Men in Gradenko's position did not climb the ranks by being combative. This had begun to change with the inclusion of "young men"—that is those who did not yet have grandchildren, but it was still generally true. As it stood, most members of the Politburo held their tongues, watching and waiting to see which side to come down on in this overt power struggle. No one was willing to stick their neck out and get it chopped.

"Minimal risk?" the general secretary asked. He was no fool, he could see through a bold-faced lie.

"Comrade," Karamazov tried, "there is *another* political cost that Comrade Gradenko may have overlooked. That is the cost of meekly standing by as our socialist brothers in Yugoslavia tear themselves apart. If we show the world we do not act now, what will we say when the cries for re-unification begin again in Germany? Or when the Polish again push for more freedoms? Will we stand by for fear of offending the West?"

Silence met him.

The general secretary, a man whose power was in question since his elevation to the post, was lost in thought. His brow furrowed, lips pursed. "If we invade we are damned in the eyes of the world. If we do nothing, damned in the eyes of our allies." He smirked to himself, "We must avoid both of these if we can." His attention went to the minister of defense. "Comrade Tarasov, I would like you to begin preparations for Blue Masquerade at once."

Gradenko's stomach fell.

"We will not yet implement it, however," the general secretary finished.

The triumphant half-smile vanished from Karamazov's lips.

"Comrade secretary," Karamazov said, "A delay in an operation such as this—"

"The operation will *not* proceed until we have deemed that it is necessary. I am not as confident as you or Minister Tarasov in your predictions of swift victory. For the time being, I would like you to draft plans to provide our Yugoslavian friends military assistance. I imagine they will welcome the assistance. I believe an army corps should do. Short of war, a demarcation of the country is all we can do. Comrade Minister Gradenko, please communicate with President Aleksic's government to arrange this."

Gradenko nodded and scrawled a note on his notepad.

"Perhaps in time the situation will improve," Kavinski finished.

Karamazov made no counter argument, he could see that the general secretary's position was solid on this.

A half-measure. It was a bitter victory for Gradenko. Military occupation of Serbia would avoid confrontation with NATO and cries of "Imperialism," but it would also leave swaths of the country open to foreign adventurism. Politics—Gradenko mused—was often a game with no victors.

"If there are no further measures, I would like to discuss preparations for the 30th Party Congress." And just like that, the matter was buried. "Unanimously" decided, as was the Soviet style.

Even though Gradenko had not gotten his way entirely, he took wry satisfaction that the general secretary had backed him. It seemed the man had the backbone of a leader after all. Who knew? Given enough time the two of them may form a power bloc strong enough to uproot Karamazov's clique, with or without the army's cooperation. So long as Gradenko had the favor of the general secretary, he and his own plans were safe.

***

2

All things considered, Jean would have preferred to drive herself. As it was, bouncing down a rutted back-country road in a rented 4x4, she'd have rather been the one in control of the vehicle's movements. Jean was never one to leave others in control if she had a choice but, of her three person team, she was somehow the only one who could properly read a map.

"This right," she said, indicating a barely-visible earth and wood bridge that crossed a deep irrigation ditch which sat half-full of tepid water. The ditch was mostly hidden by leafy foliage which was just starting to turn a dull brown in the autumn chill.

"Jesus," her cameraman Pete Owen said as he wrenched the wheel. "Hardly even a road." His heavy brow was furrowed in concentration. Despite his intimidating size, Pete always had an air of nervous uncertainty about him unless he was behind the lens of a camera. He chewed his lower lip anxiously as he straightened the vehicle out.

"You expected a ten-lane super highway?" Jean teased, gripping the "chicken handle" above her door long enough to ensure that Pete wasn't going to miss the narrow bridge and put the nose of their truck into the ditch.

"Highway my ass, *that* was a cow track! You said 'rural driving,' you didn't say it would be backwoods path finding," Pete said, leaning forward in concentration to wrestle with the wheel as the truck hit another deep rut. This one had likely been carved out from decades of the same farmer's tractor driving down the same muddy road every day. "How much farther to this place? Popovaka?" he asked, trying the unfamiliar name.

"Popovacha," their translator, Dario, said from the back. "That angle above the 'c', you see?" Somehow Dario was the only one in the vehicle who seemed untroubled. His dark, expressive eyes were open, clear, and eager.

"No, I don't," Pete said, "I'm watching the road like Jean keeps telling me."

"We're almost there," she said. "Relax. This road should drop us out right on the edge of town and avoid any militia entanglements." As she spoke, she absently turned down the volume on the radio, fading away the dance-centric Serbian pop song droning from the radio. "This is the place Novak told you about, right Dario?" Jean asked, lowering the map to look back at the Croat. He nodded, "Yes, this is the place. He says we are to meet a Croatian army unit in town who will bring us to the prisoner."

Jean nodded. An interview with a Serbian militant was worth its weight in gold right now. Her editor back home in the States was practically salivating for the chance for a candid sit down talk with one of "the bad guys."

You're gonna be talking with Darth-fucking-Vader, Jean. These guys are burning out the Croats and Bosnians and anyone who isn't a Serb. No softball questions. No bush league shit. Get me a good fucking talk and we're talking bank.

This part of Croatia, on the southern border near Bosnia and Herzegovina, had very large Serbian majorities. These were people who were happier under the Pro-Serb Yugoslavian government and would apparently rather drive their neighbors out by force and secede to rejoin the "homeland" rather than submit. So far the Yugoslavian federal government, such as it was, hadn't done anything officially to aid the Serbian radicals. *Unofficially* Jean had still seen enough aging T-55's with Yugoslavian army marks hastily painted over to know they were aiding them in some capacity at least.

The 4x4 dipped down and bounced through a rough patch in the road before cresting a hill that was flanked on either side by broad, open cornfields which framed the city of Popovača. The outskirts of the town were dominated by pastel-colored homes with the characteristic shallow angled roofs and narrow windows common to this part of the Balkans. Normally it would have been pretty, if unremarkable, but the minor cosmetic marring Jean noticed became bullet holes as they drew nearer.

Popovača was a Croatian-majority town, but it was right on the border with a Serb-majority area, making it a rife battleground. The damage to the town was minimal, mostly broken windows and some pockmarks. Here and there Jean saw the flashy silver and brass of spent shell casings lying in the gutters.

The people of the town stood about, eyeing this strange vehicle apprehensively. Jean and her compatriots had been *very* careful to mark the truck with the word "**PRESS**" in bold, black paint on the doors and hood. It wasn't foolproof, but it would hopefully ward off all but the most homicidal fighters. As they drew nearer to the center of town, bystanders became more common, many simply going about their daily routine. Even war didn't stop people from needing to buy groceries. The buildings here were an eclectic mix of styles. Many were the blank-faced, low-rise apartment complexes indicative of the country's socialist past while others were more ornate, in an almost Mediterranean style.

"Are these Novak's friends?" Pete asked.

Jean hadn't noticed the gaggle of soldiers ahead in the town square. Just over three dozen men stood idle. They were centered around a cluster of improvised combat vehicles, pickup trucks carrying machine guns on pintle mounts, commonly called "Technicals" in Jean's line of work. Paying off the warlords that often operated them was written off as a "technical expense" by aid organizations.

The technicals here were splashed with mottled green and brown camouflage paint. The soldiers were also haphazardly equipped. Some wore the cut of a Yugoslavian army uniform though the identifying patches had been removed. At a glance, they were deserters from the crumbling national army. Either that, or they were simply motivated civilians and militiamen armed with the spoils of combat or the looting of reserve centers. Others among the armed band wore civilian clothes with simple blue armbands to mark their affiliation.

"Yes, that is them," Dario said. "Approach slowly."

While Pete tapped the brakes, the soldiers' eyes were on them.

The Croats carried assault rifles and Jean had no doubt they'd used them in the recent past. Despite their roughshod appearance these men were not in fact a guerilla or warlord band, but rather the official government-sanctioned army of Croatia. A sad state of affairs, especially when stacked against the comparatively huge and well-armed Yugo-Serbian army, but they had little choice. These people were fighting for their homes after all.

The armored column was parked in the shadow of what had been a glass-fronted building of some kind. It had lost all its windows to a bomb blast long ago. The shattered plate glass crunched under the truck's tires as Pete swore and did his best to avoid it, weaving the car into the shadow of the building and stopping with a quiet squeak of brakes.

Two of the Croatians approached, one throwing a cigarette butt to the ground as they moved to opposite sides of the vehicle. Neither looked happy to be there, nor did they look alarmed. To Jean they looked tired, drained of any enthusiasm.

Pete and Jean rolled down their windows at the soldier's approach.

"Hello," Jean spoke first. "English?"

"No," the soldier on her side said. "Reporter?" The word was a butchery in his mouth.

"Yes, reporter. AP." She gestured to the camera equipment in the back at the same time she raised her press ID.

Now Dario spoke, conversing with the soldier in Croatian. "The prisoner is here," he said after a moment.

"Alive?" Jean asked.

The question was relayed and came back with a translation from Dario. "For now."

"Roses," Jean said with mock cheer. "Ask them if we can see him today."

The request triggered a back and forth exchange between the two soldiers, neither seeming sure of how to proceed. As they spoke, the rest of the men in their unit loitered around apathetically, smoking and talking amongst themselves and savoring the cool weather. The deliberation took a moment before one of the soldiers addressed Dario.

"They want us to come with them," Dario said.

"Right," Jean unbuckled. "Pete, get the camera."

The news team assembled outside the truck, Jean's tape recorder handy while Pete held the large, black video camera by its top carrying handle. He adjusted his Yankees ball cap with a free hand, ensuring it sat snugly on his head.

"I think the Serb is in that building," Dario nodded toward one of the nearby apartment blocks. "They're trying to determine how they want to do this interview."

"Right," Jean said. They wanted to show the prize they bagged and they wanted to get word out to the West about what they were up against, but they wanted the narrative to go their way and not get spun by some hopped up, over-eager journalist.

A third Croatian soldier approached from the building Dariob had indicated. He carried an AK-47 on a homemade strap hung over his shoulder. He didn't look much like a soldier, excluding his half-uniform and the weapon he carried. He was middle aged with the first hints of a gut starting to hang over his belt and his hairline was receding.

To Jean, he looked more like some balding dad who'd fit right in scooping leaves out of his pool in the suburbs back home in the States or maybe flipping patties on the grill. This illusion vanished when he drew close enough for Jean to see the barely restrained fury in his eyes.

Dario and this man spoke. Their tones were conversational despite the seriousness of the subject matter.

"We will see him," Dario said, his voice full of relief.

"Tell him 'thank you'," Jean said as the four of them moved as one into the apparently abandoned apartment building.

Ascending the stairs, she noticed that their escort, the man who appeared to be in charge of all these soldiers, wore Adidas trainers. She pointed this silently to Pete and snapped a still image with the Nikon that hung around her neck.

If that wasn't a symbol of the resurgence in Eastern Europe, she didn't know what was.

The building had once been nice enough to live in, but mistreatment and neglect had filled it with a stale, vaguely-foul odor. Paint flaked off where rain and wind had gotten in through the cracked and shattered windows. Jean saw no direct combat damage though, which she couldn't be sure was a good thing or not.

"He is here," Dario translated as their escort unlocked an unmarked apartment door and led them in.

The apartment was almost totally unfurnished, though it wasn't clear if it had been this way before the war or was the work of looters or these soldiers. Only a few spare chairs littered the room. One chair held a Croatian sentry, smoking a cigarette and watching the newcomers. The other held the object of their interest: the Serbian.

Jean stopped in the doorway and stared at the man who was staring back at her, his hands and legs bound to the chair. She was looking "the enemy" in the eye. She'd seen the grisly handiwork of his compatriots. The shallow ditches full of half-buried bodies. Men, women, children. She'd seen the black husks of burned villages left in the wake of the Bosnian Serbs trying to carve their own ethnic enclave. Now, in front of her own eyes, was one of the enemies in the flesh.

The Serb tied to the chair had short, dark hair, matching stubble on his chin, and a ripe-looking black eye on his right side. He was younger than she would have expected, maybe in his early twenties, wearing the mixed-kit uniform typical of Serbian fighters she'd seen. It was a combination of various elements of Yugoslav army gear, primarily olive drab fatigues and a mottled, woodland camo coat. A hat—presumably his—lay on the floor nearby. It was a field cap with button-up ear flaps for cold weather and a small red, white, and blue Serbian shield patch on the peak.

After a moment, Jean collected herself, feeling her heartbeat already rising in anticipation of the interview, the confrontation of evil. "Pete, set up here," she said, indicating the man's left side, hoping to hide his black eye from view. She saw no sense in making the situation any more gray than the public at home would already think it was. Jean didn't need viewers at home feeling confused about things. Reprisal killings and Anti-Serb militias muddied the waters further. This story needed clear good guys and bad guys.

Dario brought a pair of chairs, one directly before the Serbian and one slightly off camera.

Jean sat front and center, adjusting herself, clicking on her recorder and sitting it on the bare floor between them. A glance at Pete showed her the small, red, record light snap on above the lens of his camera. Showtime.

"I'm Jean Carson, Associated Press," Jean said, addressing the soldier while Dario relayed her words in real time to the young man. "May I ask your name?"

His response needed no translation, "Lazar Jelic." But he followed it up with words unfamiliar to Jean.

"Lieutenant, Serbian People's Army," Dario translated.

"You are a soldier?"

"Yes."

"How old are you?"

"Twenty."

Beside her, Pete adjusted the zoom on his camera, likely drawing in on the young man's face.

"You're a young man, Lazar. Why are you dedicating your life to war?"

The Serb scoffed once Dario finished translating.

"This is not a war we wanted," Lazar replied through the interpreter. "It was our desire to remain one nation."

"But why do you fight the Croats? The Bosnians? The Slovenes? They desire their own nations as well."

"Should I be content to be ruled by a Croat from Zagreb?"

Lazar turned to the camera to glare. "The Serbian people do not consent to be a part of this new nation."

"You say you are defending your home then?"

"Yes. This place was our home and will stay our home. Let Croats live with Croats and Serbs live with Serbs." Dario's disgust was transparent on his face, but he did his job, reciting the words given to him in English.

It was the sort of rhetoric that Jean had heard used to justify all sorts of violence from religious to ethnic cleansing: "Defending a way of life."

"How can you justify then the killing of civilians? Burning of villages?"

"Such killings do not take place," Lazar said defiantly.

"We know that they do," Jean returned, willing her voice steady to only project a calm and impartial manner. "We've witnessed the mass graves first hand. We've seen the bodies of civilians dumped in like they were garbage."

"Even if that were true," Dario said, speaking for Lazar, "The people should have known better than to stay where they are no longer welcome. They have a choice, leave to live with their own kind or be destroyed."

It was classic doublethink, the type usually confined to the most hardcore holocaust deniers: "It didn't happen, but if it did they deserved it." Jean was also distinctly aware of Dario's simmering discomfort. He wasn't from this area. Dario lived much further away in the coastal city of Zadar where they'd flown in, but he was a Croat. Croatia was his home and these were his people.

"Are you paid? For what you do?"

"Service is its own reward."

"What about the Yugoslav government," Jean asked, "Do *they* pay you?"

A distinct reaction, Lazar hesitated, collected his thoughts.

"I serve the Serbian people."

Jean decided to try a different tactic, something to break the sensation of this being an interrogation. "Lazar, I am not a part of the Croatian—or any other government. I am here to find out about you and your cause. Can you tell me how you were captured?"

"I was part of an anti-aircraft battery from Sisak," Dario repeated, "I was captured after being caught by surprise." Before letting Jean speak again, Dario relayed a question to the paunchy Croatian commander. "They found him relieving himself in the woods," he added.

"This interview may be broadcast," Jean said, brushing aside the less than dignified circumstances of his capture. "What would you want to say to your family? To the world?"

Lazar thought for a moment, choosing his words carefully before speaking. "I would want them to know," Dario said with painful deliberateness, "the lies of the Croat and Bosnian. My captors have beaten and mistreated me."

Jean didn't have the heart to tell the kid he wasn't covered under the Geneva Convention. She could see this interview was only going to receive a carefully memorized and parroted official line that could have come from any number of Serbian factions. "I think we've got it Pete. Dario, thank him." Jean stood as the camera was packed away. Jean waited until Dario and she were a healthy distance away from the others where they watched Pete carefully clip the lens cap in place on his camera."What are they going to do with him?" she asked. "Kill him?"

The translator shook his head, "No. He will probably be held like this until they can make an exchange for a Croat prisoner."

Jean looked back at the man tied to the chair. The defiance in his face was gone and he simply looked tired now, like the soldiers outside had. The Serb fighter stared at the floor of the apartment, likely wondering what lay in store for him next. Jean wished she knew, not just for Lazar but the whole of this country. "Let's get to Novi Sad," she said. "I want to get that interview with the Serbian State Department before we have to get back to Zagreb and send this footage off."

***

"A waste," Jean said, idly wrapping the phone cord around her wrist as she spoke, a bad habit she'd picked up as a teenager. "It's all trash, Tony."

"Come on now," her editor said, his voice tinny and crackling over the poor phone connection, "that's my job to say, not yours."

The hotel room was cozy enough—not up to Western standards, but decent. It had been built in the 1970s to house traveling technical experts, a throwback to Yugoslavia's socialist past. Now the Hotel Centar in Novi Sad was home to dozens of foreign journalists scouring the country like scavengers in search of a scoop. The accommodations were sparse but it had a decent view of the Danube River, a meandering blue-green concourse that framed the southern edge of the city and etched a snaking trail across the north of Serbia.

"Tony, he was just spouting the party line! No confessions, no threats, not even any waterworks, just a half-assed line about the Croats 'getting what they deserved'," Jean sat heavily on the bed and sighed.

"We can use that!" Tony returned, "Audio is useless for something like that, but a headline: 'Serb Fighter Says Croats 'Deserve' Cleansing.'"

"Jesus that's morbid," Jean said, fishing a cigarette out of the front pocket of her flannel shirt.

"Morbid sells, Jean. What about the State Department?"

"A fucking kiss off," Jean said. "I met with some aide, spoke broken English, refused to admit Dario."

"What'd he say?"

Jean put on her best Serbian accent, "The government of the Federated Republic of Yugoslavia does not recognize the Croatian nation." She sighed. "Party lines, party lines. I haven't heard an independent thought in ... oh, I don't know."

"You're running dry over there, I know," Tony said. "That's okay, Jean. We're not gonna strike gold every day. Have you talked about heading to Sarajevo? Might get at least some B roll footage of Serb tanks and shit deploying."

The thought both frightened and exhilarated her. Wasn't that why she'd wanted to come out here? To stare the sickness of man in the face? To catalog and describe it? To put a spotlight on its every dark recess? Even so, the thought of being that deep within the "belly of the beast" was petrifying, but as they say, it wasn't her first rodeo.

"If I can't get anything there, sure," Jean said. "But that's amateur hour. All the major networks have people in Sarajevo."

Outside the window, a wide, flat-bottomed barge laden with Hungarian grain cruised south, maybe intending to offload at Belgrade or continue on, back over the border into Romania. She'd gotten her first decent night's sleep in a few days here and was enjoying it. The trio had spent a week traveling and crashing on any couch that would hold them, even the bare-bones amenities offered by this hotel seemed like paradise. It was also nice to finally have a bit of privacy to herself. Being a woman gave her enough leverage to insist on her own room; poor Dario and Pete had to share. Jean lit her cigarette while Tony spoke.

"Sure they do, Jean," Tony said, "But not like you. You *dig*. You see shots fired, you're gonna be there finding out who was shooting at what, why."

Jean puffed and smirked, "Yeah."

There was a rap at her door. "Hey Tony, let me call you back, okay?"

"Don't bother. I'm gonna try to put something together from what you've given me so far, okay? Get some rest and get me some more good stuff when you've got it!"

"Bye." Jean laid the phone in the cradle and answered the door.

Pete stood, looking sheepish in her doorway. "Busy?"

Jean blinked at him, taking a long drag from her cigarette. "No, Pete. Not particularly."

Her cameraman cracked a boyish grin at her, "We got something."

"Something?" Jean asked, ushering Pete in and closing the door.

"Dario was talking to a contact of his, seeing about booking a train to Kosovo maybe, and that's when we found out."

"Found out what?" Jean asked, stubbing her cigarette butt out in a bedside ashtray without looking; Pete's discovery absorbed all her attention.

Pete drew a carefully folded map from the back pocket of his jeans and spread it out across the bed before grinning at her again. "The trains are shut down."

"So?"

"So! This is new, the government hadn't unilaterally shut down rail service until just the other night." Pete studied the map, searching for something, "And it's not all the other lines! Dario told me it's ..."

"What are you looking for?" Jean asked, impatient.

"Where the fuck is Novi Sad?"

"Here." Jean laid a finger on the city.

"Right! So look—" Pete traced a finger and read off stops. "Belgrade, Novi Sad, Subotica."

Three points in a nearly straight line running north, an arrow pointed at— "Hungary?" Jean asked.

"Right. Heavy security too, army patrols at rail junctions, blackouts around rail yards."

"Blackouts."

"Right, no-go zones. Including—"

"The one here," Jean supplied, recalling seeing a large industrial district on the map of Novi Sad.

"Ding ding ding!" Pete chimed. "What do you think it is?"

"Somebody's moving something," Jean said, squinting at the map and trying to make sense of it. "It's coming over the border, through the Iron Curtain. It's got army protection so it's important."

"And it's *big* or why bother trying to hide it?"

Jean hummed in concentration and tapped her chin. "You think we can get into that yard?"

"What, the rail yard?"

"Mhmm. If they won't let anyone nearby, then it's got to be something that we'd see, something big, like you said."

"We could just stake out the rail bridge, right?" Pete tried. "If the train continues south, then it's gotta cross."

Jean shook her head, "No good, the rail bridge is north, out of sight, too easy to cut off. I want first-hand confirmation."

Pete looked in Jean's eyes. "Jesus, you're serious."

"We're not here to *hear* about the news, we're here to report it," Jean said.

"Right. Yeah." Pete looked at the map again, as if the answers were there. "It'll be like Somalia again."

Jean nodded, recalling the gut-clenching terror she'd felt sneaking along that wadi with the rattle of machine gun fire in the dark all around them.

"I'll go blackout the camera and let Dario know." Pete said.

***

The chill of night had crept over the city in full force, blanketing everything in a cold that hinted at an early winter. It was not entirely unpleasant though, since it drove off the high humidity that came off the river and left the air smelling crisp and fresh.

The citywide curfew was usually ill-enforced, but seemed to be taken more seriously tonight.

Jean, Dario, and Pete moved on foot, sticking to back roads where they could. Normally a journey from the riverfront to the railyard was forty-five minutes at best, but at the slow pace they went with frequent sidetracking it was nearly an hour and a half before they came within sight of the rail yard perimeter.

"This is it," Dario confirmed as they took shelter in the doorway of a closed pub on the roadside. There was nothing to see yet, just a rusted chain link fence surrounding a stand of trees shielding the industrial eyesore of the railyard from the rest of the city.

"Hold tight a sec," Jean said, willing her heart to beat slower and watching for patrols. After a few minutes a pair of Yugoslav soldiers in an old, battered jeep cruised by. They danced a flashlight beam over the fence, checking for gaps. Another five minutes later, the process was repeated.

"Dario, wait here," Jean said, "and watch for trouble."

"Okay."

Truthfully, she didn't want to involve their translator if she could help it. Western journalists had a lot more leverage than a Croatian interpreter did should they be caught.

"Pete?"

"Ready." His ball cap was on backwards, snugged down tight on his head, and he had a deathgrip on the handle of his camera. The telltale record light was covered over with a patch of black electrical tape, along with any shiny and metallic components.

"Let's go." The pair rose to their feet and dashed across the deserted street. It would have been comical if it weren't so terrifying. At any second Jean expected to get pinned in the headlights of a Yugoslav army jeep barreling around a curve.

None came and they reached the fence fine.

"Ladies first," Pete whispered, interlacing his fingers into an adhoc step and bracing them on his knee.

Jean didn't argue the point, gripping the rusted metal wire of the fence and using Pete's hand to boost herself up and over.

The camera came second after a few moments of careful coordination. Jean caught it awkwardly when Pete let it fall over the fence. It was all a wasted trip if they didn't get any good footage, and that made the video camera precious cargo.

Pete exhaled hard when he landed, knees buckling.

"Come on!" Jean seized his wrist and together they pressed into the dark and tangled woods. They stopped a dozen meters in to peer back at the road, waiting until a pair of patrolling headlights cruised by without stopping, only then did they breathe easy.

For reasons she couldn't explain, Jean felt safer in the woods even though she was arguably in much greater danger on this side of the fence than the other. Still, it was easy to convince herself—just for a moment—that she was simply on a wilderness walk and not headed into danger at all. That illusion failed as soon as she heard the sounds of idling diesel engines and elevated voices. Light spilled from the yard, filtering through the skeletal branches of the trees and painting Pete and Jean in blotchy shadows. Another few meters and they reached the edge of the woods with a clear view down the length of the yard.

Jean was shocked to see that it was not a train that caused all this commotion, it was a dozen of them. Each was loaded with flat cargo beds and a few passenger cars, all of these were laden with military gear. Tanks—and not the old surplus ones the Yugoslav army used, these were modern, T-72s and T-80s from the looks of it. Accompanying them were armored vehicles of all types: engineering tanks, armored personnel carriers, BMP infantry fighting vehicles, SAM launchers, armored cars, jeeps, trucks, self-propelled howitzers. Some were covered with tarps, but their forms were easy enough to discern.

If the tanks weren't alarming enough, there were soldiers as well, hundreds of them milling about the platform, sitting, talking, smoking, drinking, all in full battle garb.

"Oh shit," Pete whispered.

Jean didn't have to be an expert to identify these as Soviet soldiers.

"It's the whole goddam Red Army!" Pete said, voice barely above a whisper. He'd already uncapped his camera and was positioning it for a shot.

"How many do you think there are?" Jean asked.

"That's gotta be a few battalions at least," Pete said, tapping the "record" button and slowly panning the lens to take in the scene, his off eye squeezed shut.

It looked like the soldiers were taking a break here, maybe they would re-load and continue on to Belgrade in the morning. If there were a regiment here, then there would probably be more at the other closed yards, maybe the vanguard of an army. Now *this* was a scoop.

"What time is it?" Jean asked excitedly.

"What? It's like three AM."

"No! In the States. East coast." Jean asked, "Nine? Nine PM yesterday?"

"I think so."

"We can make the morning news tomorrow. Let's get some good shots and get back."

"What's it mean?" Pete asked, adjusting to get some shots of a cluster of menacing looking SAM launchers that kept watch over the staging area with a waiting bank of missiles.

"Whatever it is," Jean said, "it's a game changer."

***

3

It was chilly when President Rick Simpson crossed between the White House and the West Wing. He walked along the colonnade and savored the fresh air while he had the opportunity.. Everyday he tasted the DC air reminded him of victory, even if it was normally too humid for his tastes. "My ancestors crossed the nation in search of more tolerable climes for a reason," he was fond of saying.

"Yet somehow," his secretary, Doreen, would invariably respond, "they ended up in Texas."

Simpson was usually in a good mood. He'd been in a good mood since his election victory three years back swept him and his party into the White House and the driver's seat of the United States federal government. Everything seemed to be going his way; the economy was up, crime was down. Approval numbers—while not where they were three years ago—were still good, or at least better than bad. Simpson was a man on top of his game and he was more than happy to take credit for the successes he'd engineered. The boys on the Hill were still patting each other on the back over the "Right to Work" bill they'd wiggled through. Couple that with the successful diffusal of the Ethiopian occupation of Djibouti last year through the limited "modern blitzkrieg" of the Aden Gulf War, and he had a government that was strong both domestically and internationally.

This morning, however, Simpson was not in a good mood. He'd watched the morning news.

"Good morning, Mr. President," Doreen said upon his entry into the office. He was continually impressed with her cheerful demeanor despite long hours and early mornings. That and how she somehow kept her desk clutter free, even in the cramped conditions of the chronically undersized West Wing. No matter what was developing business-wise, his secretary only ever had the most recent items out on her desk. She always handled only one matter at a time, yet she never fell behind in the day's work. "A clean desk," she often said, "is an efficient desk." Today's main business looked like a schedule for speaking engagements later in the day. For personal effects she had only a small glass bowl of mints and a photograph of her husband.

"Well it's morning alright," Simpson returned dryly, stopping to help himself to a mint from her desk. "You watch the news, Doreen?"

"I can't say I've had time, sir."

"Huh." Simpson sucked on the mint and pondered.

"Mr. Harrison is in the Oval Office, sir. I think he's waiting for you."

Simpson smirked humorlessly. "Walt? I expect he would be. Thank you, darlin'."

That little mannerism of Simpson had taken time to register with his staff. The media had tried to stick him with the "chauvinist" label but so far he'd managed to let his policies do the talking. Higher average wages for women and a female secretary of state—the first in the nation's history. No amount of "darlins'" would undo those strides forward.

Simpson pressed on through the white, paneled door, noting its surprising weight as he swung it open—the result of a few layers of hardened armor, bulletproof supposedly.

Unlike his predecessor, President Slater, Simpson actually preferred to do his work in the Oval Office itself rather than the small adjoined presidential study. In Slater's outgoing letter, he'd suggested to the incoming president that he make use of the small private space to disconnect from the height of his office and focus on the work that had to be done.

Like much of Slater's advice, Simpson had disregarded it. He liked the grandiosity of the Oval Office and the significance it carried. It was a far cry from his boxy office in the Governor's

Mansion back home, and certainly different from his modern office in a Dallas highrise, but he liked it all the same. Pomp and circumstance invigorated and compelled Simpson regardless of the flavor.

Walt Harrison, Simpson's chief of staff, half-sat on the behemoth desk, flipping through a stapled briefing report.

"Come to tell me what I just saw on the news?" Simpson asked, trying to keep his infamous temper in check.

"Rick," Harrison said, spreading his hands defensively. "We've got a security briefing in ten minutes, there's a packet about—"

"They *lied* to me, Walt!" Simpson exclaimed, driving a fist into his palm, any pretense of remaining calm gone. "That Ruskie sunuva bitch Rykov sat right there—" Simpson pointed to one of the white, plushly upholstered couches in the office "—and told me they weren't gonna go in on Yugoslavia. And we believed 'em!"

"I can get the state department to have the Soviet ambassador stop by—"

"Why!?" Simpson blurted, circling his desk to plop heavily into his seat. "So he can lie to me again?" Simpson shook his head and collected his thoughts, "How many? How bad is it?"

"Intelligence has been going over satellite recon data and we estimate forty to fifty thousand."

"It's a goddamned May Day parade goin' into Belgrade. And we believed him like a couple of Barnum-born fools!" Simpson shook his head and quoted the Soviet ambassador, "'No unilateral action in Yugoslavia.' Horseshit." The president fell silent, trying and failing to recall the exercises his wife had suggested for when he let his emotions run away from him. "How long have y'all known?"

"Rick—"

"How long?" Simpson repeated, staring down his chief of staff.

Harrison hesitated before responding. "I just found out that we'd been tracking troop build ups in Hungary and Romania for a week. We were going to brief you on it this morning."

"Well, the cat's outta the bag now, Walt! Soviets are on the move. I just watched—" Simpson gestured broadly toward his residence, "—on the TV, video of Soviet tanks and troops in Yugoslavia. How the hell does CNN find out this mess before I do?"

Harrison had no answer. He simply handed over the folder.

With practiced swiftness, Simpson flipped it open and paged through it, skimming the contents. It was a detailed breakdown of the exact Soviet forces involved. 82nd Motor Rifle Division, 5th Tank Guards, 11th Tank Division—the names meant little to a career airline CEO and governor like Simpson. He relied on other people to interpret this stuff for him.

"Cancel the morning briefing," Simpson said. "I want a groupthink on this."

"The cabinet?" Harrison said.

"Naw, what the hell good is Transportation and Agriculture gonna do us?" These spontaneous, high level meetings drove his chief of staff nuts, but Simpson liked to keep abreast of challenges as they developed. "—state, defense, the security advisor, and the chairman of the Joint Chiefs. Oh! And someone who knows the Ruskies, some intel spook."

"That sounds like the National Security Council, sir," Harrison said.

"You know best, Walt," Simpson said, hands held up in surrender. "Just get them together. Let's say ..." Simpson checked his watch, "Thirty minutes?"

"We're breaking an awful lot of schedules, Rick," Harrison cautioned. "Thirty minutes is short notice."

"Well Walt, you can let 'em know that the Ruskies broke the schedule before I did. We're racing the news cycle here. Bill—" he referred to the press secretary, "could tell you that. We don't get word out on this thing by noon and we're going to look like a preacher with his pants down."

Harrison, who had all the restrained dignity expected in a New England conservative, denied himself a smirk, "Yes, sir."

***

It took ruffling some feathers—that was part of Walt Harrison's job description after all—but he made the meeting happen. The chairman of the Joint Chiefs and the secretary of defense were both right on time, having already expected to meet with the president. The secretary of state—Wanda Shilling—arrived a few minutes late having been at Capitol Hill discussing a diplomatic initiative with Japan. Simpson's famous insistence on his cabinet "jumping on command" was well known by now, but still caused friction and some of those gathered were less than pleased to have been summoned at such short notice.

Also present at the meeting through the miracle of teleconferencing were the US ambassador in Moscow and the US ambassador in Belgrade, their images displayed prominently on two of the video monitors in the situation room. The main display, a mosaic image built from a few large television displays, cycled through satellite images of the Russian columns deploying in Serbia, secret photographs from NATO intelligence operatives, and of course images from the news media itself.

"Mr. President," General Orville, the chairman of the Joint Chiefs, spoke first. As a craggy and decorated Marine veteran, he didn't have any apparent fear of Simpson's outbursts—one of the general's qualities that the president deeply respected. "The final tally of forces is done and it looks like we're looking at about fifty thousand Soviet troops, the 11th Army and elements of the 6th Guards Tank Army with token forces from Romania and Hungary."

"And y'all saw them coming a mile away and just decided to let it slide?" Simpson said.

"Sir, Ivan can't twitch his nose on that continent without us getting word. Unfortunately, he twitches his nose an awful lot," Orville said.

"I think, General," Wanda said, shifting in her seat, "this is a hell of a big twitch."

"Yes, ma'am," General Orville allowed, "but it's consistent with the Soviets' redeployment of forces before winter garrison duty. Only in this case they shifted the forces from Poland to Romania and Hungary without rotating out the existing garrison forces. They still have about one hundred thousand men stacked up in the border region who can redeploy within a week's time."

"They've never done anything like this before," Simpson said.

"Not since Czechoslovakia, sir," the chairman said. "Six divisions in the Serbian side of Yugoslavia including Macedonia and Montenegro, four more in Romania and five in Hungary. These are mostly Class B troops with a few Class A divisions to harden them up."

"What does that mean?" Simpson asked. "Their best and brightest? Is this their Marine Corps or what?" Even now he wasn't above throwing a little flattery the general's way but if the shot landed, it didn't show.

"B Class is the last generation stuff, Mr. President," Barry Gillis, the secretary of defense said, putting on his reading glasses to pursue one of the reports. "Reservists and hand-me downs. Similar to the National Guard."

"The Class As are just that, their A team," General Orville said. "Current generation tanks, younger troops, better officers and training. They keep most of those in East Germany or watching China. We're looking at five divisions of those, the rest are Bs," the chairman concluded.

"Are they gonna follow up?" Simpson asked, "Is this part one?"

"That remains to be seen, sir," General Orville said. "There hasn't been any movement as of yet."

"And any word from Moscow yet?" Simpson addressed the video monitor of the Soviet ambassador.

"Nothing, Mr. President. I haven't asked them of course, but I think they're playing dumb. Since relations froze again in the late eighties, they haven't been very transparent about these things."

"And the Serbs— or Yugoslavs? Whatever it is they call themselves," Simpson asked the other ambassador.

"The official line is that Yugoslavia is being aided by their fraternal Slavic and socialist brothers in the struggle against counter-revolutionaries and reactionaries.'"

"Slavic *and* socialist?" Shilling mused, "Sounds like they're trying to cover all their bases. Yugoslavia has been moving away from socialism since Tito died."

"Any port in a storm," Harrison said.

Simpson looked up to the main monitor as a map of Yugoslavia flashed onto the screen. The separatist republics were marked off by a dotted white line and the Yugoslav-loyal portion shaded red. Orange divisional markers sketched out the Soviet military positions. "So what are they up to? Is this a muscle flex? A saber rattle?"

"It might be a chance to induct Yugoslavia into the Warsaw Pact," Shilling said, "After they lost them and Albania under Kruschev."

"Is Albania next?"

"It doesn't seem so, sir," General Orville said. "They've made no allowances for reserves or movement that way. Logistics doesn't indicate it."

"Albania's president has also gone on record swearing to 'fight to the last' any Soviet or Yugoslav incursion into their territory," Shilling said. "The guy'll do it too. He's been turning the whole country into one big bunker complex for the past twenty years."

"Ivan's crazy," Simpson said, "but he ain't stupid. What's their deal then?"

Gillis spoke, leaning forward on his elbows, "Two possibilities. First, he's propping up Aleksic's government so the rest of his satellite states don't catch a fatal case of nationalism. The second may be that he's trying to free up Serbian troops to move formally into Bosnia and Croatia, maybe even up to Slovenia."

"I could have sworn we got Aleksic to promise *not* to use direct military force here," Simpson said, tone dry.

"We did, sir," Shilling confirmed, her features clouded with disappointment. "This may be a game changer for him. It may not be all bad either. We *have* favored a one state solution in the past, that's why we didn't recognize Slovenia last year and why we've kept talks with Croatia informal."

It was widely accepted wisdom that it was better to make deals with one stable state than a half-dozen unstable ones.

"Sure, but that doesn't cover a resurgent Eastern Bloc," Simpson said. If Yugoslavia went commie—*really* went commie —then he could kiss any easy re-election in November goodbye. "What are our options?"

"Sanctions are on the table," Shilling said. "We could hit the Soviets with limitations on agricultural sales. We can also lean on Europe and Japan to find alternate oil and gas solutions."

Simpson dismissed this out of hand. "We're gonna tank the stocks a couple dozen points because some tinpot dictator brought 'big brother Russia' in to help clean up a mess? Taxpayers aren't gonna buy it. If I can't make Americans stomach that then I sure as heck can't get the Europeans to accept gas price hikes going into winter. The Arab states'll put 'em over a barrel."

"The Soviet Ministry of Agriculture has also reported record grain production since they privatized a lot of their farms during the Andropov reforms. Between that and their deals with the Argentinian government, we don't have a monopoly on their food supply anymore."

"We might have to take this one on the chin, sir,"Gillis said. "Europe will see this as an internal Yugoslav decision and not something we can blame the Soviets for."

It was not the answer Simpson was looking for. A big foreign blow up like this was going to wreck his approval ratings, and with it his chances at a smooth re-election in two months. That was not even mentioning the potential to destabilize the situation in Southern Europe. The Greeks already had to watch the Bulgarian border, now they'd be watching almost twice the frontage, which wasn't even mentioning Italy.

"So why did they only do half? Russians could have walked across the whole country and we couldn't say 'boo.'"

"It could be the result of internal disagreements," the Russian ambassador said. "The current general secretary is seen as a compromise candidate; maybe he couldn't get the political clout together for a full intervention. If they were proud of this choice, they would have shouted it from the mountains, not tried to downplay it."

"It may also be that they are waiting to see how we react, sir," General Orville. "International recognition of the northern republics is shaky at best. Italy has given Slovenia some informal recognition, as has Austria, but the big fish—Croatia and Bosnia —they're terra incognita."

Simpson drummed his fingers on the polished wooden table, his mind racing while he watched images of tanks and troops cycle over the monitors. "In '56," he said, not taking his eyes from the pictures, "Hungary rose up against the Russians. A few weeks around this time of year, I think." Simpson stood and paced closer to the monitors, close enough to see the individual color cells that made up the images on the screen. "Eisenhower didn't do anything then, just let 'em die in the streets. Didn't want to rock the boat." The president looked back at his advisors. "I don't want to go down in history as the guy who fiddled while Yugoslavia burned. Now's our chance to get ahead of this thing. Russians want Serbia? Let 'em have it. I want to send a clear message: 'paws off the rest.'"

"A partition?" the Shilling asked.

"Why not?" Simpson asked, "Good fences make good neighbors. Let the Serbians keep their state and we'll drop a NATO force on the others, make believe that this was the plan all along with the Russians. Joint peacekeeping duty. We save face, we don't back down on this, and we stop all this ethnic cleansing."

"SACEUR won't go for it," the chairman said.

"Who?" Simpson hated all the damn army acronyms.

"Supreme Allied Commander Europe," the chairman explained. "He coordinates all NATO military activity. It's a gray area, Mr. President, and he's committed to frontline security first and foremost."

"Frontline meaning Germany?"

"Yes, sir."

"Aw hell," Simpson said, "so we go in and strap on a few token units ourselves. The Brits'll do it."

"Yes, sir," the Chairman agreed, "I don't doubt that they will. But Italy is in an economic recession and already getting squirrely about their contributions."

Simpson looked at Wanda. "And can we put the screws on Europe? Enough to raise ... *something* to make this thing international?"

Shilling demurred, her lips pursing, "That might be a bit extreme, Mr. President. If we push Italy into this it could cause issues in the long term."

"Well who can we get? Brits and who else?"

"The Low Countries are a safe bet, Belgium and the Netherlands. If we frame it as a humanitarian action we can probably get France to chip in. The West Germans won't blink unless they think the Soviets aren't looking."

"Can't fault 'em there," Simpson said. "Okay, Wanda, Barry can you make it happen?"

The secretaries of state and defense nodded. "We'll get word to the NATO council about our intentions," Gillis said.

"Tell 'em that we're gonna jump with or without them," Simpson said, "They know which side their bread is buttered on, they won't leave us hanging." It was the same kind of seat-of-the-pants diplomacy Simpson was famous for and thus far it had gotten them what they wanted.

"When we do go, what do we have in the area?"

"We can get the Second Marine division into Split in a matter of days. 82nd Airborne likewise. We can support all this with the *Gettysburg* battle group in the Adriatic. Right now they're conducting peacekeeping operations off the coast of Lebanon."

"Get them rolling, General," Simpson said. "I want to take the initiative on this. We'll get NATO at our backs and have Bill Laursen make a statement before the evening news. We pitch this as a multilateral peacekeeping move and not as an escalation and we'll be good."

***

4

The Mediterranean sun beat down on Captain Oleg Yessov mercilessly, warming his skin the second he stepped outside. While the cool and dark of the small command shed by the sub pen was marginal at best, it was a welcome relief from the North African heat. He was lucky; he'd been on station in Libya long enough that his naturally fair skin was tanned a warm shade of bronze. The captain seated his wide-brimmed, peaked cap to provide the protection for his scalp that his short, blond hair did not. A pair of mirrored sunglasses went on next, a necessity here in the blinding sunlight of North Africa. Compared to the icy expanses of Polyarny, it was unbelievably hot here—a fact that his newest inductees were still coming to terms with.

Yessov stopped at the edge of the port facilities and watched his boat—the Kilo-Class diesel electric submarine B-218—where it sat lashed to the pier. The Kilo wasn't quite as prestigious as placement in the vaunted nuclear submarine corps, but Yessov did not mind. For one, a Kilo was a much quieter boat. With no humming coolant system to betray their position, they were as quiet as the turning of a screw when cutting through the ocean. For another, Kilos were primarily coastal defense ships and not sent on the months'-long cruises of the Atlantic and Pacific that were the bane of a sailor's existence. There was also the fact that he had no fear of a deadly radiation leak, the ever-present nightmare that haunted the minds of Soviet nuclear sailors.

The Kilo was an ungainly thing to Yessov. Even as its commanding officer he found it cumbersome and unsightly. It possessed a squared-off sail that seemed to take up fully half of the submarine's deck, and a rounded off tail with no vertical dorsal fin. It was a far cry from the graceful teardrop shape of an

Alfa or Akula-class, but he loved his boat regardless. He loved it in the same way a parent might love an ugly child.

Two metal gangplanks ran to the sub's deck, fore and aft, to permit the loading of provisions. Since no conveyor belts could pass supplies into the narrow confines of the submarine's passageways, all the work was done by hand. Two human chains of sailors were formed along the length of the gangplanks passing crates, cartons, and boxes. Many of these men were fresh conscripts, recently started in their four-year-long service; others were transferred in from service in other Russian ports. They'd been newly deployed to her premier naval fighting force: the submarine arm. It was easy for Yessov to pick these men out from the others by their pink complexion, the result of the Libyan sun's merciless work on their pale skin. The work was hard and sweat ran in thin rivers down their faces. Many of them had stripped down to only their blue and white striped undershirts, the iconic and prestigious *Telnyashka*, while they worked.

Yessov couldn't say he was sorry to be shipping out; Tripoli didn't offer much to a Russian for entertainment. He'd had his fill of strong coffee and, in a land largely devoid of alcohol and easy women, his crew were getting antsy as well. Ahead of him, the harbor was a blue-gray plane under the pitiless gaze of the sun.

From here he could distantly see an oil tanker setting to sea, laden with crude oil intended for refinement in Italy, passing a container ship bringing fresh imports into the city as it left.

"Comrade Captain Yessov," his executive officer said, coming beside him and adjusting his uniform's tunic, doing his best not to sweat. "We have received final confirmation from Moscow. The American carrier *Gettysburg* is bound for the Adriatic."

Gettysburg. It was quite the prize, a symbol of the West's long-reaching military arm. A fleet aircraft carrier like *Gettysburg* was emblematic of the primary focus of decades of Soviet naval training and strategy. It did not take an intelligence expert to put the pieces together: the Americans re-deploy a carrier group and B-218 received orders to depart port at once. While Yessov couldn't open his sealed orders until he was at sea and in the company of his political officer, he was confident of what they would say: *tail the American battlegroup and maintain combat readiness with a focus on the enemy carrier.*

"Thank you, comrade lieutenant," Yessov said, "I would like you to proceed aboard and oversee final preparations for our departure." Truthfully, his XO was a sycophantic, useless dreg and Yessov had no time for his kind. He'd prefer to contemplate the coming mission in silence than have to worry about watching his back for political opportunists.

"Of course, comrade captain." The executive officer saluted and carefully weaved his way along the gangplank back to the sub.

Gettysburg would be a tough nut to crack if it came down to it, and even with the rest of the Mediterranean squadron working toward that one unified goal, it would not be simple. American naval doctrine focused on the carrier, much as Soviet doctrine did. And just as the Soviets aimed to find ways to destroy them, the Americans intended to keep them afloat and functional. Soviet surface warships were equipped with dozens of long range missiles for this purpose. They were intended to be fired en masse and at long range to saturate American missile defenses. That sort of combat was purely a numbers game: whoever shot first generally won. Likewise whoever could put the most "birds" in the air had a better chance of overwhelming their opponent through weight of numbers. In short, it was a competition to be the first with the most.

It was the submarine fleet that was intended to break this mathematical stalemate. Boats like B-218 were able to slip within a carrier's protective cordon, past their anti-missile picket ships and drop a spread of torpedoes on the carrier like a knife in the back. Theoretically.

Army generals dreamed of recreating Cannes, air force commanders dreamed of the Israeli annihilation of the Egyptian air force on the ground in the Six Day War, and Soviet submarine captains dreamed of sinking an American aircraft carrier.

Yessov pulled himself from his fantasy; such a feat was not easy and not likely to occur in any case.

Besides, he had other matters to attend to. He saw a Libyan military delegation, a colonel and a pair of adjutant officers, arriving by jeep at the edge of the sub pen. He crossed quickly to them before they might have a chance to interfere with his sailors.

"Captain Yessov, we were not informed of your departure," one of the junior officers said in thickly-accented Russian, translating for the colonel.

Yessov's own Arabic was so broken it was better left unused. "I have only just found out myself. We are to put to sea at once." He neglected to remind them *again* that he had no obligation to keep them apprised of his plans.

"What is your destination?"

Yessov gave the colonel a tight smile. "I'm afraid I have not yet read my detailed orders. I will discover this at sea."

The Libyan chuckled. "Such is a soldier's life then."

"We all do what we are asked," Yessov replied. The Libyans were allies in everything but name. Supposedly their own brand of Arab Socialism was meant one day to coincide with the Soviet version of Communism. Until then, the Soviet Union equipped their dictator's flagging military, trained his engineers and pilots, bankrolled his economic problems, and fed his vices with gifts of jewels and Cuban cigars. In return the Libyans were meant to offer a friendly shoreline to operate in the Mediterranean.

In practice Yessov found that the Libyans adhered to socialism as closely as the Americans did.

"Your government tells you as little as they tell us." The colonel's grin was meant to color his statement as a joke.

Yessov wasn't laughing.

"I will order my men to provide you with every assistance," the colonel added through his translator.

So they can get their hands on our technological advancements no doubt, Yessov thought. Although Libya was as of yet ill-equipped to construct their own warships, he had no doubts they'd love to try or, at worst, sell the secrets to any nation that would pay. Even setting aside basic operational security and regulations, Yessov would not tell them his mission. Any one of these uncouth mercenaries would sell the secret as easily as they would eat or breathe. "I thank you for your consideration, but my men will be sufficient for this task." Even as he spoke, he saw the final crates come off the waiting trucks and pass down the human chain into the submarine. "I should be aboard. We will depart momentarily."

The colonel didn't hide his indifference. He'd seen his game was useless. "God go with you."

Yessov was unsure if this was an oversight or an intentional slight to his atheist background and so only returned a tight smile before saluting and turning on his heel to return to B-218.

An intensely sunburnt sailor stood guard at the end of the gangplank and saluted Yessov by presenting the AKM carbine he carried, eyes fixed dead ahead and unmistakably terrified. His sailor cap provided precious little protection from the sun.

"If any of those Arab dogs try to come aboard," Yessov said in a low tone, "you are not to allow them under any circumstances. Shoot them if you must. Clear?"

"Yes, comrade captain!"

Yessov nodded with satisfaction and continued on to the sub, passing a saluting petty officer, and descended into the Kilo through a hatch in the main deck. The interior of the submarine was a metal rat's warren with cramped, pipe-lined passages and low bulkheads to duck beneath. Yessov had heard that the Soviet Union's mighty Typhoon-class ballistic missile submarines had gymnasiums, arcades, and even a miniature swimming pool on board. His ship had no such luxuries and every possible area was functional.

Already unglamorous work, a further complication was brought about by B-218's station. The heat and humidity of the North African coast was not accounted for by the designers of this submarine. It was like living in a gym locker room, Yessov mused. The boat's climate control simply could not keep pace with the press and bustle of humanity on board, not least with the sun beating down on them. Things would improve, he knew, once they took her to deeper water and dove.

Moving through the submarine was made easier by the respect that rank brought, seamen and officers scrambled out of the way regardless of what they were doing—but Yessov took the opportunity to ensure the latest class of conscripts was being broken in well. Work was being conducted swiftly and orderly. There was no loitering, no meandering, and no shirking under his watch. These men would bend to the expectations of the Soviet Navy or they would be broken.

Upon reaching the bridge, Yessov let out a breath he'd subconsciously held in the narrower parts of the boat.

Here the bridge crew were undertaking final checks of the Kilo's systems and preparing to ship out.

"Tea, comrade captain?" a yeoman prompted, offering a delicate china cup and saucer. It was entirely too hot in the submarine for tea but Yessov was a man of culture.

"Thank you," he sipped the warm beverage and winced at how little it helped soothe him. He had heard it said that in the American south they commonly drank *iced* tea. The very concept puzzled Yessov, but then again, much of what the West did confused him.

"All sections report ready, comrade captain," the XO said, puffing his chest proudly as if this simple accomplishment left him worthy of the Order of Lenin.

"Very good." Yessov was ready to take her out, but he knew better than to act as lord and master of his ship. In some cases it was proper to show deference. "Comrade commissar, B-218 should—with your permission—take to the seas."

The political officer, a quiet man with sunken eyes nodded approval, not feeding Yessov's penchant for drama. The commissar was a popular man with the men, it would do well to stay in his good graces.

"One third ahead," Yessov instructed. "We'll take her out past the minimum safe diving distance before going down."

"Yes, comrade captain."

Yessov sipped his tea again and imagined he could feel the thrum of the engines despite the sound dampening in place. He'd been a sailor for over a decade and yet every time they took the ship down he had a niggling fear that some careless sailor had left a hatch undogged and the sea might come pouring in. It would only take one time for it to be the last. Still, Yessov resisted his urge to order the hatches checked again, lest the commissar take him for an incompetent or a coward.

As the boat went out and eventually dove, no seawater flooded her compartments, the hatches had—as always—been sealed properly. Another exhale of relief, one carefully hidden from the commissar and crew. Yessov hadn't read the orders yet but was still confident of their contents. He could imagine that *Gettysburg* lay ahead; every turn of the submarine's screws brought him that much closer to it. Maybe this time—of all his many deployments—maybe this time greatness awaited.

***

Captain Don Vance always hated the stifling Floridian summers and so was grateful to see fall approaching in force. The latest weather development was that he could stay in direct sunlight and not immediately begin sweating or feel like his skin was burning off.

It was unbecoming of an officer, he'd been told, to seek out every shady patch he could find during field exercises.

Vance thought it was probably more unbecoming to sweat bullets and pass out, though.

His heart wasn't in it. Even now, in the commander's cupola of an M60A3 "Patton" main battle tank, he was elsewhere. Vance was designing bass riffs and drum loops in his head while his eyes were sweeping the field around him through a pair of binoculars.

The field they were in was one carved straight out of the swampy Floridian wilderness, ringed with pine and moss-covered oak. The open area ahead was a churned morass of sandy earth and scrubby grass. Bravo Company's dozen tanks were holding the firing positions ahead, main guns thumping intermittently to unleash a burning round down range. Bravo was Victor Benyo's unit—Benyo, of course, being the battalion favorite

Vance's view gravitated to Benyo's tank—"Bad Time"—in time to see it fire, the muzzle belching smoke.

The round moved faster than the eye could follow. It was marked only by a briefly glowing tracer that arced out of sight and by the dust impacts on the ground a few hundred yards from the tank where the discarding sabot petals were flung aside.

"Good shooting, Red!" Captain Benyo declared over the open channel. "That's a kill."

Vance sighed and lowered the glasses, squinting up at the sun and wondering how much longer they'd be at this today. Alpha and Bravo companies had both qualified at the gunnery range with no issues so far. Vance's own Charlie company was next. It was Charlie Company officially; unofficially, it was Cutoff Company.

"What the fuck does Cutoff mean?" Vance had overheard a fresh reservist asking one of his NCOs on the first day of the two week field training exercise.

"Charlie is the dividing line between 'pass' and 'fail.' If you do better'n us then you're A-OK. You do worse and you're gonna get your ass reamed by Battalion HQ. You score like we do? You're on the cutoff."

The nickname had bothered Lieutenant Gentry, Vance's First Platoon commander. "You're gonna let 'em call us that to the new guys?"

Vance had grinned, "Dunno, I think it's kinda cool."

Now he lowered himself back inside his command tank and tuned into the company-wide frequency. "Alright guys, we're up next. Let's make those shots count, okay? Uncle Sam doesn't pay us by the hour."

He barely heard the half-hearted replies before he was tuning out, eyes going to the picture of Molly taped onto the side of his radio set. Another shot weekend, one that Vance should have been at home helping her study for her upcoming exam or cleaning up their place, not out here losing his hearing in an old rustbucket.

"Captain," the radio crackled. It was Major Esposito, the battalion commander. "Get your company hot, you're up."

"Set the bar low," someone else said on the radio.

"Clear the channel," Esposito replied sharply.

Vance ignored the jibe and adjusted his own helmet mic, "Charlie Six copies." With a flick of his wrist Vance toggled from battalion net to company net. "All platoons advance to phase line Echo."

His own tank was the last to move and he used this fact to oversee each of his platoons as they advanced. The tanks' diesel engines roared as their treads chewed up the earth. Only once the last tank was rolling did he ensure his own command vehicle was moving. When they broke this exercise he'd have to sit down and write out the set idea that occurred to him. He had a new turntable at home that he'd been experimenting with.

Benyo's tanks fell back in good order, allowing Vance's to pass between the gaps with a minimum of maneuvering. He caught sight of Benyo himself, beaming triumphantly and speaking to someone on his helmet radio. On catching Vance's eye he raised a hand in greeting, a signal Vance returned. "Good hunting!" Benyo shouted.

Vance returned a thumbs up. Music production wasn't his profession actually, just his hobby. Vance made a living as a show promoter and part time DJ when the situation called for it. Weddings, bar mitzvahs, field parties, whatever. He was working on his own album though, nothing fancy, just a few simple tracks and remixes made on school studio equipment in off hours. It was a dream project, something to noodle around with.

His tank reached the pre-prepared firing position, really just a hull-down scrape in the earth with a few half-sincere protective measures scattered around the top, sandbags and splintered logs. From here he had a clear line of sight across the shooting range to the targets, ostensibly Soviet-made T-72 and T-80 main battle tanks, in reality just simple two dimensional pop-up targets like the kind you might find on an infantry firing range but blown up.

Vance sighed again. *Let's get this over with.*

"At this time, First Platoon, load sabot," he said on his mic. "Scan your lanes. Weapons tight."

"Sir!"

The guns began to boom.

***

All things considered, Vance would rather have been back out in the Floridian heat rather than where he was now standing in Major Esposito's office. He was conspicuous of the dirt on his uniform as he stood at attention, not daring to speak while Esposito looked over paper reports of the range test. Vance saw his on top. He was sweating despite the air conditioning running at full blast.

"Vance, how'd you do?"

"We passed, sir."

"Passed," the word was a curse in Esposito's mouth. "Took you guys two tries."

"Yes, sir."

The major looked up at Vance finally and leaned back in his chair, crossing his arms imperiously, a judge deciding a fate. "Captain, why exactly are you here?"

"Sir?" Vance broke his stony facade and looked the major in the eyes.

"In the Army, Vance."

"I ... want to serve my country, sir."

"Don't give me that bullshit," Esposito said. "Name one guy

who is here for his country. Guys are here for the GI Bill, guys are here for a paycheck, for the bragging rights. We *all* believe in the mission, but so does your average Joe on the street, but they won't be out here in the mud bog with us without something tangible."

"I ... I guess I'm here for the money then, sir."

"Right," the Major looked at the report again. "Vance, do you know why *we* are here?"

Vance did not like this game. "Weekend training, sir."

"No, captain. We're here because a great big shit pot is brewing over in Yugoslavia. The commies are getting uppity, and you know what happens when they do that."

"Yes, sir."

"One day, when those paper targets are shooting back, Ivan isn't going to give you and your guys a second chance to qualify."

"Yes, sir."

"You've *got* to come down on your guys, Vance. When the *other* company COs find time to coach your soldiers, it looks bad."

"Permission to speak openly, sir?"

"Go ahead."

"I don't think I understand. My men have always done well enough-"

"Well enough," Esposito said, "doesn't cut it in the field. We're moving into a higher action period and division is looking for heads to crack and knuckles to rap. The battalion is solid, but you're an outlier, Vance. Your men are just barely qualified, the lowest scores in the battalion."

"But not the lowest in the brigade," Vance said.

The Major shook his head, "Vance, I'm *not* going to be the nail that gets hammered because you stuck out. 'Good enough' isn't good enough anymore. I want *best*."

"Yes, sir."

Esposito stared at Vance as if daring him to speak in his own defense. "Tomorrow," he said, "the battalion is doing land nav. We'll be on long range maneuvers, road driving. I'm putting your unit at the head."

Vance's heart sank. If he was at the head of the column it meant he was going to be the one double checking navigation for the battalion so not to get turned around. "Sir."

"I was going to have Benyo do it, but I *know* he can do it. You … we'll see. Anything else, Captain?"

"No, sir."

"Dismissed."

***

We'll see. Vance swore as he drove and clicked the volume on his car stereo up just a couple ticks so the rhythmic pounding bass vibrated his rear view mirror. He'd never excelled, he'd never been a gung-ho type like Benyo, but he'd *always* done the job. Even during the next day's land navigation he'd been haunted by Major Esposito's words. Black marks didn't wash off easily in the Army, and marks like that would hamper any chance he had of moving beyond captain, which he was going to have to do if he ever wanted to make serious money off his time investment.

Truthfully, he needed this extra income if he was going to keep his dream job afloat.

Headlights passed in the dark while he squinted, looking for the trailer he shared with his girlfriend. His company had caught the brunt of it from him though: terse commands, snippy corrections to mistakes, and extra demands on his platoon leaders. A miserable experience made worse when his fears had been realized and his unit had taken a wrong turn. It was only when Bravo Company caught up with them that they realized the error. Benyo had set everything straight, of course. When the company had debriefed with the rest of the battalion, none of his men were speaking to him.

All his problems seemed to evaporate away though when home sweet home fell into his headlights and he pulled off the main road and into the gravel parking pad in front of his house. The problem was not insurmountable; Vance didn't need to break his back. The goal posts had moved was all, he just had to catch up with them and then things could settle down like normal.

The interior of the trailer smelled like cooking meat.

"Hey, love!" Molly called from the living room.

"Hey," Vance dropped his gear by the door with a muffled rattle, stretching his aching back.

"Steak and fries for dinner, your favorite!" Molly burst into the room like a sunrise, beaming and glowing. Her dark, curly hair bounced with each step. She stopped at once on seeing the strained look on his face. "Oh, bad weekend?"

"It was training," Vance replied. "It's always bad."

"Aw, Don." Molly put an arm around him, guiding him into the trailer's small dining area and easing him into a seat. "What happened?"

"Nothing much. My CO thinks I'm a moron and my company hates me."

"You're their boss, love. Aren't they supposed to hate you?"

"That's what NCOs are for," Vance replied.

Laughing, Molly brought over the plates she'd prepared, laying one in front of Vance and sitting beside him.

Vance's frown vanished after a bite of steak. "Wow, babe!"

"Uh huh," Molly said proudly, "I've been studying up. I picked up a cookbook with recipes and seasoning tips and things."

"Well it's working." Vance leaned in to kiss Molly on the cheek before digging into his meal.

After dinner, they retired to the den where Milly put on the news and Vance noodled with his new turntable, mixing records with his headphones so not to disturb her. Without the sound he could still read the storylines on the news. US Airborne land in Zagreb Airport. NATO peacekeepers deploy to Split.

He removed the headphones and looked at Molly.

His girlfriend was transfixed, eyes wide at the sight of soldiers in battle gear marching and armored vehicles deploying in the lush Yugoslav countryside. She looked to him, "Do you think they'll call up the Reserves?"

Vance looked at the news as if evaluating and then put on false bravado. "A little thing like this? Nah. This is the kind of thing we have the Marines for."

"You're sure?"

"Yeah," Vance said as the news switched to cover the latest tax reform bill being pushed through the House and Senate. He picked up the remote control and clicked off the TV. "Come on, let's get to bed. I've got to get up early tomorrow to set up a venue."

***

5

Gradenko was not expecting good news from this week's Politburo meeting; after all, he'd seen the reports of NATO troops in Yugoslavia. French, British, Dutch, and American "Peacekeepers."

The statement from President Simpson had been translated by the Foreign Ministry shortly before he'd made the trip here and it left him hollow. Simpson had called the Soviet maneuvers a "bi-lateral occupation" of the region to "stop the sectarian violence." Gradenko had called Simpson a "cunning bastard" to his deputy ministers. The American businessman was a difficult party to work with. He seemed to have a knack for dealing with the Western news media to spin a situation. What should have been a tough sell to his allies seemed to go through smoothly.

Gradenko dreaded the humiliation the general secretary would face for this botched compromise plan. The Soviet Union's worst fears had been realized and Gradenko had slaved his cause to that of the general secretary. What he found in the meeting chambers was somehow worse.

The committee was just beginning to come together and take their seats, but already Gradenko knew something was wrong. Both Tarasov—looking restrained in his highly decorated military uniform—and Karamazov—in a well-fitted suit—were already present among a handful of other Politburo members. Each was seated silently facing the other. So the KGB and Army were coexisting peacefully. Why did that disturb Gradenko so?

"Good morning, comrades," Gradenko greeted his fellows, pleased not to be late this time as he took his seat.

The meeting room doors were closed by waiting aides after the last members had filed in.

"I believe we should begin with the news of the latest developments from China, Comrade Gradenko," Karamazov said, looking over the agenda for the meeting.

Gradenko felt his pulse quicken. Karamazov was running the meeting and Tarasov was not objecting. Why wasn't—his eyes fixed on the general secretary's empty seat.

"Comrade minister?" Karamazov tried again.

"Should we not wait for Comrade Kavinski?" Gradenko suggested. His voice sounded meek even to himself.

"Ah." Karamazov lowered his paper agenda back to the table. "Comrade Kavinski has fallen ill and has retired to the countryside for his health. Unexpected surgery. The doctors expect a long recovery."

Gradenko willed himself not to look to the only member of the Politburo who might stand in the way of this obvious coup, but he needn't have bothered.

Tarasov was silent and compliant. The only reason that old war horse wouldn't raise a fuss was if he himself was a part of this coup.

And a coup was what it was, there was no doubt about it. Kavinski was—relative to some of his peers—young. He had no outstanding health conditions that would require such a drastic medical step.

"My apologies, comrade," Gradenko said, voice betraying no emotion. He flipped open his own notes and tried not to let his fear show. "The situation in China continues to deteriorate alarmingly. The president's 'Reform and Clarity' program has opened the doors to radical elements in the country and we believe that the military is contemplating a coup."

"A coup?" Karamazov asked, "What reason do we have to suspect this?"

Without the general secretary to stabilize the Politburo, it meant that the KGB and Army, evidently cooperating in his disposal, could run the show as they pleased. It meant the men that opposed them—men like Gradenko—were a liability.

"The Tibetan uprising," Gradenko explained. "Tibet has

declared their independence and we have—as of yet—seen no major military action to return them to the fold. It is the opinion of the Foreign Ministry that China's president does not trust the military in these matters."

"A disloyal military is not automatically evidence of a coup, comrade," Karamazov explained patiently.

Gradenko really wished they'd stop using that word. "Of course, comrade chairman. I merely mean to suggest that it seems the president fears employing them, suggesting disunity in the government."

"This has fit with what we've seen from our agents. Local governments are strengthening their own power as the central government struggles to maintain hold," Karamazov said. As the chairman of the KGB turned his questions relating to trade and industrial production to another Politburo member, Gradenko's heart raced.

If they wanted him dead, then Karamazov's men would have dealt with him when they 'retired' Kavinski. Clearly he was being kept around for something, but what?

"Comrade Tarasov," Karamazov addressed the minister of defense.

"The Chinese military is in a similar state of disarray. Our units on the border have been moved to a higher state of readiness after reports of mass army movement in Manchuria. Recon satellites suggest they are disorganized deserters, but it may be something more."

Karamazov gave a nonchalant reply of agreement before turning his head to Gradenko. "Comrade Gradenko, what is your forecast on the political situation long term?"

Gradenko snapped from his doomsday thoughts. "The nation's radical political and economic reforms, on the heels of stagnation brought on by the 'Cultural Revolution', have left the central government weak. I predict their total collapse within six months to a year. Western forces, the United States, the Nationalist Chinese, and the Japanese will all seek to hasten this collapse and likely wish to see a return to Republican rule."

"An unacceptable situation," another member said.

"Yes, but one which I believe can be staved off for some time. As China falls, we will be there to help rebuild. My recommendation is continued economic and military support to our socialist brothers in the region: Vietnam, Korea, and Mongolia."

"We are all in agreement then on the proposed aid packages?" Karamazov asked. As was tradition, there was no dissension. "The measure is passed."

A nearby clerk silently recorded the result.

***

After the meeting Gradenko held tight to the handle of his briefcase to stop his hands from quaking with fear. He'd long planned for this moment, the moment his government tried to turn on him. He wouldn't go meekly to his death or be transferred into an "early retirement" like Kavinski. No, Gradenko had a country dacha outside of Vyborg near the Finnish border and a set of—up to date—passports for himself, his wife, son, and daughter hidden there. He could cross under darkness and then use a second set of passports to travel to Stockholm, Bern, or even Paris. Wherever he chose.

Gradenko was no traitor. He was a patriot of the truest kind but, more than his country, he respected his own life. If only his driver would bring the car around quicker! The foreign minister checked his watch again. Five minutes standing in the car park was five minutes too long. The Soviet Union had an unemployment rate of zero. Those who had no work could be found a job. Maybe his driver needed a transfer—he was a KGB plant after all.

Gradenko's thoughts were interrupted as the glossy, black Lada rounded the corner, coasting to a stop before him. "Anton," Gradenko opened the door to scold his driver and stopped mid sentence.

"Comrade," Minister Tarasov greeted, sitting peacefully in the back seat. "Come for a ride with me."

Any thoughts in Gradenko's mind of escaping or fighting back were blown away by the mere presence of Tarasov. The old soldier stared fixedly at the rear of the headrest in front of him as they left the security cordon around Red Square.

"Anton, the Foreign Affairs Building, please," Tarasov said, before looking at Gradenko. "I apologize for the subterfuge. I hope that Anton has been a good driver for you. He is a good man."

So Anton wasn't on KGB pay after all.

"Where is the general secretary?" Gradenko said, his mouth forming questions his mind was too terrified to put forward.

"Resting," Tarasov said, lighting a Cuban cigar with a match and cracking the window slightly. "At a dacha near Omsk."

"Omsk," Gradenko said, almost dead center of the Soviet Union.

"It is regrettable. Kavinski was a good man, but he has outlived his usefulness in his role. The Yugoslav Compromise sealed his fate. He will live in obscurity, an early retirement like was done to Kruschev."

"And me?" Gradenko asked.

Tarasov fixed him with a stare, puffing a cloud of aromatic smoke from the cigar. Those azure eyes were cold. "You will live as well, comrade. Mother Russia has use of you yet, as she does us all."

"What is this about?" Gradenko asked, trying to force himself to relax. "Yugoslavia?"

"Yes. In part," Tarasov said, blowing more smoke before coughing softly. "You give the Chinese government six months, yes?"

Gradenko nodded.

"I believe we ourselves will be lucky to have five years."

The admission came as a shock to Gradenko, hard enough that it shook him from his mortal terror. "Five years?"

"Look around, Gradenko," Tarasov gestured to the window, bidding Gradenko to look. "What do you see?" The minister of defense answered before Gradenko could. "McDonalds. Movie theaters. Arcades. Teenagers on motorcycles. Drunks in the gutters. The Soviet Union is cracking, Gradenko, and the West is seeping in."

"This was expected," Gradenko returned, "the Reforms—"

"The Reforms are all that has saved us," Tarasov replied, "But is it not another half-measure? Much like Yugoslavia? We give the West a new market, we take their money, we invite their press, and they corrupt our youth in return. We are rotting, Gradenko. Complacency will destroy us as it did the Chinese."

"China is falling," Gradenko explained, "because they radically liberalized. It could have happened here if we did not draw a hard line in the sand. We take the Wests' money but not their ideology."

"They are one and the same," Tarasov sighed. "General McDonalds has taken Moscow where Hitler and Napoleon have failed. Yes, we drew a line, but at what cost?"

Gradenko remembered the dark, grainy news footage of Soviet tanks firing on unarmed student protests in Poland. He remembered the bleak days of suppression and occupation in the Baltic states. Firelit streets filled with dashing figures and the strobing flash of machine gun fire. Tear gas billowing and monuments to democracy torn down. A line had indeed been drawn, demarking what the new government was willing to tolerate and what it was not.

"One crack in the armor is all it will take to bring the whole system down."

"You mean Yugoslavia," Gradenko said.

Tarasov nodded.

"Then what hope is there? You are saying Marx and Engels—Lenin—they are wrong?"

"The first lesson we learned after the revolution," Tarasov said, "is that we are writing our own rules. Comrade Trotsky discovered this, as did Comrade Khrushchev. Communism is ever evolving, comrade. The goal is always the same, the path different."

Gradenko was too fascinated to be afraid now. "What are you saying?"

"I am saying that things will need to change. Economic reform is necessary. Collectivizing the farms was a mistake—"

The admission was a shock even to Gradenko, who had always known it to be true. Soviet agriculture had languished for decades behind the rest of the world, not that they would admit it. The failure of socialized agriculture was an open secret in the Soviet Union.

"Privatization has helped, as has budgeting for our industrial sectors. We are trying to expand into consumer goods production—to bring the sort of casual luxury expected by a socialist utopia—but it is hard to switch from making steel pipe and cement to circuit boards and denim." Tarasov chuckled, his chest phlegmy, before trailing off into a soft cough. "Karamazov is of the same mind on this matter."

They *were* cooperating.

"You are surprised?" Tarasov asked.

"I ... only thought—"

"That old ghost is a bastard to be sure. I'd as soon trust him as trust a wolf. I don't like him, but we need him."

We.

"A power of two men cannot remain. One will come to dominate the other and neither of us will allow that."

"A troika," Gradenko said. A triumvirate government. The Soviet Union had experienced a number in its time, alliances of convenience that usually ended in one member seizing control over the others, sometimes bloodily. The last time it had happened was after Brezhnev's assasination in 1969. It had ended when Andropov consolidated his control of the Troika and became general secretary. "That is it? I am to be the third?"

Tarasov smiled, "You would complete our party of three. KGB, Defense, Foreign Ministry. The others are complacent enough." The defense minister must have registered Gradenko's confusion. "Comrade Karamazov and I dislike one another, but we can both agree that you are acceptable as a third—despite your attempts to derail our plans."

Gradenko's face flushed with heat. "I was acting in the best interest of the people of the Soviet Union!"

Tarasov laughed deeply again, "Yes, comrade. I am sure you thought so."

"Let us say," Gradenko said, licking his lips and sparing a glance out of the car window at the cityscape crawling by, "that I agree to this. What is your plan?"

"War in Yugoslavia."

"Are you mad?" Gradenko demanded. His own outburst came as a surprise to him, but he let the words come. "War with the West? For what?"

Tarasov's good humor strained and his bloated face reddened. "Don't forget, comrade, that you are speaking to an equal."

Gradenko reminded himself of his own very real mortality; being invited to the Troika was not itself a guarantee of safety. If anything it might only paint a bigger bullseye on his back. "Tell me then what you intend."

"The plan is simple," Tarasov said. "A partition of Yugoslavia cannot happen. We will manufacture an incident and use it as justification to take control of the occupation from NATO. They will be compelled to withdraw." Tarasov puffed on his cigar again before grinding it out on the ashtray mounted to the door. "Our buffer will be secure and our people will be re-invigorated by victory. A swift and bloodless win over our hated enemies. They will see that the West is *not* the future. We will be there to bury them when the time comes."

They were words that had been spoken before. Almost one hundred years ago the Tsar had believed a "short victorious war" might turn the favor of his people.

"You forget the lessons of the past, comrade," Gradenko said. "Your 'little war' may grow larger than you are prepared to deal with."

Tarasov laughed again, "I have stared war in the face, comrade. I have no fear of war. War birthed our nation and war made it strong. Another war may usher us to greatness. If the

West wishes war, let them come."

The boldness of the statement shook Gradenko to his core. Tarasov was out of his mind, and Karamazov *agreed*!?

"Preparations are underway," Tarasov said. "Insurances of our victory. We *will* march on Yugoslavia and we *will* confront the West. I simply ask—" Tarasov fixed Gradenko with that deadly gaze again. "—will you support your comrades?"

Gradenko thought of Switzerland and Sweden. He thought of the Finnish border. All so far away. If what Tarasov said was true, then the actions had already been set in motion, and no one man could stop it. Maybe his place was at the helm of the government, in place to prevent the war from tipping over the abyss into annihilation. Tarasov was right in part. The Soviet Union was born and forged in war. The Great Patriotic War had unified the nation—but it had unified it in suffering. "I will help you," Gradenko said.

"Then all that remains is our brothers in the KGB to create the justification for our intervention."

Tarasov did not yet know that ultimately their meddling wouldn't be needed.

***

6

The Croatian highway the Marine patrol traveled down was virtually deserted. With no vehicle traffic anywhere in sight and open farmland ringed with trees extending almost to the horizon, Lieutenant Williams could imagine that the entire country was deserted. The truth was almost worse somehow. Since the arrival of the multinational NATO peacekeeping force, much of the domestic violence had dialed back to the point of near nonexistence. This peace came at a cost however. Virtually the entire nation was in lock down. People avoided traveling, they avoided anything beyond what was necessary for their survival. It was a country devoid of life.

Williams himself had seen the Serbian militias standing bitterly by, holding their perceived turf until some kind of permanent settlement could be drawn up. So far, at least in Croatia, the Serbs had been smart enough not to challenge NATO directly, while in Bosnia the British Marines and French Foreign Legion had been facing fierce resistance.

Williams unbuckled his chinstrap and removed his helmet, enjoying the cool breeze that ran over the LAV-25 as it moved, its massive wheels rumbling along the pavement. Squinting up at the sun he marveled at how unlike the Mediterranean it felt here. Really, this could be any stretch of land in the Midwest back home. Flat farmland, cornfields, and highways stretching to the horizon.

"Shouldn't take your helmet off, sir," his platoon NCO, Sergeant Washington said, "Not on patrol." Washington hadn't been in a good mood since they'd gotten here.

Williams knew his sergeant had been involved in the punitive action during the Aden Gulf War, but felt the sergeant was being overly cautious. He didn't want to argue with him though. It wouldn't look good to the men to contradict the sergeant. Williams put the helmet back in place and refastened the chinstrap before taking a laminated map from his breast pocket. He held it flat on the vehicle's armored roof as he tried to read it. "Quiet here, so far," he observed, speaking up to be heard over the roar of the engine.

"So far," Washington agreed.

Williams was disappointed. When he'd found out that rather than policing some remote dirt hole he'd be going to Europe to stop a genocidal civil war he'd been apprehensive. Even so, he couldn't help but be exhilarated at the same time. His grandfather had been in much the same situation fifty years prior and had taken a stand that had liberated Europe. Williams didn't see his role as quite so grand, but he was gonna be damned if he watched one Serb or Croat butcher another on his watch.

Williams looked up and to his left—north—squinting. "That treeline," he said, gesturing so his sergeant could see, "that's the Bosut River. It runs west to east just north of Lipovac." He didn't hear Washington respond, but didn't need him to. Lipovac was their destination, another border town on the new frontier that bisected what had been Yugoslavia.

"Yes, sir," Washington agreed.

They'd been in the country a matter of weeks now, just enough to get comfortable, though Williams' battalion had only recently been deployed from the interior near Zagreb to the border out here. It hadn't felt real until the patrol yesterday. That was the first day Williams had seen the enemy.

They were honest to God Soviet troops on patrol—just like he was—on the other side of the border. He'd watched them from a distance. Tracked vehicles and wheeled APCs roving the countryside as they staked out their corner. One of them— probably a lieutenant like him—had been watching him back with a pair of binoculars whose lenses flashed in the sun.

Williams looked behind himself at the rest of his patrol force: two armored fighting vehicles—LAV-25s, and a trio of Humvees sandwiched in between. The center of the trio mounted a bulky TOW missile launcher. If the Russians wanted to cause trouble, he was ready to deal with anything they could throw his way. He ducked back down inside the armored vehicle and picked up the microphone that was patched to the vehicle's own intercom.

"This left, sir?" the driver asked, referring to an approaching turn off.

Williams poked his head up to squint down the upcoming road way. Frowning, he consulted his map. There was meant to be a town beside the road but he saw no sign of it.

"Negative, the next left."

"Yes, sir."

Sergeant Washington looked to Williams. "You sure sir? I thought the turn off was just ahead."

"Positive, sergeant," Williams replied. "These maps are all suspect anyway. We didn't have a lot of lead time to prepare for this operation so we're operating on borrowed intel."

"Yes, sir."

Navigating a strange and semi-hostile country was only the first challenge in a long list that faced the Marines.

The convoy passed through a dense wood that hemmed in all sides of the highway. Williams' men were on high alert, rifles and machine guns trained on the trees around them, ready to light off in the event of an ambush, but none came. Instead they came up to their turn. The path they needed to take was not a designated road but instead it was a steep, grassy slope that led up to a highway overpass.

The vehicles each took it in sequence, one by one. Williams and his men clung tight to anything they could as the APC pitched backward and ground up the incline.

When the rear LAV finished the climb, the grassy slope was a bare dirt patch, churned up by off road tires.

"There she is, sir," the sergeant said. Lipovac was like most of the towns they'd seen, colorful and condensed without the kind of suburban sprawl Williams was used to back home in the States.

"Take us in," Williams said on the intercom before clicking the radio to the group channel. "Watch spacing. We're in the Wild West now, boys."

The column slowed and the distance between vehicles increased. The gunners of the Humvees kept their eyes peeled while the LAVs' turrets rotated to each cover one flank of the convoy.

The town's streets were lined with parked, Eastern European compact cars in need of a fresh coat of paint. Like most other towns in the region this one was centered on a pastel-colored Orthodox church with the traditional "onion-bulb" steeple.

The people here mostly watched openly, standing along the side of the road or leaning out of windows. At first, Williams had been amazed by the apparent lack of fear the locals displayed, but soon learned that they were simply used to these sorts of things and would passively welcome anything that wasn't there to kill them. In fact—he thought—they should actually be happy to see US Marines. They were safe as long as he was on the job.

Still, the town looked smaller than he'd expected from the map. Williams peered down at the small black squares on the laminate sheet to try and determine where exactly they were.

As he searched, the convoy rolled to a halt by the church and disgorged a few marines to secure the area on foot.

"Get the men deployed, sergeant," Williams said, looking up from the map which he tucked carefully back in his breast pocket. "We'll make a show of force here before we move on. Get one of the LAV's on the road north and one looking east—" the two most likely avenues of approach. "I want the TOW Humvee here in town to shift either way, the other two can cover ..." Williams looked around, still trying to get his bearings, "One south and one by the highway."

"Yes, sir." His sergeant hopped off the LAV and marshaled out its squad of soldiers, ushering them to the points Williams laid out.

The lieutenant likewise dismounted and watched the LAV rev its engine up and roll out to the north. He saw that a small crowd of puzzled civilians was gathering before the church, watching the marines hustle about. The crowd was mostly women, children, and the elderly. Civil war seemed to suck up young men wherever it went. Whether they were dead, hiding, or off fighting, Williams couldn't be sure.

Williams adjusted the sling on his rifle, making sure it was still there and strolled toward the people, giving them a broken greeting in Croatian—"*Zdravo!*" He'd studied up on this region and knew that it was predominantly Croatian, the border delineating where it became primarily Serbian to the east. Conveniently the languages were similar to the point of being nearly identical from what Williams could tell, meaning that he only had to really learn "Hello" and "throw down your weapons!" in one language.

A handful of broken greetings met him from the group and he smiled warmly, surveying them. They seemed amused by his presence and demeanor. His eye caught a young boy and girl in the group, both holding onto their mother.

"Ah!" Williams said, like a brilliant idea appeared to him. He unclasped a pocket flap and produced a chocolate bar which he waved at them, the international signal for "treats."

With some reluctance, their mother walked with them closer to Williams who had unwrapped the bar with care.

"Here," he said, breaking it in half to offer half to each of them, "chocolate."

"*Čokolada!*" their mother explained to them, forcing herself to sound cheery. "Mmm!"

The children each took a bite and their apprehension melted like the chocolate in their mouths. Soon both were returning toothy smiles from chocolate smeared faces as they ate.

Their mother said something to Williams that sounded like thanks.

"No problem, ma'am," he said, waving and backing away, still smiling when he saw the runner approaching.

The marine courier did not look happy at all. "Sir! Sergeant Washington wants you at the north post ASAP!"

Williams' own grin evaporated. "Let's go."

The trip by Humvee took less than a minute. The ill-maintained country road threw up a plume of dust behind them that was likely visible from miles away.

Though he could hear the river nearby, Williams wasn't able to see it and so the rush of water was simply distant white nose.

The LAV was nestled in a small nook by a hedgerow It's barrel poked through the shrubbery to the north, pointing across a series of cornfields that ran along the edge of the road.

"How long have they been sitting there?" Williams asked. He tried to get a better look at the row of pickup trucks lined up along the road about a kilometer and a half away. He stood on tip toes beside the LAV and squinted north.

"They stopped when they spotted us pulling in, sir," Sergeant Pulaski, the LAV's commander said, leaning out of the hatch to make himself heard..

The pickups were civilian models but had been crudely painted with camo paint and carried machine guns on pintle mounts welded to their roofs. Technicals, civilian militia.

"Serbians?"

"Can't tell, sir," Sergeant Washington said, likewise observing the men.

"Not supposed to be any Croatian army forces operating around here," Williams said.

"Should we send a messenger?" Washington asked.

"You speak, Serb, Sergeant?"

The sergeant smiled humorlessly, "No, sir."

"I don't like them watching us like that," Williams said.

"I can drop a few dozen rounds over their heads," Sergeant Pulaski said coolly, "or on them."

"Hold fire," Williams said, "I'm not going to start icing people for looking at us funny. We'll just play it cool." He looked around until he caught sight of the nearby radio operator. "Get Second Squad back up this way. I want some firing positions along this whole row." Williams gestured to the hedgerow that ran perpendicular to the main road for at least another kilometer.

"Just extend the line enough that we'll know if they try to come this way."

"Expecting trouble, sir?" a corporal asked.

"Always."

A short radio call back to battalion HQ confirmed no friendly militias were operating in the area. They also confirmed Williams' standing order not to start a fight. Concluding the call, he'd been promised backup in the form of a British infantry platoon in about an hour, as well as alert air assets from *Gettysburg*.

As it was, the apparent Serbian militia did nothing but sit and watch the Americans watch them.

"They're over the border, sir, aren't they?" Washington asked.

"They sure are, sergeant." The militia was indeed on the wrong side of the river. "But they don't look like Yugoslav Army so who knows where they belong." Williams had taken to crouching in a half-concealed fighting position in the hedgerow, close enough that he could make it to the LAV in a few seconds in a dash. To his right, 2nd Squad extended along the hedge. A man occupied a makeshift fighting position every fifteen meters.

Williams' sergeant shared his lieutenant's fighting position for the time being, periodically making the rounds to check the deployed troops. "We might want to get you back to that farmhouse, sir," Washington indicated a nearby structure, "Something more secure so we can plan our next moves."

"I'll stay here," Williams said, "Gives me front row seats." Williams couldn't stomach the idea of missing something. If lead was going to start flying, he had to be there.

"Movement! Movement, sir!" the commander of the LAV shouted, standing excitedly so he was halfway out of the top hatch.

Williams started and his men hunkered in more, readying weapons.

"Check the squad!" Williams slapped the sergeant's back as the NCO ran off to see to the men. Williams himself raised his field glasses and sighted the Serbian column. There was indeed movement, fresh arrivals of heavy vehicles. Wheeled Soviet APCs.

Williams' heart was hammering as he watched the 8x8 vehicles rumble into sight, belching exhaust, before spacing out and proceeding down the road. Each was laden with Soviet troops, riding on the outside of the vehicles as their grandfathers did in the Second World War.

"Ah, shit," Williams said, "Here they come." He looked around and spotted the radioman hunkering nearby before frantically waving him over, not wanting to take his eyes from the enemy.

The radioman reached Williams and crouched in the sparse cover of the hedge beside his Lieutenant.

"Get me the platoon net." Williams picked the phone off the receiver and the radioman patched the channel.

"Deadly Two this is Deadly Two-Six," Williams said, addressing the platoon. "We have unidentified infantry and APCs approaching our position. Deadly Two-Two is holding the line, Deadly Two-Three hustle up here with Ajax Three—" the anti-tank Humvee. "All units on alert." As he instructed the radioman to dial into the LAV. Williams noted that he didn't feel fear, just a sort of calm drive.

"Sergeant," he addressed the LAV commander, "what do you see?"

"They're definitely Soviets," Pulaski replied. "I can practically see the red banners from here. BTR-80 carriers and those Serbian technicals."

"AT weapons?"

"Just whatever those infantry are packing."

Williams swore again.

"Sir, I have 'em dead to rights. We can plaster 'em on this road."

"Negative, hold fire," Williams said.

"Sir, there's at least two platoons of guys coming this way," Pulaski said, more insistently.

"You're to hold fire." Williams wished more than anything that he could get a signal to the Russians, tell them to turn back or else.

"They're not stopping, sir. How long am I holding fire?" Pulaski pressed.

Williams bit his lip and looked up, eyeballing the distance between him and the advancing exhaust cloud. "Five hundred yards, when they cross that second hedgerow."

"That's real close, sir. Point blank."

"Five hundred yards," Williams repeated, unyielding, before dialing into battalion HQ.

"Deadly Two-Six actual, we've got Soviet infantry approaching my position, less than one thousand yards now, requesting orders."

The reply took a moment as unseen panic occurred at HQ. "Deadly Two-Six, this is Deadly Six actual. Can you confirm Soviet infantry?"

"That's a big affirmative sir, BTR-80s and infantry. It's them."

"Over the border?"

"They're on our side of the river, sir. No other possibility."

"Deadly Two-Six, you are authorized to defend yourself and position. Weapons hold, how copy, over."

Williams grimaced. Weapons hold: fire only when fired upon. "Solid copy, Deadly Six." He glanced up at the Soviets again, they were barely visible this far away.

"Sir," the radioman cut in, "Sergeant Pulaski—"

"Deadly Two Six out," Williams gestured to be connected to Sergeant Pulaski in the LAV.

"Soviets dismounting, sir. They're spreading out. Just under seven hundred yards."

"We are weapons hold," Williams said. "We fire when fired on," he released the transmit button before adding a "Goddammit."

The Soviets advanced in a loose line, their BTRs fanning out to shadow the infantry squads. Individual figures dashed across the open fields between parallel hedgerows, moving closer to Williams and his men.

The roar of a Humvee engine drew Williams' attention. Turning, he saw Ajax-3 arriving on the scene with the Marines of Third Squad. They deployed from the Humvee to rush to join

Second Squad in their positions.

A burst of gunfire cut the air, tracer rounds flashing overhead.

Williams turned, dumbfounded, toward the Soviets and saw the BTR fire again, stitching bullets over the heads of his unit. "Shit!" he scooped up the radio handset again for the LAV. "Sergeant Pulaski," he said, feeling the weight of the words, "permission granted. Weapons free, open fire."

Pulaski wasted no time. Within a heartbeat the LAV was rocking back on its suspension as it belted out rounds from its autocannon with a dull "chuff-chuff-chuff" sound.

Twenty-five millimeter projectiles arced out and danced across the lead BTR. The shells punched through the Soviet APC's light armor with ease, detonating inside and around it with flat bangs that echoed across the farmland.

Now the roar of small arms fire joined the booming autocannon as the Marines delivered precision rifle and machine gun fire on the advancing Soviets, dropping a dozen soldiers in mid stride and sending the others diving to the ground. Tracer rounds swept across the Serbian technicals, one of which burst into flames.

Return fire was swift but inaccurate. The telltale rattle of Kalashnikov rifles was unmistakable. The Soviet infantry spread out, trying to get a cohesive fighting line together in the face of overwhelming American fire superiority.

Williams tried to pay attention to all aspects of the unfolding battle at once but found himself stretched thin. The LAV had held them in place for now and the infantry attack was breaking up, but he caught sight of more dust in the distance. North. It seemed more Soviet reinforcements were likely.

"Deadly Six, this is Deadly Two-Six. We are under attack, I repeat, under attack. Taking fire from Soviet infantry advancing on Lipovac. We're holding for now, requesting urgent fire support, over."

"Affirmative, Deadly Two-Six, the British are on the way, hang tight. I'm detailing a pair of Hornets from *Gettysburg* to your position, ETA fifteen minutes, copy?"

"Copy!" Williams shouted, pressing the earpiece tight to be heard over the gunfire around him. "Have those flyboys hustle!"

***

Two hundred miles southwest, the Antietam-class aircraft carrier *Gettysburg* turned into the wind and accelerated to launch speed. Steam-hydraulic catapults fired, hurling a pair of F-18 Hornets into the sky, laden with bombs for ground attack. The slate-gray fighters circled *Gettysburg* once before banking sharply northeast and engaging their afterburners.

***

The intervening fifteen minutes felt like hours to Williams. He struggled to replace the magazine in his rifle while a corpsman treated a shrapnel wound on a wailing Marine nearby. Williams could handle the whizz and snap of bullets and the shriek of mortars, but it was the screaming of the wounded that really got to him. Throughout it all the LAV's autocannon laid down a devastating barrage on the advancing Soviet infantry. Spent shell cases the length of William's hand were strewn across the grass around it, with more coming all the time.

The AT rocket that destroyed the LAV moved faster than Williams' eye could follow. One moment the wheeled fighting vehicle was dealing death, the next it was a flaming husk. Its remaining ammo stores cooked off with a sound eerily similar to firecrackers. Williams felt the concussion of the blast in his chest hard enough to catch his breath.

Recalling that Sergeant Pulaski had been in that LAV, Williams found renewed vigor. He slapped his rifle's magazine home and propped himself up in his fighting position, looking for more targets.

A trio of drab figures rose up and moved across the smoke-shrouded field a few hundred yards away.

Williams lined them up in his sights and fired two bursts, unsure if it did any more than keep their heads down.

"Sir!" Sergeant Washington scrambled up beside him, "LAV's down. We oughta bring up the second one."

"We can't," Williams said, shouting through his own deafness. "Soviets will plaster it with those AT missiles. We need it on the flank!"

The sergeant nodded, "Then we should fall back, sir! They're zeroing that mortar and the Brits aren't here."

Williams checked his watch, wiping a streak of dirt from the glass face, "Air assets will be here soon!" He thought of the children in the town and wondered what the Serbian militia might do to them if left undefended. "They got my blood up, we're not giving up this town!"

Despite his bravado, the position was coming apart. Weapons fell silent as their operators were overwhelmed by the weight of the attack. It looked like a full Soviet motor rifle company deploying in the fields to the north. Williams could just barely see the low, boxy-shapes of BMP tracked fighting vehicles inching across the cropland, itching to bring their own autocannons to bear.

"Lieutenant!" The radioman handed Williams the headset.

The lieutenant pressed the plastic receiver against his ear hard enough that it hurt, ensuring the volume was at max, and struggled to listen through ringing ears.

"Deadly Two-Six, air assets are in the area, callsign 'Sawhorse.' They're carrying rockeye cluster bombs. We need you to guide them in."

"Right!" With Sergeant Washington's help Williams produced his map as the pilots were patched into his channel.

"We're two minutes out, Lieutenant. Mark your position with smoke and let us know what to hit."

Williams signaled his men to pop smoke and waited to ensure the green clouds were billowing high enough to be seen from the ground. "We're grid reference 57-24!" he shouted. "Our lines run along a hedgeline south of the river, north of the town. Enemy is advancing in the open parallel to the river. I need you to flatten everything north of the smoke. A-fucking-SAP!"

"Copy, Deadly Two-Six, standby one."

Williams braced himself for the deafening scream of jet engines tearing overhead but nothing came. Instead the rattle of gunfire droned on and a nearby mortar burst cut short a despondent wailing.

The radio fuzzed in his ear. "Deadly Two-Six, confirm that smoke has been deployed at your location."

"Fuck!" Williams swore and looked left and right to visually re-confirmed the nebulous green smoke clouds at either end of his line before toggling the radio again, "Confirm! We have popped green smoke—repeat—*green* smoke! We're north of Lipovac!"

Ajax Three unleashed a TOW missile to the north moments before it was chewed up by autocannon fire. Its windows exploded outward, the crew dying in an instant.

"Deadly Two-Six," Sawhorse said, "we have no visual of green smoke, we don't see any activity at Lipovac, over. Confirm your location."

Williams felt his heart sink amid the pressing certainty that something was very, *very* wrong. He looked at the map again, scrutinizing the area around Lipovac, the fields to the north. Something was wrong. The map only showed a half kilometer between town and river to the north, while here there was definitely a two kilometer stretch that ran alongside a bend in the river. So this town *couldn't* be Lipovac. Williams broadened his search, looking for other towns nearby, somehow he'd ended up—

Williams felt nauseous. It couldn't be right. It wasn't possible. The town he was at was four kilometers further east on the highway. Just a few kilometers past the turn he'd missed. Two full kilometers over the Serbian-Croatian frontier.

"Deadly Two-Six, this is Sawhorse, we can't loiter too long, please confirm your position, over."

"Sawhorse, proceed four kilometers east," Williams said, knowing this couldn't be real. He couldn't have made a mistake like this. "North of Batrovci."

"Deadly, that's Serbian airspace, that's over the demarcation line. Can you confirm?"

The chaos of combat raged around Williams. Everywhere was the sound of men fighting and dying desperately trying to defend a town that wasn't theirs. Fighting to defend it against men trying to clear them back over the border the Americans had violated.

"Confirm, Sawhorse."

***

7

It was a nightmare—one that Simpson couldn't wake from. As usual, the news cycle dominated the events of the day and the headlines were not flattering.

Skirmish at Batrovci! Sixteen marines killed, twenty wounded in a pitched firefight in Serbia.

Simpson banished the paper to the far corner of the Oval Office desk, as if that would rid it from his life.

The cover picture showed the burned out husk of a marine combat vehicle wedged into the charred foliage of a hedgerow.

The door to the office opened and his secretary stuck her head in, "Walt's waiting to see you, sir."

"Send him in," Simpson said, careful not to let his temper loose on her.

Simpson's chief of staff entered a moment later, looking as unhappy as Simpson felt.

"What in the hell was this Williams guy thinking!?" Simpson demanded, jabbing at the paper on his desk.

"In debriefing he reported a navigational error, sir."

"Navigational my ass! We gave some boys some shiny toys and told 'em they were cowboys, so naturally he saw the Reds as the goddam Indians."

The door opened again and admitted Bill Laursen, the White House press secretary.

"Bill!" Simpson said, "How are we gonna ride this bull?"

"We're calling a press conference at eleven. We're labeling this a tragic accident and saying the Soviets reacted aggressively to a navigational error."

"No one'll buy that," Simpson said heavily. "Have you seen what the Soviets are saying?"

Laursen was taken aback. "No, sir."

"'Imperialist aggression.' They are calling for NATO forces to withdraw to permit unilateral occupation to avoid another incident."

"Christ," Laursen said.

"I want you to try to hold this thing down, but it's gonna blow up. What are we doing about Williams?"

"He's looking at a court martial," Harrison said. "Drum him out of the service and make an example of him."

Simpson shook his head, tapping his fingers on the polished surface of the desk. "Naw. Can't do that, makes us look like the bad guys. I don't care how much this buckaroo screwed up, we blame him and we look like a buncha clowns. We should say he responded reasonably when fired on by the Russians. Anything else admits blame. I'd like to run this clown through the ringer myself but we gotta keep appearances up."

Laursen hesitated. "Mr. President, we can't do *nothing*, sir. People are worried about another Vietnam. They don't want to get dragged into something."

"But we back down," Simpson said, "and walk away from this thing and the Soviets spend the next fifty years reminding the world of the time they sent us packing, not to mention we'd lose Yugoslavia to the Russian bloc."

"Rick," Harrison said, "they're talking about unifying the country. If we stay we're going to be risking conflict."

"Hell, Walt, we *got* conflict! Boys are dead over there."

"You know what I mean."

Silence lapsed in the oval office as Simpson considered his options. He was used to making tough calls. One of the first things he'd done upon becoming CEO of Texas Air was to lay off five thousand under-performing employees. It was a move the media tried to crucify him for at the time, but a decision he stuck with all the same. It gave the company enough liquid capital to acquire some other struggling regional airlines and expand operations. That choice let him hire on ten thousand new employees over the next few years. In Simpson's world sacrifices were sometimes necessary to move things forward. Being president was no different. There were no "right" answers, some were just better than others.

"It's the same old game," Simpson said, "They got that rumpled suit in charge—Kavinski. He won't say 'boo' without doing the cost-benefit analysis first. Truth is, Yugoslavia ain't worth dying over. They'll rattle the saber at us and call us names, we'll knuckle down and tell 'em we're not giving up, and things'll blow over. No, Kavinski isn't a fighting man." Simpson was confident in his read on the Soviet general secretary.

Harrison and Laursen nodded. "What's the call then, sir?" His chief of staff asked.

Simpson cleared his throat, "Tell the folks at home this was an accident, blame high tensions and Cold War rhetoric—not people. Tell the Russians they have our answer."

***

"America will not bow," Gradenko sighed, laying down the diplomatic letter from the American embassy. While his own office was quiet save the hum of a fan, the "bull pit" of desks just beyond his door in the Foreign Ministry building was alive with activity, the sound of keyboards clacking and papers shuffling as aides and deputy ministers bustled about, scrambling to contain the fallout of the American declaration.

The minister stood, his chair squeaking on the yellowed linoleum floor. He paced to the windows at the rear of his office, passing bookshelves laden with literature from the world over. Gradenko had always believed that if you understood a culture's stories then you understood that culture.

There was precious little fiction from the United States here. All of their heroes—it seemed to Gradenko—resided on the silver screen, recorded on celluloid. They were cowboys and soldiers: men who shot from the hip and asked questions only after the gun smoke had drifted away.

The view from his office looked out to the east toward the

city center. From the Stalinist-era highrise he occupied he saw the white stone facade of the Cathedral of Christ the Savior shining orange in the fading daylight. The church's golden domes glinted red. The church, an artifact of the city's distant Tsarist past, was sandwiched between the shimmering blue of the Moskva River and the barely visible green path of Gogolevsky Boulevard. Gradenko had walked with his children along that very path when they were young, smiling as they ran and played in the dappled sunlight that filtered through the trees.

President Simpson had—through an official press release—called the violation of the border a "tragic accident" and laid the blame on "the epidemic paranoia and mistrust of the Cold War." Paranoia would not pay the pensions of the Soviet soldiers killed and maimed in that battle. The Soviet declaration of Yugoslav integrity had been all but ignored. It seemed the Americans and their allies would only respect force.

There was some good news, however. The Soviet embassy in Rome had reported the Italian government was backing away from any involvement with the Yugoslav intervention, declaring it to be "ill-conceived and misguided." With Italy out of it and Austria maintaining its official neutrality, it meant Yugoslavia was virtually entirely isolated from the rest of NATO, an advantageous military situation—one that Gradenko aimed to make a political victory as well.

Back at his desk, Gradenko picked up the receiver of his phone and dialed his deputy minister of Balkan affairs. "Gregor, it's Andrei. We will proceed with diplomatic cables to the governments of Greece, Albania, and Italy, informing them that we will respect their territorial integrity including airspace and water. Inform them of our intention to wage war on hostile—do not use the term 'NATO or Western'—*hostile* shipping in the Adriatic sea up to the Straits of Otranto. A combat zone like existed around the Falklands, understand?"

"Yes, comrade."

"Please work quickly. I must call a compatriot in the Politburo now." Gradenko hung up and dialed again, punching in the secure code for Chairman Karamazov's direct line. Ironically, Gradenko knew that his office was likely bugged and so a direct phone call felt like a mere formality.

"Comrade Karamazov," Gradenko began, "the Americans are not going to fold without pressure."

"Yes, I saw the reports. Your suggestion, Comrade Gradenko?"

Could it be possible that if Gradenko advised *against* military action that he could stop all this? He was one third of the primary decision making of the entirety of the Soviet Union now after all, a fact that was only now beginning to register to him. He'd always had a high degree of freedom for diplomatic action under Kavinski, but with the formation of the Troika it was clear to him exactly how little oversight he had. No one save Tarasov or Karamazov would challenge him, but on the other hand, another act of rebellion to the other two members of the Troika might finally culminate in his disposal. There was always the Finnish border...

"Blue Masquerade should be put into full effect," Gradenko said, purging his voice of emotion. "I have given our comrades in the military a perfect stage for this. We can declare our intention to fight a war limited to Yugoslavia and avoid unleashing Armageddon."

"You believe this will prevent the war from spreading?"

Gradenko would not let Karamazov put this choice squarely on his shoulders. Instead he quoted Machiavelli: "'Wars begin when you will, but they do not end when you please'. You can have this war but I cannot promise anything outside of that."

The KGB chairman made no reply for a moment. "We will execute the plan. The Western powers will be given twenty-four hours to withdraw. Please release this statement."

"Yes," Gradenko said, wondering how many would die by his lack of resistance.

"I will inform Comrade Tarasov to make the necessary preparations."

***

The mechanical efficiency of an army on the move never ceased to amaze Major General Pyotr Strelnikov. What had been nothing but a rye field to the east of the train depot at Nagykanizsa, Hungary had been utterly transformed with the relentless work of the Soviet engineering corps and labor battalions. The crops had been plowed under and the ground packed flat. Neat rows of tents and makeshift motor pools had been set up with row upon row of idling combat vehicles. The smell of diesel exhaust was thick in the air despite the constant breeze.

Currently, General Strelnikov rode in the back seat of a UAZ 4x4 moving north through the makeshift camp and closer to the city of Nagykanizsa itself, in the direction of Lieutenant General Gurov's headquarters. He tried to read the expression of the private who drove the truck, trying to gauge his emotions. Soldiers, Strelnikov knew, were complex creatures, not mere machines like their weapons or vehicles. They were much more difficult to maintain, their needs more complicated.

Napoleon had said that an army marches on its stomach, but Strelnikov knew they fought with their hearts.

In Iraq he'd seen well-trained, well-equipped armored divisions panic and crumble when confronted with fanatical Iranian teenagers armed with nothing more than Kalashnikov rifles and faith. The Iraqis didn't have their heart in the fight. Did his men?

The 121st Motorized Rifle Division was in a sorry state of readiness by Strelnikov's estimation. One of his regiments had only recently been fully supplied with the new BTR-80s and his mechanized regiment still had a few older BMP-1s in use. He had those units currently conducting maneuvers to the west of the city, crushing Hungarian wheat beneath their treads and tires much to the consternation of the local farmers.

War was a beast, Strelnikov mused, one that fed on men and crops alike. Rommel had said that sweat saves blood and Strelnikov intended to save as much of his men's blood as he could. As members of the 10th Army, they'd been tasked with deploying at staging grounds along the Hungarian-Yugoslav border in preparation for an anticipated intervention in Yugoslavia.

No official word had been given, but ammunition and fuel allowances for training had been dramatically increased and all furloughs had been cut short. That was as clear a sign as there would be.

The men in his division were woefully unprepared. This was despite the best efforts of Strelnikov and his subordinate commanders. In part, he blamed the Soviet military system itself. Military service was compulsory in the Soviet Union. It was something to be endured, suffered through, and put behind you as quickly as possible. Men did the least possible and shirked duty when they were able. It was only through harsh punishments and the threat of firing squad that the whole thing was bound together.

Strelnikov had been a soldier a long time. He had seen the best and the worst it had to offer. He had been there when the Soviet warmachine crushed the Warsaw protests beneath metal treads and boot heels. He knew that the Army—like the nation and system it upheld—was deeply flawed and imperfect. Were he in charge things might be different, but wishes and hopes and dreams only carried so far in the face of reality. The reality was that he was merely a lowly divisional commander and the weight of duty trumped any idealist fantasy.

Movement in the sky to the west caught his eye. Strelnikov saw a trio of dark specks fluttering just above the horizon, lumpy attack helicopters laden with anti-tank missiles thundering along and practicing attack runs. It was likely Gurov's aviation battalion, preparing for the sort of rapid hit and fade thrusts at which helicopters excelled. Strelnikov was taken from his thoughts as the UAZ bounced through an unfilled pothole in the makeshift road, lurching him in his seat.

"In one piece, if you please, private!" Colonel Mishkin snapped at the hapless driver.

"Yes, comrade colonel!" the driver replied.

Strelnikov's chief of staff had been irritable since their division had been transferred south from Poland and into Hungary, leaving behind a fairly tense occupation mission for an even more tense potential active combat situation. It could not be helped; Mishkin was a natural worrier which was what made him an excellent chief of staff—one that Strelnikov wouldn't trade for another tank battalion.

"The 322nd Motor Rifle Regiment has finished practicing with their new anti-tank missiles?" Strelnikov asked, knowing the answer but wanting to distract his subordinate from his own mind.

"Yes, comrade general. Their performance was adequate."

"Only adequate?" The Soviet Army in peacetime had a tendency to overstate its own effectiveness, a consequence of a military culture that demanded perfection even as the ingredients provided were less than satisfactory.

"Yes, comrade general. The men still engage their targets at maximum range. We've been trying to instill in them the virtue of patience. The closer their target gets, the less time it has to respond."

"Years of occupation duty have dulled them," Strelnikov said, though this could be true of the Soviet Army as a whole. "Policing counter-revolutionaries in Poland is quite different from fighting NATO armored divisions."

"Yes, comrade general."

"War is a harsh teacher," he continued, "I expect that the lessons we drill into them will be applied when the time comes."

"Of course, comrade general. " Here, Mishkin hesitated a moment, "Do you think that we will be fighting the West in Yugoslavia then?"

Strelnikov smiled to himself. There was not much point to an army if it was not used. "I suspect we will soon see."

The UAZ reached the small parking area before Gurov's makeshift command post, currently just a plain prefabricated shelter with a radio communications suite deployed within it.

As they entered, Strelnikov took note of the anti-aircraft gun batteries and missile platforms scattered around. The rotating radar dish of the SAM's targeting radar was particularly conspicuous. Such rough preparations would make do for now but would likely prove inadequate against NATO's vaunted airpower. On the battlefield the general expected that the true threat would come not from the ground before them, but from the skies above them.

Inside the command post, an imposing sergeant checked their identification papers and waved them through into a darkened meeting area, cleared save for a large map of their focus of operations spread over the table. At the head of the table was Lieutenant General Gurov, who nodded to Strelnikov at his entrance. Gurov was short—nearly a head shorter than Strelnikov—and where Strelnkiov was gaunt, he was round. A soft chin and ruddy cheeks belied hard, steely eyes.

"Comrade Strelnikov, welcome."

The other division commanders from the 10th Army were present save for one.

"We await Comrade Dmitriyev," Gurov explained.

"No need to wait any further," Dmitriyev said, blustering into the room and removing his cap. "I apologize for my lateness, comrades. Gunnery practice ran long and I lost track of the time."

Major General Dmitriyev of the 111th Motor Rifle Division was—like many here—a man with some political connections. His father was a prominent party member in Minsk which afforded him some leeway in placing his son into a high-ranking army position. Unfortunately for him, his son's own playboy persona grated many of his more traditionally-minded counterparts. The result was that, rather than looking dashing in the cupola of a factory-fresh T-80 battle tank in the illustrious Tank Guards, he was confined to a non-descript motor rifle division.

From the look Gurov gave Dmitriyev, Strelnikov imagined that the old man was longing for the days when insufficient officers could be killed on a whim. "I should like to begin then. Time is short," Gurov said, turning to the map. "Operation Blue Masquerade is to commence in less than twenty-four hours."

The mood in the map room couldn't be called shock—no, everyone here was smart enough to see this coming. It was more akin to realizing that a terminally ill loved one was finally going to pass: Inevitable and terrifying.

"This news will be disseminated by the party to your political officers who will inform the men. We will be avenging the debacle at Batrovci and driving all the remaining hostile powers from Yugoslavia, restoring the sovereignty of our socialist brothers."

Strelnikov recalled that it was only a few years prior when the Yugoslavians were dangerous counter-revolutionaries rather than socialist brothers. He didn't like to involve himself in the machinations of the party, but at times he found it impossible not to reflect on the bold-faced hypocrisy.

"The 10th Army will advance southwest to the border and cross it at 0400 hours," Gurov said, not giving himself any further preamble or allowing his officers to dwell on it any further. "Spetznatz commandos will secure the bridge crossings over the Mur with support from our airmobile battalion. Here, the 105th Motor Rifle Division will punch through the enemy lines with the support of army artillery assets and airstrikes to set the enemy running." Gurov struck the map with a finger like a fire support mission from god. "Thirty kilometers to cover against stiff NATO resistance," Gurov explained, eyeing the commander of the 105th. The city of Čakovec must also be secured."

Strelnikov noted only blank-faced acceptance from the division commander assigned to serve as the spear-point of the attack. It was the only face a true officer could put forward. Fear and apprehension were carefully scrubbed out of officer cadets in their education. Fear spread from an officer to his men like a virus and would destroy any unit just as surely as enemy fire would. Just the same, Strelnikov felt an echo of the same fear his fellow officer must have experienced. To be used as the shock troops for the attack was tantamount to a death sentence for the division. No modern military planners expected the breakthrough troops to remain combat effective for any longer than twenty-four hours before they would be relieved by follow up forces. A short, lethal, baptism by fire. A single moment in a fiery crucible to pave the way for those to come.

"The 121st and the 111th will then exploit the gap and cross the Drava where a complete breakthrough is expected allowing the 88th Tank Division to drive for Zagreb."

The coup de grace. Perhaps the Hitlerite Heinz Guderian said it best: *If the tanks succeed, then victory follows.* Soviet doctrine held the tanks in the highest regard: they were the decisive blow, the killing thrust to annihilate their opponents. Of course, they could only be employed *after* the infantry had ground the enemy to dust.

"We will have air assets from Praga Air Force Base on access to the army," Gurov continued, looking over the map. "Questions?"

"What of the enemy, comrade general?" Strelnikov asked. "What are we to expect?"

"Renegade elements of the Yugoslav army, American and British airborne and marine units, and some light armor. With Italy refusing to support the rest of NATO, our biggest threat —" Gurov said, looking at each of his division commanders in the eyes, "will be NATO air assets, launched from Bosnian and Croatian airbases and from their carrier in the Adriatic Sea which will be out of the effective reach of our air forces. We will have an advancing SAM umbrella to protect us, as well as our own fighters. The Air Force will take care of the enemy air bases, and our comrades in the Navy are also working on a permanent solution to our carrier problem."

***

"Brace for impact! All hands brace!" the shipwide alert blared out, barely audible over the collision alarm that sounded throughout the vessel. While the bridge crew gripped tight to their stations and any other conveniently stable surfaces, HMS *Somerset's* captain ran the length of the bridge, trailed closely by his executive officer. The two officers weaved around crew and their stations as they ran trying to keep the Soviet frigate in sight. *Somerset* maneuvered hard to port coming about in a tight arc in a desperate attempt to avoid ramming the oncoming Soviet Krivak-class.

Somerset heeled over hard enough to send someone's tea mug sliding from a workstation to shatter on the deck. The ships were going to miss. Barely.

"Mad bastard!" the XO swore. He stared gape-mouthed at the Russian ship as they came within a mere dozen meters of one another. It was close enough to make out the Krivak's distinct tangle of girders and dishes that made up its radar sensor suite. "Damn near hit us!"

At this range, *Somerset* was also close enough to deliver a likely fatal blow with her onboard 40mm guns, if she were authorized to fire, that is.

"Be grateful," the captain said.

"What? That he missed?"

"That he's trying to ram us and not shoot us," the captain replied, lifting his binoculars to his eyes to sweep the Soviet warship, now moving away at a narrow angle. He could only just make out the silhouettes of men on the other ship's bridge watching him back.

"It's a Krivak, sir. She's not well-equipped for a surface fight." The XO said, his tone dismissive.

"No, but her sisters might be," the captain said. He'd been a line officer in the Falklands and knew full well that it generally only took one hit to spell doom for a warship.

The Straits of Otranto had become a dangerous place to be lately, doubly so after the Soviet foreign minister declared virtually the entire Adriatic Sea to be fair game once their countdown ended. Just under sixty miles wide from Otranto to Vlore, the strait was usually calm as far as sea lanes went, but today it was home to dozens of ships maneuvering aggressively at one another. NATO tried to deny the Soviets access while the Soviets did their best to force passage through, like teenagers playing chicken.

"They're outnumbered three to one," the XO said. "If it does come down to a shooting war, they're going to be badly positioned in the open like this."

After guided missiles replaced high-caliber guns as the king of surface warfare, naval combat became less about chance and more about hard numbers. In this case, the Soviets were sacrificing stealth for aggressive positioning. It was a suicidal strategy, unless it belied their true purpose. "I've got one concern, Mister Smith."

"What's that, Captain?"

"We're not bloody likely to hear anything on sonar in all this mess, are we?"

***

The crew of B-218 were very aware of the intense—but so far bloodless—struggle taking place on the surface of the sea some 300 meters over their heads.

"Ahead ten knots," Captain Yessov said, refusing to show the fear he felt. The shooting hadn't started yet, but it certainly would, and there was always some poor dumb bastard to take the first shot. History didn't tend to focus on them, but they existed all the same and he'd be damned if his boat was going to be that historical footnote.

"Ahead ten knots," his executive officer repeated to the helmsman.

"Ten knots, comrade lieutenant," the helmsman said, throttling forward just slightly.

To the uninformed, the bridge of a submarine looked something like a cross between a commercial airline cockpit and a boiler room. Every available inch was covered with readouts and control switches. Indicator lights blinked statuses to the men who read them. Dim computer displays were mounted to walls and analog dials fed details about the boat and its functions to the nerve center of the ship. Anything not taken up by these vital control components housed cables, piping, tubes that held the nerves of the ship themselves: the wiring that connected all the systems to this single location.

The bridge was cool and dark. The bridge lights were kept dim in situations like this so as to preserve the crew's night vision in the event of a po-er failure. When coupled with the fact that they'd left the baking heat of North Africa far behind for the chill of the deep sea the result was a bridge that was still intolerably cold and humid. Cool, clammy moisture condensed on any bare metal surface leaving a glistening sheen. The humidity was complicated by the exhalations of the dozen or so men working their stations and sweating bullets.

Despite the prevailing silence it was tense rather than calm. The Soviet submarine arm was the cream of the crop as far as the Navy went, but even the best of the best could feel fear.

Yessov pretended to sip his tea. The captain of a vessel, beside simply deciding its course of action, was also responsible for maintaining crew morale. A nervous captain was the fastest way to destroy that. So, while Yessov was nervous enough that the tea tasted like warm battery acid to him, he was conscious enough of his crew's fear to pretend to enjoy it.

"Sonar, what is the status of the vessels we've detected?" Yessov asked.

"Two surface contacts, comrade captain," the sonar operator said. He reviewed the data feed from the "waterfall display". The display matched the sound auras produced by each contact to a database of pre-recorded and identified audio signatures. "One matches a *Krivak*-Class, the second a *Sheffield*-class. British." The operator pressed his clamshell headphones over his ears, struggling to listen. "They are each making about twenty knots and keeping close with one another."

"You can make them out distinctly?" Yessov asked, knowing the answer.

The operator failed to hide a wince. "No, comrade captain. The targets draw too near one another."

Passive sonar and audio detection equipment was one of many areas where the Soviet Union lagged behind their Western counterparts. It was only in the 1970s, when an American spy had defected, that the true deficiency of the Soviet submarine program had been brought to light. Before the Americans developed near omnipotent passive sonar, active sonar pings were thought to be the best and only way of detecting submarines; consequently, Soviet active sonars were among the best.

Imagine the surprise when it was discovered that the Americans could listen to passing Soviet submarines as easily as one might watch a sunset.

The drawback of utilizing active sonar was that it worked both ways. Like most modern electronic detection methods at sea, it was like a game of flashlight tag in the dark. The player who turned on their light had a reasonable chance of seeing their opponents, but it also meant they would be seen by everyone around them.

"Take us down another thirty meters," Yessov said, allowing his XO to relay the command to the planesman. It would dip B-218 just below the thermal layer of ocean water, where the ambient temperature fell off dramatically. The Layer acted as a sort of curtain or shroud against sound waves, meaning that anything above the Layer generally could not 'see' below it, and vice versa. "Sonar, inform me once you lose contact with the surface ships."

"Yes, comrade captain."

Yessov took another mock sip again before handing the cup and saucer to a yeoman—carefully so as not to betray his shaking hands—who he hoped would not notice the lack of change in the volume of liquid.

"Our surface fleet comrades are putting on quite a show," the XO said, puffing out his chest. "Let the British see if they can hear us with their engines up to speed."

Yessov would just as soon not find out if their gambit worked. While the Americans and their NATO allies espoused "lone wolf" hunting tactics for submarines, the Soviets had continually experimented with interarm cooperation and "wolfpack" type approaches to ship hunting. Modern communication challenges made direct cooperation all but impossible, but it still gave opportunity for maneuvers like this one.

"Do you think any other submarines have made it through undetected?"

"Lieutenant, we ourselves don't know if we've made it through undetected," Yessov said wryly, savoring his XO's red-faced embarrassment. "And we most likely will not know. Not until it comes time to strike." It would be all too easy for a detected submarine to be shadowed and destroyed by a sneaking surface ship.

While the Adriatic was a narrow and shallow sea, fortunately the Straits of Otranto ran down to almost 1200 meters in places. After they cleared the mouth they would pass through the South Adriatic Pit which afforded them plenty of deep water to hide in, but further north, where *Gettysburg* and her escorts operated, they would be working in water less than 200 meters deep.

Yessov would not allow himself to think of it as a suicide mission.

"Contact with surface ships lost, comrade captain!"

Yessov resisted the temptation to assume that because he could not hear them, they could no longer hear him. With NATO dipping sonar and passive sonobuoys likely littering this area it was a long shot that he would make it to the target completely undetected.

"Wonderful," Yessov gave the operator a tight smile. "Straight on, hold at ten knots." Yessov looked to his XO. "We will go above the Layer to check passive sonar again in thirty minutes. Once we reach the Pit we'll take the boat down to wait until hostilities have officially commenced." Yessov spared a glance at his watch. It would afford his crew a few hours of rest at least before they'd be called upon to act. "No sense getting caught before we can shoot back."

"Yes, comrade captain."

"Watch things here. I'll be in my quarters." Yessov knew that while his temptation was to personally oversee every movement of his ship, it put the crew on edge. Giving the XO the helm would show that he was unconcerned.

"Yes, comrade captain." The XO delivered a salute that Yessov returned as he left the bridge, heading aft. He wondered how much sleep he could manage to steal before the deadline.

***

"Here, right here!" Jean shouted, tapping the glass of the passenger-side window. Pete laid on the brakes and the passengers all braced as the 4x4 rocked forward on its suspension. Fighting against inertia, Jean rode out the increase in G-forces until the truck stopped on the overpass. She felt Dario thump into the back of her seat just before she began to unbuckle.

"Here?" Pete asked in disbelief, "We're in the middle of an overpass!"

"They're coming!" Jean insisted, "and there's no one else on the road, come on!" She threw her door open and nearly hit the guardrail that lined the edge of the highway overpass. Just as she'd said, there was no one else on the road but them. After the arrival of NATO troops most of the fighting in Croatia had died down across the board. It had gotten to the point that they'd been preparing to travel to Sarajevo once more. They'd hoped to see the French Foreign Legion trying to put down the Serbian militias that had secured huge stretches of the country.

Dario and Pete got out behind her. Pete doubled back to the rear of the vehicle to shoulder his camera gear. The small news team fanned out to stretch their legs in the few free moments they had.

Jean squinted south and saw the hazy line of vehicles just coming around the bend a few kilometers away. "Get set up, I want to see them all passing by."

"Which is this?" Dario asked, "Which unit?"

"Americans," Jean said, checking both directions out of habit before crossing the road to the opposite end of the overpass. "So ratings will be high. People back in the States love a good show of force. It's the 82nd Airborne, I think." Before she could say anything else, a pair of attack helicopters crested the treeline behind the convoy and thundered overhead. Their rotors blurred as they came in low. Both swooped close enough for Jean to make out the shark mouth motif painted on one of the Cobras. Before she could direct Pete's camera, they were gone, continuing north toward the Hungarian border.

A third helicopter was not far behind them. This one was a smaller, bulb-headed scout helicopter of some form. It whizzed overhead before hauling back and circling around, intending to get another look at these strange onlookers.

"Act natural," Jean said, loud enough to be heard over the chopper, and waved up at the bird. She wasn't sure what "natural" was in these circumstances but opted for "friendly".

The helicopter hovered for a moment as if unsure of how to proceed. A second later, Jean saw the co-pilot give her a small wave and then continue on after its more heavily-armed brothers. Yet again Jean was glad to have "PRESS" painted on every flat surface of their truck.

Within a few minutes, the ground convoy reached the overpass where Jean made sure she looked inconspicuous by waving at the passive vehicles. If the paratroopers didn't like being watched, they didn't act like it. Most just stared up at her curiously while a few soldiers actually waved back or mugged for the camera.

The convoy itself was impressive, taking up both sides of the freeway. It was spearheaded by Humvees and fast scout vehicles that moved in pairs. Later it was followed with small, short-barreled tanks, boxy APCs, and armored fighting vehicles. They were all painted in standard green/brown woodland camo patterns and further decked out with bushels of native foliage spread liberally over them. In this way they mirrored the men who crewed them. The visible soldiers poking out of hatches and cupolas were green and black like their vehicles, and some sported vegetation stuck in their cloth helmet covers.

"Magnificent," Dario said, awestruck as dozens of tanks and trucks passed under the bridge. These were followed shortly by logistics trucks and engineering vehicles. There were anti-aircraft missile launchers and gun batteries, self-propelled artillery pieces and towed howitzers; it was a self-contained fighting force on the move.

"They're going for the Mur or Drava River, I bet," Jean said, calling on her own limited Yugoslavian geography. "Try to discourage the Soviets from crossing over."

"Will it work, do you think?" Dario asked, a hint of hope in his voice.

Jean often had to remind herself that this was Dario's home, not simply another third-world country torn open by the superpowers of the Cold War. What happened here would be intimately personal to him, not a scoop he would one day fly home from. "God, I hope so," she said.

Pete lowered his camera after the last truck of the convoy had passed. "Are we following them?"

"Yes," Jean said. "As close as we can."

"Have you heard anything from Tony?" he asked before carefully powering the camera down and applying the lens cap so that it clicked in place.

Their editor had been desperately trying to help get Jean in touch with the 82nd Airborne's public affairs officer, the person who could get them "embedded" with the unit. It was the last thing Jean wanted. She'd seen embedded reporters get placed in hotels a dozen miles from the combat, given scraps and morsels of insider info from the Army. It was pathetic. She wasn't going to be eating under the table. She was going to sit at the table like everyone else.

"Nothing," she said. "We're going to tail them for now, see how close we can get without stepping on their toes."

Pete frowned at her, "The Army doesn't usually like snoops, Jean. They have a three letter word for people who prowl around military activity without permission."

"We won't get in the way and we won't be divulging any secrets. We're just going to get the real deal." And if she *had* to, she'd make the call to the public affairs officer herself.

"Boy," Pete said, adjusting his ball cap to point forward again, "Who would have thought that what we caught at that train depot ..."

That had registered with Jean too. What if what they'd sent back home had helped shape some policy decisions? She wondered how much of it had been inevitable and how much of it had been ushered in because of her. The debate about right and wrong was best left up to others. Her game was about transparency. The world had a right to know what was happening in this corner of existence.

"We changed the game alright. The shot seen 'round the world." Jean agreed. "We can collect our Pulitzers after this is all over. For now, we have a convoy to catch. Dario, how fast can you get us to Čakovec?"

***

8

President Simpson scowled at the floral wallpaper that covered the interior of the presidential bedroom. He was told the color was "powder blue" but to him it looked like someone had left a respectable color in the sun for too long until it faded down to the ghost of a color that haunted his vision. He didn't think it was possible for a single color to upset him more than a floral pattern did, but somehow the carpet was worse. It was a rosy shade of pink that made Simpson think of old nursing homes. It clashed ferociously with the cream-colored plush furniture and the gold trim around the fireplace.

He had been informed that First Lady Slater had made renovations upon her husband's election. He wished the old bat had left it alone.

The thing Simpson hated most about occupying the White House—by far—was occupying the White House. Harrison had told him at least a dozen times that he had no obligation to actually live in the White House. He was welcome to stay on his ranch in Texas or even to stay in a highrise penthouse in Dallas for most of the year. "They'll bring the government to you," he'd said.

"Well what the hell'd I fight to win for if I wasn't gonna enjoy every second of it?" Simpson had retorted. Now he was eating those words. His wife, Dahlia, wasn't much for homemaking either, despite her "Betty Crocker" public image. She was more at home in a courtroom than a kitchen.

"Senator Dewitt is rumbling about running again," she said, not looking up from the newspaper in her lap.

Simpson was looking in the vanity mirror and fighting for the perfect tie. Harrison told him they paid people to do this kinda stuff for him, but what good was a man who couldn't even tie his own tie? "Election's a ways off, hun," he said.

"November's right around the corner," she replied, turning the page. "Dewitt's talking about more 'Simpson-style' tax breaks," she said.

Simpson snorted, "Flattery, huh? Well I'm tickled pinker than this here carpet, but he's crazy if he thinks the party will switch horses right now. He's welcome to try again in '96, after I get my next four years."

Dahlia looked up into Simmon's cocky grin, rolled her eyes at his bravado, and returned to reading, but not before a smile escaped her careful mask.

"If that old mule is even still kicking then," Simpson added.

"Still kicking?" Dahlia gave her husband a sidelong glance. "He's fifty-nine for christsake."

"The man was born in the damn Depression," Simpson said. "He'd be sixty-four by the time he's ready to run. Older than Ike. Too old."

"Sixty-four is *not* too old, dear," Dahlia replied. "Besides, people like him."

"He reminds them of grandpa." Simpson tightened the knot slowly, carefully until it was perfect. "There. They like Dewitt because he's old, harmless, a jolly coot. No one wants a coot with the missile codes. Americans want youth, they want panache."

"Panache?" Dahlia was amused. "Like what you've got I expect?"

"A lot like what I've got." Simpson met his wife's eyes in the mirror and flashed her a grin.

"I like that uh … Kahelae fellow from Hawaii. Bright eyes, good tan, looks like he could take you surfing at nine and teach you about local politics at noon."

"You think Kahelae has a chance?" Dahlia asked.

"Not in hell. Most Americans can't point to Hawaii on a map unless it has its own inset. I'll endorse Wilks when the time comes."

"*Wilks!?*" Now Dahlia was stumped. "You know he spent the

whole Christmas party half-drunk, right?"

Simpson looked at her again, "Panache," he said, much to his wife's amusement.

The election was closer than it seemed, a looming obstacle, but one Simpson was confident he'd overcome. The economy had grown, he'd kept the US clear of any quagmires overseas, and he'd looked damn good doing it. Even so, four years was gone in a flash; the next would likely be just as quick. There was no harm in looking to legacy now, premature though it may be. Solidifying power in the party and reaching out to moderates who might cross the aisle for him had seemed awfully important just a few weeks ago. It seemed so important to secure the next four years and build that legacy he was thinking about. Now—

Simpson glanced at the TV that he insisted stay running at all times he was awake in this room. Twenty-four hour news was a blessing and a curse. Right now the footage was of Marines driving inland, moving to defensive positions along the Yugoslavian demarcation line.

"Damn that Williams," he said. "That little weasel. I ought to have him shot."

"You're the President, dear. I think you can make that happen," Dahlia said.

Simpson sighed. "And what good would that do? We're not the goddam Reds."

Dahlia laid down her newspaper. The light caught her dress while she looked her husband over. "You look good, dear. Very presidential."

"Thank you. I oughta. I've got a meeting with NATO and then a national address to do at dinner time. Trying to keep Janey and Johnny Public informed."

Dahlia stood and approached the bulletproof glass window that looked over the immaculately mowed lawn of the White House. Thanks to strategically placed trees and landscaping, the nearby DC traffic was merely a suggestion in the dark. Only the hint of flashing headlights could be glimpsed through trees.

Beyond that manicured perimeter burned the lights of a dozen government agencies that never slept.

"Good luck, dear," Dahlia said. "Kiss me goodnight, will you?"

Simpson couldn't help but grin and obliged his wife. Crossing the plush carpet to give her a soft peck on the lips, he undid the zipper on the back of her dress with one hand, more a favor than flirtation. "Night, hun."

"Goodnight."

Simpson tried to hold onto that feeling of marital bliss. He and Dahlia only had one child, a daughter, who was off running her own law practice in Tucson. He and his wife had both worked while she was growing up and consequently Simpson knew more about profit/loss margins than he did about being a dad. A goodnight kiss with his wife was a small slice of that domestic heaven that he'd never really had.

As the night of briefings before the conference wore on, he found it harder and harder to maintain that simple happiness. By the time he'd finished the teleconference with the heads of NATO, he'd forgotten it entirely.

"Italy is a no show," Simpson said, his temper rising.

"De Vasco has trouble with the voters," Harrison explained. "There's a large liberal-socialist minority in that nation that sees our intervention in Yugoslavia as trying to meddle in the affairs of a sovereign nation."

"Like the Yugoslavs were saints," Simpson said, sitting once again at his familiar desk in the Oval Office. The windows around him only showed the light reflected in the interior of the room, casting the illusion that there was nothing beyond their panes. The phone on his desk rang and Simpson picked it up. "Hello."

"Mr. President, it's Vice President Bayern for you, sir."

"Yep, put him through."

There was a series of soft clicks as the call was connected across the country.

"Rick? It's Jerry. I'm getting on a flight back from Tacoma right now."

"How was the speech, Jerry?" Simpson asked, there was always time for politicking.

"Fine. Washington will be going for us next election I suspect, but I heard bad news about NATO."

"Goddam Italy," Simpson said, "They're saying we started this war so the treaty doesn't hold."

"Our guys did fire first, Rick," Bayern said with an excess of patience. Jerry Bayern was a "ticket balancer" of sorts. He was Californian with connections to the youth of the country—more than a millionaire airline CEO and governor at any rate. He'd been a Navy man in his younger years before retiring to work in politics. They'd been called "the Western Wave" in the elections and had been portrayed—for better or worse—as a couple of old west gunslingers: sheriff and deputy, here to bring the country back to order.

"It's all a buncha crap," Simpson said. "But no reason to rush back here. I want us doing 'business as usual.'"

"Been watching the stock market, have you?" Bayern asked slyly.

"Dropped fifteen points when the Soviets gave us the timeline and another eight when Italy backed out. Bad news on Wall Street."

"I think the boys will pull through after they scrape their co-workers off the streets."

Simpson snorted, a rare moment of levity before he quieted. Bayern was ten years his junior and something of a maverick in the field of politics. Still, Simpson liked him. If Jerry Bayern had another ten years of experience under his belt, he'd be Simpson's next choice for president. As it was, he knew Bayern needed a bit more tempering. He had a tendency to leap without looking, a tendency to react rather than lead. There would be other chances. "I told our NATO pals that the Russians were throwing us a bone by making this a limited affair. If we can kick their ass out of Croatia or wherever they should call it quits, no harm no foul. No risk of this thing going nuclear."

"We're at a disadvantage here, chief," Bayern said. "With no

Italian air bases and an Austrian-no fly zone, we'll be flying out of old Yugoslav airstrips and off *Gettysburg*."

"We're trying to get *San Juan Hill* out of the Red Sea and moved north, but with the Suez backed up like it is, it's gonna be a photo finish if they make it in time."

"Maybe we ought to call this one quits," Bayern said.

Silence lapsed on the call long enough for the long distance crackle and pop to be audible.

"You know we can't do that."

"Why not?"

"We can't blink! We blink and the commies'll start pushing us at every turn," Simpson said. "They'll get on us about Israel again, or about India, or Iraq. If we let them have Yugoslavia— lock, stock, and barrel—then where do we draw the line? We got the chance to stop them cold here and now!"

"You think Kavinski will blink first?" Bayern sounded skeptical.

"Hell, he'll just about have to! That little fish doesn't have any pull in the Politburo. They'll kick him into Siberia so fast you'll faint. Besides, I've got a 'walk point.'"

"Walk point?"

Simpson often forgot that despite his agreeable attitude, the Vice President didn't share his business background. "It's an old negotiation policy. You don't start a talk without a 'walk point.' Some call it the 'limbo bar '; it's as low as you'll go before you walk away."

"What's ours?"

"Zagreb," Simpson said, having already given this some thought, "or Sarajevo. We lose one and I'm not gonna tear the country apart to get it back. We'll take 'em to the boardroom. Make some kind of a deal."

"And what's their walk point?"

Simpson was speechless. He somehow hadn't considered the Soviets' position in all this. It was a classic negotiation error. Seeing a deal only from your side left you liable to be blindsided when the other party wanted the prize more than you, or was willing to go farther than you. There was a moment where doubt tightened in his gut. Had Yugoslavia been a mistake? For Rick Simpson an answer was never long in coming though. "Ivan's playing on credit," he said. "Political credit. If we rough him up bad enough over this, then he'll *have* to take his hand out of the cookie pot. We make Yugoslavia into a bear trap and he'll know better than to go ape over it."

Bayern looked unsure. "You trust them not to escalate?"

"Hell, why would they? We both know what this is about and we know the stakes. *They're* the ones that drew up that limited warzone plan. We'll play ball with them for now. I'll call their bluff, but I'll fold before we see this thing become a third world war."

"Alright," Bayern said, clearly unconvinced.

"Look here," Simpson said, "You stick out your speaking tour. Don't want to raise any eyebrows about what might be brewin in the Oval office, right?"

"Yeah. Fine," Bayern said, "Just keep me posted on what happens, okay? I'll have reporters frothing at the lips for an inside scoop on anything that makes the front pages."

"No surprises," Simpson promised.

"Works for me."

"I'm going to make a national address in just a minute here," Simpson glanced at his watch. It was getting into the early evening hours. The camera crews were just beginning to arrive in the hall outside his office.

"Alright, I'll tune in and let you know how you did."

Simpson laughed, "I appreciate it. Night, Jerry."

"Good luck, Rick."

President Simpson rested the phone on its cradle and let out a deep breath before looking up at his waiting chief of staff. "Okay, send 'em in."

***

The rhythmic thud of bass from the dance floor was still

sending imaginary vibrations through Vance's body during his commute home. It had been a long day breaking in audio equipment for a show this weekend. Vance had fun all the same, practicing his scratching and mixing for the handful of sound engineers present. It was important to him to take his mind off tonight. The presidential address was tonight and for better or worse, Vance expected it would shape the course of his future.

The topic was no surprise. Everyone knew it would be about Yugoslavia. The Soviet deadline for the withdrawal of NATO forces was public knowledge by now and it was hot news. The deadline ran out early tomorrow and so far the government had made not one step to move any forces in or out as far as anyone could see.

A confrontation was coming: a meeting of East and West and the whole world felt it. Was fifty years of tension finally about to boil over?

It mattered doubly so to Vance since there was a very real possibility he would get called up. It had almost happened during the Aden Gulf War before the Ethiopians backed down after a military sucker punch, and now it looked like it might happen again.

Vance parked the car in a hurry, the parking brake ratcheting loudly into place. He thumped up the rickety wooden steps to their trailer and rushed inside where Molly was already tuning in to the news. "It's starting," she said.

The two of them sat together on the couch, dinner forgotten, and held hands.

The image resolved to President Simpson, his characteristic smirk gone and replaced by a stony seriousness. "Ladies and gentlemen," he began, "there's no need for formality here. You all know me, and—if polls are to be believed—about half of you hate my guts."

Vance could always tell when Simpson went off script, which was often. Personally, he hated the clown. Simpson had axed so many social programs that it made his head spin. Things working Americans counted on to get by were trampled in the name of profit. Even so, normally it was entertaining to see him go off the carefully laid rails.

"But today, that doesn't matter. I'm not coming to you as a politician or a leader, I'm coming to you as an American. You all watch the news so you know about the conflict brewing in the Balkans." He paused. "To someone who declines to look further, this is 'more of the same'; some far away battle in a war that's been going on for close to five decades. A war of ideology, a war we all pretend doesn't exist but not one of us can ignore."

Molly tightened her grip on Vance's hand.

"You see, this one is different because the true face of totalitarianism has been shown. For all of the Soviet Union's talk of peace, cooperation, and 'liberalization,' we see now that no amount of economic development can prevent them from rolling out the tanks to enforce their will. Recently, the United States took a stand. We stood—alongside our brave European allies—"

***

"Except Italy," Pete said with a snort.

Jean hurriedly shushed him and turned up the volume on the small TV in the hotel room, wishing the picture were less fuzzy so she could make out the expression on Simpson's face.

"—for the right of the people of the Balkans to follow their own path, free from tyranny and death. Slovenia, Croatia, and Bosnia: all chose to be free. It was a decision that the Soviets have not respected. They insist we want a war. They insist we are trouble makers and that we want nothing more than to gobble up these little states."

Simpson folded his hands together on the desk, "Well, I know my people. Americans don't want war. We love peace and we've fought *damn* hard to keep it. The Soviet government has set a deadline for us: a deadline to leave these people to their fates or they'll enforce their decision with military power."

To Jean, it felt like Simpson was looking right at her.

"I can only say this: America doesn't back down from what's right. We've never shied from conflict if the cause was just, and I believe this one is. Currently, our soldiers, sailors, and airmen stand along the Yugoslav frontier as a vanguard against communist oppression. A line has been drawn in the sand."

"He's doing it," Pete said. "Crazy bastard is calling the Soviets's bluff."

"A line that the Soviet Union will have to be the one to cross." Simpson paused, folded his hands together and looked into the camera. "Consider this broadcast a dual purpose communication —"

***

The ordinarily boisterous bullpit of the Soviet Foreign Ministry was silent save the tinny buzz of a lone television broadcasting President Simpson's speech. A dozen diplomats, clerks, and deputy ministers stood around watching and waiting.

Gradenko chewed a wooden pencil as he watched, a nervous tick he'd thought he'd lost in primary school.

"—the first part," President Simpson continued, "is to inform you, the American public, of my decision and my reasoning. The second—" he leaned back in his chair and collected his thoughts, "is a message to my Russian counterparts. This war will only happen by your hands. You hold the sword and the decision is yours to draw it or let it lie. Because once it's drawn I think we're gonna find it's mighty hard to sheathe. I hope for all our sakes you make the right choice." Simpson let the words rest and nodded slightly to himself. "God bless you all, and God bless the United States."

No sooner had Simpson ceased talking than the American news broadcast cut straight away to news anchors in a press room speculating on what could happen next.

Gradenko didn't have to speculate, he knew. It meant one thing. "War."

T.K. BLACKWOOD

***

9

"Vandal One, clear for takeoff."

The pilot of Vandal One gave a thumbs up through the cockpit out of habit, though it was largely too dark to see, and throttled up his craft. The plane itself wasn't as flashy as the Navy's Tomcat fighters or as sleek as the venerable F-15 and F-16, but it was no less deadly. An A-10 Thunderbolt—commonly called a Warthog—was a plane built around a weapon which itself was built around killing Soviet-made tanks.

The plane's turbojets revved up and lifted the attack craft into the starry night sky. Behind Vandal One, the airbase rapidly shrank away, disappearing into the dim, rolling Yugoslav countryside.

The base itself, Zeljava Air Base—codenamed Asgard—was unlike any other base Vandal One had flown from. He had flown in from Aviano Air Base in Italy which was ordinary in every way. Zeljava, originally built by the Yugoslav government and later seized by the Croatian rebels, was the world's largest underground airbase. While its runways were of course open air, they proceeded, fan-like, from a central hub that was buried in the base of a mountain. Fuel, control, maintenance, and repair facilities were all safely encased in hardened concrete which was layered beneath hundreds of tons of rock and earth, out of touch of all conventional weapons including the most dedicated bunker buster bombs. Even a nuclear bomb would have a hard time gouging it out of the mountain range.

As Vandal One peeled into the sky, he glanced out of the bubble canopy to his left, to the peak of the mountain. There —he knew—an array of search and targeting radars were positioned, controlling the air bases' extensive surface-to-air missile batteries that ringed the perimeter. It was a hell of a position—one that was going to be instrumental in keeping the Soviets out of Yugoslavia should they attack.

"Vandal One, you're good on our scopes. Stay low and keep your eyes open."

Vandal One grinned behind his oxygen mask. "Roger, Asgard."

"Be advised, friendly air cover over Zagreb will be escorting you to your patrol sector. Watch for Eagles."

"Copy."

"Good hunting."

The phrase haunted him. Hunting implied killing, and Vandal One hoped he wouldn't be doing either of those anytime soon. Yet even as he hoped against it he knew time wasn't on his side.

Vandal One had been briefed on the ground before this mission. It was a standby assignment in case the Russians went through with their attack plan. He was proceeding north-north-east for 115 miles to engage targets of opportunity, specifically advancing Soviet armor columns should they materialize. It was the task this plane had been built for, and one he'd trained for his whole flight career. It was the task that he was now dreading.

***

A few kilometers north of the Croatian-Hungarian border, Soviet artillery batteries were arrayed in neatly echeloned lines across empty fields. What crops had been here were trampled and flattened, ground into the dirt. Depressions were gouged in the earth to protect the guns, and camo netting strung above them. Each gun's crew stood at the ready, loitering nearby, silent and anxious.

The battery's commander paced, surveying his men, who were doing their best not to stare at him too obviously.

It would be his first shot fired in war. Maybe the first shots of the entire war. It was a lot of pressure. Checking his watch, the commander saw that the deadline was sixty seconds out. The official given deadline for NATO withdrawal was still an hour away but this way there was still some semblance of surprise for Soviet forces.

"Radio channels are still clear?" he asked the radio operator who sat nearby in the command dugout.

"Clear, comrade major."

The major wiped his forehead. Despite the cool night air he was sweating. If there was to be a change in plan the orders would come by radio. He imagined they would have come long before now.

Thirty seconds.

The major checked his firing tables again, reviewing a list of targets and timetables. They'd ranged out NATO's positions already; the coordinates had been fed in by advanced recon teams. In war he'd been trained to fire and maneuver. A stationary gun battery was a sitting target for NATO aircraft and counter battery fire. He would fire five rounds at his primary target and then re-deploy the entire battery to a nearby field which had been pre-prepared. From there he could engage the second target. The towed guns would be hooked to trucks and moved within a minute or two. It was a well-drilled ballet, one he and his men had endlessly practiced, a ballet that was about to debut for the first time.

Ten seconds.

He watched the hand of his watch tick down the last remaining seconds. The major cleared his throat, turning to his nearby subordinates. "Commence firing."

The command was relayed in an instant and a second later the first volley fired. The guns barked in near perfect unity. A single deafening bang sounded and night was lit with the collective muzzle flash of an entire artillery battery firing at once. The chirping insects fell silent as the sound reverberated through the night.

Hot, smoking, brass shell casings were ejected as crews worked their guns, ramming fresh rounds home and adjusting elevation. The second volley was staggered as each gun's ready time became dependent on the skill and speed of the crew. They fired off a third volley, even more broken than the second. By the fourth volley the barrage was just a continuous, thumping roar.

The major looked on, mentally counting down the seconds to a potential NATO counter-battery barrage. He eyed his watch, noting the unceasing tick of the second hand. Each moment that passed brought inevitable retaliation closer.

The fifth and final volley came a second later. The men instantly transitioned from working their guns to packing them. Trucks rolled into position and teams of men muscled the guns into place, hitching them up.

The entire process had taken less than five minutes.

***

The countryside north of Čakovec was flatter than a pancake: cornfields from horizon to horizon, broken here and there with small clumps of woods or towns. Jean had clear visibility nearly halfway to the Hungarian border even at night. The border was close enough that she saw the flash of explosions in the dark. Within seconds the echoing booms caught up with them, the sounds of war. Initially, each sound was individual. Unique, booms and bangs echoed back and forth. Soon enough these noises merged together as one, like a continuous roll of thunder.

Fireballs flickered and climbed into the sky. At this range they blossomed in the dark, rising above the distant treetops. Each explosion momentarily lit a section of the night sky before fading away, leaving only dark plumes of smoke.

Pete said nothing, just panned his camera across the rolling barrage the Soviets were laying down on the front. Firelight reflected in miniature on the camera's lens.

Soon American guns were replying. Their own sharp barks were heard over the bass rumble from the north. It didn't fade; if anything, the sounds grew more intense.

***

The men of the 105th Motor Rifle Division were not

much different than Strelnikov's own men. They were nearly universally conscripts built around a solid officer corps and semi-professional NCO force. They were young men in the prime of their life, and they had to be terrified.

Even here, kilometers from the fighting, Strelnikov could hear the boom of the guns. Though he couldn't see the men of the 105th, he could follow their progress via the radio. In the cramped command BTR, he and his small staff listened to their efforts.

"Forward recon and AT teams in position. Engineering battalions advance," a regimental colonel's orders crackled over the radio. The men and machines of the 105th went forward with the same solid determination that had carried their grandfathers and great-grandfathers to victory. With a flurry of shellfire raining on the enemy, they advanced in a great wave on the Mur River. The river was a slow-moving and relatively shallow body of water which separated Croatia from Hungary. In normal circumstances it was no great obstacle to travel, but for an army on the move it was a formidable barrier. The bulk of NATO's combat forces were arrayed well behind the river, intending to catch the Soviets at their most vulnerable as they tried to form up after crossing. Even so, they left a token picket force to harass the engineers.

American sharpshooters and tank hunter teams took shots at the exposed assault engineers as they crossed the river in inflatable boats and moved pontoons into position in the dark. Even worse, these forward observers called down precision fire support missions on the exposed engineers. Bridging under fire was a well-practiced exercise in the peacetime Soviet Army, one they had honed to an art. With a doctrine that focused entirely on securing forward momentum for victory, there could be no allowances made for natural obstacles. Rivers would have to be crossed with breakneck speed.

Assault engineers, moving with startling rapidity, crossed the river in inflatable rafts and makeshift ferries, bringing with them both the weapons they needed to clear the far bank and the equipment to begin bridging operations. These men took heavy losses from the waiting American Marines who put their famed rifleman skills to work. They picked off the engineers in the open as they struggled to advance. The entrenched Marines peppered the Soviet engineers with machine gun fire and grenades, slowing their work and exacting a bloody toll.

Strelnikov folded his arms and tried not to let emotion show as he listened to the back-and-forth exchange between a regimental colonel and the 105th Division's commander. The colonel's men were struggling across the river now. Amphibious armored vehicles swam or waded, while follow-on forces crossed the pontoon bridges left in the wake of the initial assault.

After thirty minutes, there were no more radio reports from the first regiment. The whole HQ, or at least the transmitter, was likely a casualty of NATO's precision air forces. Soon a new officer had seized control of what was left of the lead regiments and resumed the attack.

"We must have more field hospitals," he said, "Those we have are inadequate. I also have an urgent need for a dedicated burn unit to treat my men."

The division commander himself was quick to respond, the transmission quality robbing it of any emotion. "All the division's medical assets are tasked. Press the attack."

"Comrade general, my men are dying untreated in the field! Where are the triage stations we were promised?" In peacetime such insubordinate responses would never be tolerated. Here, with the dead and wounded mounting around him and his command being chewed to pieces, it was hard to fault him.

The division commander's response was no less emotional. "Then attack, damn you! There are no more medical units to spare! Leave your men where they fall and drive!"

Strelnikov caught an uncomfortable glance from some of his staff. Before long it would be their division going forward. If the Americans were not broken by that point, then they would be marching into the same deadly jaws as the 105th. It was a worry for the future. Right now, he was struggling to glean what insight he could from the deaths of his comrades.

Their American Marine opponents put up fierce resistance, but they were ultimately overwhelmed by the weight of Soviet firepower. Pre-sighted howitzers called down a blizzard of shells against their prepared positions and prevented swift reinforcement of their line. It was a textbook Soviet attack, though hampered by a major river: pin the enemy with firepower and strike in force to seek and exploit as many breakthroughs as possible.

The Americans had made one mistake already. Opting to maximize the defensive position of the river and surrender as little territory as possible, they had left themselves vulnerable to exactly the sort of battle the Soviets wanted. A forward defense meant that their depth of deployment was limited and many units were destroyed where they stood. In particular, those units tasked with guarding bridge crossings took horrendous losses, many being annihilated to the last man; the survivors—mostly wounded—were taken prisoner by the advancing enemy. Reports filtered in of American prisoners here or there, but it seemed many simply fought to the end.

"Čakovec is in sight, comrades!" a regimental officer reported. "We will take the city by dawn!"

***

Unfortunately, NATO's commitment to keep the battle contained to Yugoslavia meant they could not conduct deep air raids against Hungarian positions. This gave the Soviets a large advantage in terms of their ability to stage aircraft right over the border.

It was something Vandal One was cognizant of as he flew through the contested skies. After verifying he was on the propper flight path he tapped into friendly radar coverage provided by a circling Boeing AWACS plane. Such third party coverage was the best way to get a clear picture of the battle raging in the air around him.

The AWACS plane was a jet the size of a civilian commercial airliner, and it mounted a large, circular radar disc on top that provided intensely accurate radar imagery of all the craft in the air. In short, nothing could move without being seen by the AWACS and its crew. Using the data the plane picked up, its crew of combat operators and analysts could direct interceptor aircraft to cut off any enemy incursion. Having such near-omniscience on the battlefield was a huge force multiplier, but it wasn't limited to NATO. The Soviets fielded their own version of the AWACS plane which circled just on the Hungarian-side of the border.

Vast flocks of Soviet aircraft were visible on both sets of radars as they zipped over the border. The proximity of their bases to the battlefield enabled them to conduct short aerial operations before retiring when sufficiently harried by NATO interceptors. It was a tug of war as NATO aircraft sought to do the same.

It was into this electronic no-man's-land that Vandal One dove, his wingman—Vandal Two—just off the starboard wing. Together they both passed over a large, artificial lake created for a hydroelectric dam, bringing them into range of Soviet airborne radar.

"Bring it to the floor, Vandal Two."

They both descended, their altimeters dropping until they read just under twenty meters to the ground. It was low enough that stray power lines or a rogue treetop were just as capable of taking them out as a Soviet missile. Flying low was the only realistic defense when moving into such a densely monitored area and hoping to come out alive without the protection of electronic-countermeasures. It made them that much harder to detect and track. The denser air close to the ground also grossly limited the effective range of anti-air missiles and made engagement windows for anti-air guns much smaller.

The night was so dark that Vandal One couldn't see his hands on the control stick save for the light from his consoles. He was flying by instrument, relying on a high-tech, ground-mapping radar system to avoid plowing his fighter into a hillside. The light, drizzling rain made their task no easier, but posed no insurmountable challenge.

"Vandal Team, this is Oxide, we have a platoon on the main highway west of Mura calling for danger close on an advancing tank column."

"Copy, Oxide," Vandal One said, acknowledging the intel from the AWACS. "We'll be there in five." Vandal One adjusted his stick and foot pedals slightly, angling his craft eastward and matching his new heading to the location indicated on his map.

This part of the country was mercifully flat, near perfect for aerial ground attack. Vandal One took an extra moment to line up on the right heading before coming in straight and level. In seconds the thermal sights on his wing pylon-mounted missiles relayed targeting data to his onboard computer. A string of heat signatures on the main highway resolved into Soviet T-80 main battle tanks, advancing in a staggered column. To either side of this push were scattered APCs with dismounted crews moving forward, visible only by the flashing of automatic weapons fire in the dark.

"Rifle!" Vandal One said, the codeword for an air-to-ground missile launch. His clutch of thermal-guided missiles indicated a firm lock on their targets and dropped clear before engaging their rocket motors to zero in on the distant tanks.

He could have left it there, but there was no sense in not ensuring as many kills as possible. With a few taps of his foot pedals he yawed the attack craft to angle it nose-on to the enemy battle tanks. "Guns, guns, guns!" A stroke of the trigger on his control stick revved and fired the main rotary cannon embedded in the nose of his aircraft. The force of the recoil was great enough to actually slow his forward progress, and he had to fire in bursts to avoid stalling the plane. The incandescent stream of depleted uranium spewed out, dancing across the lead elements of the armored column even as the burning pinpricks of his missiles struck targets across the convoy. The missiles hit just after his guns, blasting turrets from armored vehicles as their ammo stores cooked off, or knocking out engines and forcing the crew to bail out. After the lead elements of the attack force were savaged, Vandal One started walking his fire back along the length of the column.

Beside him, Vandal Two mirrored the attack, obliterating another dozen Soviet vehicles.

The two Warthogs screamed through the rising pillars of smoke. The smoke was invisible in the dark except for the flickering light of the flaming vehicles beneath them. The scattered fires cast an eerie red glow on the billowing black smoke. Scattered small arms fire rattled harmlessly off their armored fuselages as the Soviets fired up at them in impotent rage.

Vandal One took a grim satisfaction in his work. "Looks like we bagged a whole tank company in that run."

A second later he spotted the flash of missile launches from the woods behind the attacking column. The burning streaks of missiles climbed from the forest to meet him and his wingmate. "SAM north!" he called out. "SAM north!"

As Vandal One heeled his craft over and goosed it for every ounce of thrust, he also punched the key to deploy countermeasures. The A-10 appeared to grow a fiery set of wings as a spray of flares launched out to either side. The white-hot flares were intended to give heat-seeking warheads an overload of targets, drawing them in and giving the pilots breathing room.

The tactic would have worked if the missiles were keyed to home in on heat rather than radar signatures. As it was, Vandal One was simply lucky.

The first Soviet missile detonated with a flat bang a few meters from Vandal Two, throwing deadly shrapnel that severed electrical cables and burned out one of the A-10's two engines, causing it to roll over violently and pitch straight down into the ground, turning a grove of trees into a bonfire blazing in the night.

The second SAM locked on to the dying A-10 as well and

followed it to the ground where it detonated pointlessly in the trees, more than guaranteeing Vandal Two's death.

It was over in an instant and Vandal One was racing back south, away from the fighting. His next stop was Asgard air base to rearm and refuel.

"Vandal Team, Oxide. We've got another platoon in danger of being overrun, requesting urgent fire support."

"Oxide, Vandal One. I'm down a wingman," Vandal One replied, unnecessarily; he knew the AWACS had to be aware of that if they were monitoring radar. "And I've shot my ordnance here. I've only got guns left."

There was a beat of silence before Oxide responded, "Sorry to hear it, Vandal One. These guys are in a bad spot. Guns may be enough to get them out of it."

Vandal One wanted to argue, wanted to point out how suicidal it was to press his luck but he knew things had to be even worse on the ground. He took another look at his wingman's gravesite and toggled his radio, "Copy. Guide me in, Oxide."

***

The near-silent hum of the ventilation fan in Yessov's cramped quarters brought in cool, metallic-tasting recycled air. Yessov always found the downtime on a submarine relaxing. He relished his ability to lay in his bunk and read or write letters to his wife. The letters would not be delivered until he was back in port, of course, and he usually made a habit of delivering them himself. Still, it was nice to take the time and build a habit. In the few short minutes he would write to his wife, he could imagine they were back at home, watching the Dnieper River flow into the Black Sea from the windows of their apartment.

A submarine was not normally the space for personal contemplation and isolation; only his rank as captain afforded him such luxuries as a private room and time to himself. In peacetime he would take this time to read, but he was too nervous to read. Yessov had been a captain for years now, but never once had he fired a shot in anger, or even had to maneuver for his life. Now, here, three hundred meters beneath the surface in the South Adriatic Pit, hovering just above the Kilo-class's maximum depth, he was enjoying what may be his final moments of peace. He'd taken the time, along with the submarine's political officer, to review the orders for this sortie. They were simple enough.

PROCEED NORTH TO ADRIATIC. AVOID CONTACT WITH HOSTILE PATROLS. ON COMMENCEMENT OF HOSTILITIES PRIMARY OBJECTIVE:

> **1.   SEEK OUT AND NEUTRALIZE CARRIER USS GETTYSBURG**
> **2.   ENGAGE ENEMY SHIPPING AND TARGETS OF OPPORTUNITY**
> **3.   AVOID DETECTION AND DRAW OFF ENEMY RESOURCES**
> **COMBAT OPERATIONS TO COMMENCE ON CODE PIKE.**

In the otherwise rigidly structured Soviet military, the submarine arm was granted a great degree of freedom in executing their orders. A submarine captain had to be free to carry out his will as he saw fit, and not be beholden to inflexible commands from higher up. A submarine was a precision tool, not a crude weapon that could be hurled at the enemy en masse like so many tanks or APCs. It required finesse.

Yessov shifted slightly in his bunk, trying to make himself more comfortable on the thin foam mattress. He could have closed the curtains and sealed himself off from the rest of his room if he'd wanted the dark, but he knew sleep was an impossibility. He would sleep only when he needed to, at least until they were out of this sea.

A subtle change in vibration told him that the submarine was moving, changing its depth. He was already on his feet when the intercom chirped at him.

"Comrade captain, we have passed the deadline and are rising up to signal depth," his XO said.

Yessov depressed the "talk" switch. "Thank you, comrade lieutenant. I will be there shortly." After a brief check of his uniform in the small, dingy mirror on the back of his cabin door, Yessov stepped out into the passageway and had to make room for a sailor hustling by. Outside of his private refuge, he was reminded that B-218 was a living thing in a sense: an organism that never slept. Returning salutes as he moved, Yessov ascended a ladderway and entered the bridge of the submarine.

His executive officer stood in the middle by the periscope station, and beamed at his commander. "All systems nominal, captain."

"Thank you." Yessov took a moment to compose his thoughts. He was careful to put forward an air of calm control, even though his own thoughts and feelings were turbulent. It was the moment of truth for their coming operations. A submerged submarine had no easy way of communicating with the outside world, and so was totally cut off from the events outside. His orders were clear: if he picked up the appropriate codeword with the extremely low frequency radio, then his mission was a go.

"Comrade," Yessov said, turning to his radio operator. "Can we detect the ELF transmission?"

"Yes, comrade captain." The radioman shared the same nervous energy as the others on the bridge.

"The codeword?"

"It is 'Pike,' comrade captain."

Yessov's heart skipped a beat, but he betrayed nothing, instead only nodding slowly and turning to face the helm of his ship again. "Then our mission proceeds."

There was no cheer but the bridge crew expressed some relief all the same. In a way, knowing they would fight was better than knowing nothing. It allowed them to steel their nerves and bury their fears.

Yessov momentarily closed his eyes and relaxed his mind. He visualized the submarine itself, turning it to a living thing in his mind. He was the brain of this vessel as much as the bridge was the nerve center. He was the one who chose its course and action. Any mistake in command would be his own, and his crew would live or die by that. His task was to find the carrier *USS Gettysburg* and neutralize her. It was impossibly unlikely that he would manage to find, let alone sink her, but his orders were clear enough and he was going to execute them as best he could.

"Current depth?"

"Holding at eighty meters, captain."

Yessov hid a wince. That was dangerously shallow, but the ocean was only about one hundred and fifty meters deep outside of the Adriatic pit. Hardly enough water to hide in, and dangerously close to the bottom, closer than they would dare get in peacetime.

"Layer strength?"

"It's weak now, captain. We expect it will increase as the sun rises."

Yessov nodded to himself. "Sonar? Contacts?"

"One contact, comrade captain, bearing 080. I believe it to be a *Henry J. Kaiser*-Class Oiler."

"Escort ships?"

"None, comrade captain."

This piqued Yessov's interest. An oiler was no aircraft carrier, but she still fit his second standing order. Alone she would be a juicy target, ripe for the picking. "What is our confidence and range?"

"Eighty-five percent confidence of target, we have a bearing but ..."

Range was a tricky thing in the ocean where sound traveled much further than air. The oiler could be many kilometers away or nearly on top of them. The former was more likely than the latter though.

"Set condition one," Yessov said, his soft tone belying the serious nature of the order. "Battle stations." The lights in the bridge were dimmed to combat lighting and throughout the boat, sailors raced to their action stations.

Within moments, the XO hung up the ship-wide phone. "All sections report combat-ready, captain."

"Good." The crew had maintained its swiftness even after the stress of a real combat deployment. "Conn, take us up to periscope depth. Let us see what is on the menu." The three-thousand ton Kilo-class ascended slowly and purposefully through the water, her screw turning silently behind her until she was shallow enough to raise periscope.

"Radar mast first," Yessov said, moving over to the electronic intelligence section of the bridge.

The mast, a sort of periscope for detecting radar signatures, came up and was bombarded with signals right away. They resolved on the sailor's screen as bearings, ranges, and frequencies. There was lots of military noise, primarily from the south, which was to be expected; likely a surface group still patrolling the Straits of Otranto. There was something faint further north as well. Yessov imagined it was the carrier group. "No reading from the oiler, captain. Shall we go active?"

"No." Yessov tried to hide his horror. To switch on his own active radar would signal to every nearby ship that he was here, and it would likely spook the prey. "I will get visual confirmation. Up periscope." Sometimes the oldest methods were best.

The command was echoed by a junior officer and Yessov stepped to the viewing station. He rested his hands on the cool steel handles and pressed his face to the leather-padded scope.

Around him, the sea was calm, a blue-black plane that matched the early morning sky, just beginning to purple with the rising sun. A calm sea meant it would be easier to spot a ship, but it also meant it would be easier in turn to spot the white-feather wake of a periscope. He would keep this brief. Rotating the scope until it was pointed along the bearing that his sonarman had picked up, Yessov spotted the ship a few kilometers distant, making its best speed north east, for the Dalmatian coast. The vessel, a fuel-supply ship for warships and aircraft, was big: just over two hundred meters, nearly three times the length of his own boat. It had a high superstructure marked with parallel rows of gantries and cranes for handling fuel lines and supply pallets. It looked something like a cargo-container crane crossed with an oil tanker. Its light gray hull caught the early morning light and winked tantalizingly at him. The ship likely intended to hide among the shallows and islands that dotted the coastline as it worked north for the fleet. He wasn't going to allow that. "New heading," he said, motioning to lower the periscope. "Come about to 090 and increase speed to two-thirds."

The commands were relayed by junior officers to their subordinates as B-218 adjusted its course to advance and close on the oiler. With visual confirmation, their confidence of the target was now full. There would be no chance of misidentification, or of the torpedoes hitting a neutral vessel by mistake.

Yessov watched the video replay of his periscope sweep on the small black-and-white monitor beside the station. In the replay he could see that the ship was not at full steam, moving at a quick pace but not sprinting away. Even so, a ship like that could easily outrun his Kilo-class if it came to it.

"Captain, shouldn't we deploy our anti-ship missiles? At this range a torpedo will take some time to close the distance."

Yessov shook his head, "We have only four to use. You propose we use one on a defenseless oiler?" That shut his XO up. After a moment the submarine had finished adjusting its course, coming in perpendicular to the ship. "Range to target?"

"Four kilometers, comrade captain!"

They were close enough for the torpedoes now. Conversely, as they had risen to the very edge of the Layer any transient noises from loading and firing torpedoes would likely be heard in the water. The very act of preparing to fire might give their quarry warning, providing them a chance to outrun or dodge them, or —even worse—call for help.

"Helm, come to port fifteen degrees, slow to one-third speed."

"Yes, Captain!"

B-218 turned her nose from the oiler, instead presenting her starboard face.

"Flood tubes one and three. Open outer doors."

As the command was executed, the port-side launch doors were opened, the ones on the opposite side of the boat from the oiler. This allowed the hull of the submarine to deflect most of the noise opening the doors brought.

"Fire one and three."

"Firing!"

There was a vibration as the two torpedoes lept from their bay, turning at once to round the nose of the submarine and close on their prey. Since the torpedoes were launched with the submarine still undetected they could afford to be guided by wire. Each of them trailed a multi-kilometer long wire spool behind them that allowed remote guidance by the weapons officers on the submarine. A miss was impossible unless Yessov had to maneuver suddenly or otherwise cut the cables.

Yessov waited impatiently while the torpedoes steadily closed distance.

"Distance to target, fifteen hundred meters."

The bridge held its collective breath, Yessov mentally counting down the range. He longed to watch through the periscope as the torpedoes closed. He wanted to see the oiler's back broken, but he would have to settle for acoustic confirmation

"One thousand meters."

Yessov met the eyes of his XO and saw equal parts exhilaration and fear. They had fired their first shot in this war.

"Signal change," Sonar said, "Target is accelerating, twenty-five, thirty knots!"

"They've heard them," the XO said.

"It doesn't matter."

"Range to target, five hundred meters. Four … three—"

Yessov gripped the nearby guard rail tighter.

"Torpedo one detonation! Torpedo two-! It's a hit!"

"Sonar?" Yessov asked, forcing his own voice to be calm and level.

The sonar operator kept his headset clamped firmly to his

head, struggling to make sense of what he heard. "Engines have stopped, captain. I get a lot of transients. I think she is breaking up, comrade captain."

A mute cheer went up before a pair of junior officers put a stop to it.

"Forty-two thousand tons," Yessov said, brushing an invisible speck from his uniform. "Sent to the bottom of the sea."

The faces of his crew were all the reward he needed: relief, excitement, pride. Decades of preparation had finally come together in one pristine moment. Still, he knew the fat smoke plume from the burning oil slick that marked the ship's grave would likely draw lots of unwanted attention. They would be looking for a submarine fleeing south, back for the straits. They would hopefully not expect a submarine to sprint north in this confusion, further into enemy-controlled waters. The sounds of the oiler's collapsing hull and escaping air pockets would make the perfect cover for a submarine running at top speed.

"Make depth sixty meters," Yessov said. "Increase speed to flank."

"Flank speed at sixty meters will allow for cavitation, comrade captain," the XO said, as if Yessov did not already know that.

Yessov simply looked at his subordinate, face blank. "We will sprint for five kilometers, just beyond the wreck site and then resume two-thirds speed."

The XO hesitated, "Yes, comrade captain."

"Lieutenant," Yessov addressed his XO, "you have the conn." He had a ship's log to update.

***

10

By the time the 121st Motor Rifle division was allowed onto the main highway by the Military traffic controllers, it was well past daybreak. The air still tasted of exhaust and diesel fuel. It was the consequence of the unending flow of traffic that had been steadily pouring southwest for the last six hours. The 105th division, which had led off the attack, now lay in ruins around them across the Croatian countryside. Obliterated vehicles dotted the farmland surrounding the road. Villages were crafter-pocked, ashy wastes. The bodies of the dead lay where they fell, sometimes scattered about, other times in small piles where they'd been collected or been killed as a unit. Much of the 105th was seen in triage stations. The seriously wounded were treated by overworked doctors and medics. Others, only lightly injured or simply unable to advance further sat dejectedly in the shade. Recovery vehicles dragged disabled tanks and APCs from their resting places so they could be hauled back to motor pools, repaired, and then sent forward again. The men of the division who could still fight pressed on ahead, trailed by Dmitriyev's 111th and then Strelnikov's 121st.

The mid-morning sun cast a soft, golden glow across the expansive countryside, highlighting the leaves only just starting to turn to shades of amber. The grass that lined the fields they passed still remained a vibrant green.

General Strelnikov himself rode in the back of a command BTR, a wheeled APC with an expanded troop compartment holding an advanced radio section and a small command staff, including his chief of staff Colonel Mishkin. The general stole glances through the hull-mounted periscopes when he could. A more gallant part of him would rather have ridden in style from the commander's station of a T-80, but knew that giving orders from a battle tank was less effective than from a mobile HQ.

From the rear periscope he could just make out the tail end of his advancing columns, his reserve regiment and auxiliary forces like bridging supplies and logistics trucks. Most of his view, however, was blocked by a tracked SAM launcher. The SAM's triple-stacked missiles poked skyward, alert for airborne threats. Flanking his BTR on either side were AA guns likewise mounted to tracked platforms. Their gunners thrashed the sky with radar waves and kept a watch skyward for aerial attack.

It was more than casual paranoia; the evidence of NATO bombing lay all around them in the broken remains of the 105th.

T-80s sat burst like rotten fruit, gutted and charred from fires that had long since burned themselves out. Wrecked APCs had been bulldozed off the road, blackened bodies lay scattered around them. The cost of a modern advance was laid bare in broad daylight.

It was some time later that he started to see evidence of NATO's presence: Gaggles of US prisoners being marched to the rear, destroyed armored vehicles and wrecked planes and helicopters. It was coldly satisfying to see they were hurting the enemy too; he just wished the damage was less lopsided.

The radio crackled and its operator listened intently, jotting details down onto a slip of paper before passing it to a staff officer who read it and glanced at the map spread across a central table in the interior. Strelnikov eyed the radio suspiciously. NATO SIGINT—signal intelligence—was rumored to be the best in the world. The old joke in Frunze Military Academy had gone: "to locate the enemy's air forces, just use a radio twice." The joke held a degree of truth, though. The Western allies were no fools; anyone could see that the Soviet military operated in a highly centralized manner and so they could cut off the head to kill the body. It was something Strelnikov had long attempted to drill out of his own men, always trying to encourage individual initiative. It was a crusade unappreciated by the old guard, men who preferred structure and order to the chaos of war.

"The 105th Division reports they have taken Čakovec, comrade general."

Strelnikov nodded and followed along the map. Čakovec itself, while important for rear area control, meant nothing in terms of long term victory. If anything more than a recon platoon were used for this task, it would have been a waste. It had always been stressed that victory lay in movement. The breakthrough, once achieved, must be fully exploited without hesitation. There were only two objects in Strelnikov's mind: the city of Varaždin which sat behind the Drava river, and the foothills south of the city.

Soviet doctrine had long emphasized cutting off and bypassing urban centers where possible—a lesson learned in the Great Patriotic War at the fascists' expense—but Varaždin still would make a tempting defensive position for the enemy. It had to be screened before it could be bypassed. Beyond that, only the city of Zagreb interested the general. Sitting astride the Sava River which bisected Yugoslavia, it controlled vital crossroads and—really—the interior of Croatia itself. If Zagreb fell there would be nothing between the Third Army and the Adriatic Sea.

"Send no reply," Strelnikov returned. While he was grateful for the 105th's sacrifice and hard-earned advance, he dared not risk giving away his own position for a simple congratulation.

"Yes, comrade general."

"Things proceed well," Mishkin said, his voice low so only his general could hear him, "for all the fuss these Americans make about their Marines."

"And still, a reinforced division slows an army," Strelnikov said. "It is true they are outclassed, but they are not to be underestimated." As he spoke he continued to survey the countryside through the periscopes, trying to get a feel for the land.

"Comrade general, General Gurov has informed us that the 105th Division will be wheeling to screen Varaždin," a staff officer said, reviewing a message from the radioman. "Comrade General Dmitriyev's division will take the lead in the advance south."

Before the general could answer, he and the other contents of the APC were pitched forward as the vehicle stopped dead. Pencils and map cases scattered forward while Strelnikov grabbed a handhold. Mishkin failed to catch himself in time and fell onto the map.

The swearing of the driver told Strelnikov that they had maybe only just missed hitting the vehicle before them. "What's the problem?"

"A traffic jam, comrade general!" the driver called back.

Brushing past Mishkin, Strelnikov gestured to a junior officer and then the roof hatch above the radio man. "Get this open."

With some effort, the hatch was lifted and thrown open, allowing sunlight to spill in and Strelnikov to climb out. With a bit of careful maneuvering, he wriggled himself up and onto the roof of the armored vehicle, peering ahead to see the source of the sudden traffic jam. A slowly rising column of smoke ahead on the road told him all he needed to know. Poking his head back down he addressed his radio man, "Find the cause of this jam. I want to know when I return."

"Y-yes, comrade general!"

"Return?" Mishkin asked.

"Yes. I am going—" Strelnikov pointed to the west "—to that tank."

The general managed to drop from the top of the command APC and land awkwardly by the time Mishkin and an armed soldier had gotten out to follow him. When his chief of staff caught up with him he was walking with determined strides across a dew-wet cornfield, the crops flattened by treads, tires, and bombs.

"General, it's not safe out here."

"It's not much safer in the car," Strelnikov returned. "A guided missile won't find us as easily as that radio box either."

"Comrade general, enemy soldiers may still be about." As Mishkin spoke, he laid a hand on the submachine gun fastened in its holster at his hip.

"I assume that's why you brought him," Strelnikov indicated the rifle-armed trooper tagging along with them.

As they got farther from the idling column of vehicles, the distant rumble and boom of artillery fire became more apparent, sometimes intercut with the scream of overworked jet engines. The clear blue sky above them was cut with a criss-cross of contrails from high-altitude sorties advancing and falling back.

Strelnikov was grateful he'd opted to wear the camouflage coat of a standard infantryman rather than his stiff and formal dress uniform. The flak vest was heavy, and the helmet rattled awkwardly on his head, but it did provide him with a modicum of protection and anonymity in the field. Even so, his shoulder boards displayed his full rank for any who might stop to note it.

A few dozen meters away, across the mushy cornfield, was the target of Strelnikov's determined march: a pair of T-80 main battle tanks idling in the shade of a lone tree. The commanders of these two tanks were out of their hatches and visible from the waist up.

"You," Strelnikov pointed at the closest man as he neared. "Sergeant, is your tank disabled?"

"Are you mad?" the sergeant asked, incredulous, "There's a war going on!"

"So, I ask you why you are sitting," Strelnikov returned, his two escorts fanning out slightly to be seen.

It was at that moment that the sergeant's perplexed face shifted to shock as he realized the rank of the man he addressed. "Comrade general! No, our tanks are in working order."

"Then why do you sit?" Strelnikov demanded.

"Our platoon leader," he stammered, "had given orders to advance to this position."

"And where is he?"

"Dead, comrade general."

"Dead," Strelnikov repeated.

"We have not been able to raise the company on our radio. I think it was damaged from a shell hit."

Strelnkiov pointed toward the sound of battle, "And where do you think your lieutenant would have you go if he were alive!?"

"I-I, comrade general—"

"One more excuse and I will order this man to shoot you dead," Strelnikov pointed to his startled escort. "Unless you wish to follow your lieutenant more closely, you get these tanks moving, sergeant."

"Y-yes general!"

"You have a brain, dammit! Use it!"

At once the sergeant ducked back into his tank, barking orders, and the engine roared to life. The vehicle lurching into gear, followed shortly by its companion. Their treads ate into the soft earth and threw up a rooster-tail of mud as they raced forward.

"General, you have subordinates to worry about details such as this," Mishkin said, exasperated.

"I thought I had sergeants to command tanks and lieutenants to command *them*, Colonel Mishkin, but it seems that today the entire Soviet Army has forgotten how to function without a kick in the ass." The general patted his stunned guard on the shoulder as he passed, trudging back for his command vehicle.

"If every man fought with his all, we would be at the Adriatic by now." An exaggeration, certainly not something that Strelnikov actually believed, but such bluster suited his public image.

"Yes, general," Mishkin agreed.

Back at the command APC, Strelnikov received the report about the traffic jam.

"A pair of NATO airstrikes, comrade general. The first stopped the column and the second destroyed the engineering vehicles intended to clear the road."A well-coordinated attack to slow down the second echelon of the attack as much as possible.

"Our men or Dmitriyev's?"

"Our men, comrade general."

"Time is not to be wasted," Strelnikov said as if lecturing a pupil. "Inform company commanders that if they cannot clear the road they are to go off road. The big fancy wheels on these carriers are not for show."

"General," Mishkin said, "many of our logistical vehicles don't have such refined off-road capabilities. Our rocket artillery battalion—"

"Then they will have to wait for the engineers to clear the road. The engineers can't get here until we make way for them," Strelnikov replied firmly. "I will not have the entire division stopped because of some mud. Those who can advance will."

"Without adequate fire support, what progress will we make?" Mishkin asked.

"We have our comrades in the air force, and the artillery assets of the 105th Division already in position. We *will* advance."

"Yes, general."

Strelnikov knew scattering his units like this would play holy hell with logistics later but, for now, they had to push. The 105th had burned themselves to a husk to drive back the enemy. They were stretched thin and battered bloody, but they were not broken. Not yet. Now it was Dmitriyev's turn to try to clear a hole in the NATO lines.

***

The orderly drawback of the Marines was in danger of becoming a retreat. Now that she was more accustomed to the savage sound of furious combat, that idea more than any other shocked her. Jean sighted her telephoto lens on a pair of cement pylon bridges which crossed the Drava River. While they were far away, her camera lens made them appear much closer as she snapped pictures. The bridges which led into Varaždin were full of withdrawing American forces. One after another, pair by pair, trucks and armored vehicles raced south. To someone higher up, with both more professional experience and big-picture information than Jean, this was probably a well-considered move. To her it just looked like retreat.

"Jean," Pete said.

"Hang on."

"*Jean.*"

Jean lowered her camera to give Pete a withering glare. "They're going to blow the bridge, Pete, once they get the last guys over—and I want to get it."

Conversation was momentarily impossible as a flight of attack helicopters thundered overhead, flying low and weaving around the tall trees that lined the far side of the river. Dario watched them anxiously as Jean and Pete waited for the sound level to drop off again.

"Jean, think about *why* they're going to blow the bridge. Think about what is *right* behind those guys."

A few dozen meters further down the riverbank was a Marine Humvee parked in the shelter of some low shrubs. A soldier with binoculars watched the far bank, scanning for threats.

"We've got time, Pete. We—"

The scream of mortars was unmistakable.

The AP news team threw themselves flat in the dirt. Jean covered the back of her head with her hands, interlacing her fingers and squeezing her eyes shut. Her breath kicked up dust which tickled her nose, but she ignored it.

Mortar rounds exploded in Varaždin behind them. The sound was muffled, the blasts hidden by the city's buildings.

No more rounds came in.

"They will stop them, won't they?" Dario asked, his face streaked with dirt. "This river. The soldiers."

Jean knew that the last river had only slowed the Soviet onslaught and she had her doubts about the soldiers. Bravado can only carry you so far. At a certain point reality kicked in. The Marines were fighting hard, but they were grossly outnumbered and on the verge of being outmaneuvered.

The Marine patrol nearby was also apparently unharmed, and mounted the Humvee which started up with a roar. The lookout shouted something to his companions and pointed across the river. With a spray of dirt from its rear wheels, the Humvee peeled away, racing from the river back into town.

Jean followed their gaze and saw movement on the far

bank. Boxy armored shapes were lumbering into view. Soviets. Though almost two hundred meters away, their military purpose was unmistakable. Her breath caught a moment, as if they might notice her if she breathed despite the intervening distance.

"Jean!" Pete broke the spell.

"Okay, we're going."

Missiles swooped across the river on trails of smoke before striking the Soviet vehicles and obliterating them. The bangs echoed across the river, smoke obscuring the far bank. Jean saw debris raining down on the river water in a semi-circle of splashes.

Rising to her feet, the three of them scrambled to the waiting 4x4. Pete jumped into the driver's seat and started it.

"Drive! Drive please!" Dario shouted from the back in rising panic.

More precise fire support rained down on the Soviet platoon that had dared tried to make its river crossing here. Artillery and mortar rounds burst in the woodland canopy, toppling trees and splintering trunks.

Pete threw the vehicle into reverse and floored the accelerator, whipping the truck back onto a neighboring road where they could join the Marines in retreat.

***

The retreat back from Varaždin was a chaotic and confused mess. Humvees and deuce-and-a-half cargo trucks were intermixed with M60 main battle tanks and LAV-25s on the road south to Zagreb.

Lieutenant Williams was just one of thousands of Marines now moving south, trying to draw up a fresh defensive perimeter against the Soviet onslaught.They'd underestimated their foe, expecting them to come on in textbook formations and have the decency to stand and be killed. What they'd gotten instead was a fierce and determined attack.

Williams was the only man left of his platoon. After the chaos at Batrovci and the humiliation of the fighting there he'd been pulled from the line by the brass, his fate uncertain. Court martial was discussed and then dropped. Williams wouldn't be made an example of, he would just be left to fade away.

His men who'd survived the fight were sent to the border while he'd been held behind. Now hostilities had commenced and he had no idea where his platoon might be, which was just as well to him. He wanted to be forgotten now that he saw himself in the face of every wounded soldier and corpse. He'd misread the map, he'd sent the balloon up. Was there any man who deserved more of the blame for this whole mess? From the top of the LAV he rode on, Williams held tight to an outcrop of metal, careful not to jostle the other marines that rode with him. Looking backward as the armored vehicle ascended a rise in the highway, he could see the vast plains of northern Yugoslavia stretching near to the border. Thick black smoke plumes dotted the horizon and the flitting shapes of attack aircraft buzzed and dove in the sky.

They passed a road sign for Čakovec and Varaždin, back in the direction they were fleeing from. There was nothing behind them now but a few recon platoons and some tank-hunter teams buying time . The teams were made of volunteers who worked in pairs, armed with Dragon anti-tank missile launchers and operating from hidden positions. They stayed behind to sow chaos among the advancing Soviet ranks. Their chances of survival were slim to none.

Division command was trading space for time. The sheer volume and intensity of the Soviet attack had taken everyone by surprise. They'd thought they could hold them at the Mura River for at least twenty-four hours. They'd thought they could slow them down at the Drava. Ivan hopped it so fast that it might as well not have been there. The new defensive line was just over this wooded ridgeline, on the opposite slope of a narrow river valley. With the attack aircraft operating from Zeljava Air Base —Asgard—they could hopefully blunt the Soviet attack badly enough to stall them here.

Who would have thought that the poorly-trained, ill-equipped, unmotivated, half-hearted conscripts that Williams had spent his career training to defeat would turn out to have fight in them? Williams and the others had underestimated the tenacity of their opponent, his skill, his cunning, but most of all they'd underestimated his will to fight. A Soviet armored formation moving in the open might lose an entire tank company to anti-tank guided missiles and airstrikes. An entire company dead in an instant—and yet they would advance. Their bloody-mindedness made it nearly impossible to shock them into defeat; this was going to be a struggle to the death of one side or the other.

As the Marine convoy ascended a ridgeline, entering a wooded area, Williams saw a half-dozen high-turreted M60 tanks scattered in the woods, half-concealed with camo netting, a pair of TOW-mounted M113 carriers among them. It was a reinforced platoon deploying to slow the Soviets. While the upcoming river valley was to be the divisional stop, this prime killing ground couldn't be sacrificed. Every meter would be paid for in blood.

Williams saw a Marine officer step into the roadway in front of the LAV, holding up a hand to halt it, certain that the twelve ton war machine would stop before him. There was a squeal of brakes and Willaims nearly lost his hand hold, but the officer proved correct.

"What unit are you boys?" the officer—a first lieutenant—asked.

There was no response as the marines looked at one another uncertainly.

The lieutenant scowled, "Who's in charge?"

The others looked to Williams, the only officer among them.

"We're elements from D Company, sir," Williams said. Among the men in and on this vehicle were cooks, drivers, clerks, and engineers, as well as a pair of anti-aircraft gunners who'd lost their gun battery.

"And you?"

Williams swallowed. "Second platoon, Lieutenant Williams."

"Lieutenant, we're setting up here to buy time for the engineer battalion south of us to finish preparing fighting positions and sowing mines. I've got tracks, but I need boots. Get your team set up in the village to the east," the first lieutenant gestured to the collection of white-washed houses not far away.

"Sir, these aren't infantry," Williams explained, "We're—"

"Not infantry?" the first lieutenant asked.

"Yes, sir."

"Hell," the first lieutenant spat on the ground, "You're Marines! You're *all* riflemen! Now are you gonna do your part or not?"

Williams knew that in the Marine Corps there was no "or not." He looked toward the village the first lieutenant indicated. It had good fields of fire and the buildings offered good cover. The other men on his vehicle were beaten, he knew that. Most of them hadn't fired a rifle in anger and even fewer had expected they would ever end up in a situation which might require them to. But, as the first lieutenant said, they were Marines.

"Yes, sir!" Willaims climbed from the LAV and looked to the others. "Let's get a move on!"

With mercifully little hesitation, the other marines clambered off of and out of the APC. The first lieutenant gestured to turn toward and proceed into the nearby village before turning to Williams.

"Get your people organized and get in position. Our AT teams are holding for now, but it won't last forever."

Williams glanced north again, watching a pair of Cobras following a smaller scout chopper as they buzzed over the plains, hunting for targets. "We'll do our best, sir."

"You have a radio?" the first lieutenant asked.

"No, sir."

The first lieutenant nodded. "The withdrawal code will be yellow smoke then. I'll pop a grenade at my position—" he gestured toward the TOW M113s "—and then I want you to load your people up and continue south toward the next defensive line. We need to buy a little more time. Every minute counts."

"Yes, sir." The first lieutenant didn't offer any more motivational words. He turned and continued on toward his command section, waiting for a gap in the withdrawing Marine column before crossing the road.

Left alone with his thoughts, Williams walked to the waiting makeshift infantry team he'd been given. There were a dozen of them altogether. He indicated two sergeants and divided the men among them. "First squad leader, second squad leader. We're holding down this village until we get the withdrawal code. When you see the first lieutenant pop yellow smoke, haul ass back to the LAV."

"Sir," a private said, "do we have any AT weapons or rockets or anything?"

"There's two AT-4s in the APC," second squad's new sergeant replied.

"One per team," William said. "Ivan won't get close enough for us to use them though." Williams looked north again toward the distant banging of high-velocity guns. Two portable anti tank rockets wouldn't do much against the weight of steel the Russians were calling down on them. It would mostly be up to the tanks on the ridgeline and any fire support they might get. The hopelessness of their current situation momentarily drowned out the intense overwhelming guilt he felt. Being active was better than being sorry for himself.

The makeshift combat team proceeded on foot into the village. Long since evacuated by anyone who could leave, it occupied a Y-shaped intersection. Williams put half his men in a wooded band to the left of town and the rest, with himself, in the section north of the road. The LAV remained idling in the intersection, partially concealed by a low-stone wall and brush thrown on top of it.

The view was incredible: two straight kilometers of unbroken visibility before being interrupted by a thin strip of trees. The Russians had a lot of open ground to cover if they hoped to make it.

The men were tense, uneasy, each left only with his own fears and the certainty that the fight was coming here, sooner than later. Williams didn't dwell on it, he dwelled on the past. That field outside Batrovci where so many of his soldiers had died holding the wrong town. He didn't know for sure, but based on the carnage he'd witnessed so far, Williams was fairly sure that what remained of his old platoon—and likely most of D Company— had been annihilated at the border. He was glad for anonymity now. He knew that soon enough he would have to face up to what he'd done—what he'd failed to do. More than just a court martial or a discharge, Williams would face the court of public opinion and the judgment of history.

Almost twenty minutes later, one of the M113s in the wooded ridgeline fired. The TOW missile streaked out almost faster than the eye could follow, leaving just a thin smoke trail behind and trailing a long filament of wire. A wire-guided missile was impossible to dodge at almost any range, and now was no different.

The missile's target, a squat armored recon vehicle, was struck head on. At this range, the explosion sounded more like a pop as it detonated against the vehicle's armor. A second later black smoke started curling into the sky: a kill.

A man hunkered near Williams' left began to swear rhythmically, like a prayer or chant. "Oh Christ, oh shit. Oh Christ, oh shit."

The rest of the Soviet advance guard soon came forward, just hazy wobbling dots at this distance; they were APCs or tanks from the way they moved, fanning out into a line. Williams made out six of them, and then six more emerged. The front rank stopped and flashed with the launch of their own wire-guided missiles in a ripple volley. These shots mostly found nothing, detonating in the woods. One struck a nearby farmhouse, blowing it apart. Another missile found and hit the M113 that had launched the first shot of this engagement.

The results of the hit were more dramatic given the closer range. There was a bang that Williams felt in his chest that made him flinch. He saw a crewman bail out, pulling himself from the commander's cupola, legs limp and useless, his fatigues in flames. The fire spread to the other evergreens of the ridgeline as the aluminum-armored track burned.

Now the M60s fired. The big guns barked and sent rounds down on their targets, detonating a pair of the Soviet troop carriers in brilliant fireballs.

Williams could see the enemy fighting vehicles were leap-frogging forward, alternating lines of fire and advance. Some of them had popped smoke grenades and the lead units were billowing a thick smoke screen from their exhaust. A steady breeze kept the smoke from doing more than slightly interfering with vision, and the thermal sights on the American tanks and APCs would see right through it anyway. Behind the Soviet APCs came larger vehicles, tanks that joined in with their own big guns.

One of the M60s took a hit. A shell glanced off its turret making a sound like a giant, off-key bell. Williams shuddered to imagine what that felt like inside the turret.

As the Soviet tracks drew closer, Williams could make out details: the ad hoc application of branches and shrubbery for additional camouflage, the narrow missile tube that sat atop the round turret of each vehicle, and their own distinct, angular camouflage pattern.

Unseen artillery came into the fight minutes later. American howitzers erupted pillars of black earth into the sky. The second salvo burst just overhead and scattered anti-tank bomblets across the ground, forming an ad hoc minefield. Some of these bomblets found Soviet tracks as they advanced, tearing their armor open or catastrophically igniting the volatiles within them. One BMP struck an artillery-deployed mine and exploded into metal scrap.

One of Williams' men cheered, but it was premature. The Soviets were still coming. With the front rank of BMPs savaged, the rear advanced aggressively. Their autocannons spat shells that burst in the smokey pine forest, toppling a tree across one of the tanks and scattering wooden splinters. Other rounds came toward the village Williams and his men sheltered in, bursting across the face of a building, collapsing its north side.

The enemy tracks paused momentarily in a low gulley before continuing forward, this time shadowed by dozens of shapes slouching across the trampled cornfields. Infantry. Williams mentally gauged the distance, just under a thousand yards, almost in firing range of his rifles.

With no radio, and a voice not capable of being made out over the din of battle, Williams signaled the attack by shouldering his rifle and firing. He didn't aim for individuals at this range, but clusters of shapes. The signal given, the entire team began to fire. The staccato rattle of gunfire was picked up by the LAV, directing its fire against the BMPs rather than their accompaniment.

The enemy infantry faltered and went to ground, their tracks brewing up left and right from precision fire coming from the first lieutenant's tank section, now down to four vehicles.

A pair of F-16 Fighting Falcons came screaming from the south, causing Williams to roll onto his back in alarm. Their bomb-covered bellies just barely cleared the treetops before they hauled back, unleashing a spread of Rockeye cluster munitions that rained down on the nearest Soviet forces. Explosions blanketed their position and turned multi-million dollar fighting vehicles into twisted scrap. Perhaps more dramatically, Williams saw men tossed like ragdolls, their bodies at the mercy of physical forces beyond the ability of any human to withstand or survive.

When the smoke cleared, the Soviet spearhead was decimated, most of their vehicles burning on the field, adding to a haze of gunsmoke and missile trails that reduced visibility from thousands of meters to hundreds. Here and there scattered Soviet infantry squads or lone BMPs fought on, their shots snapping over Williams' head or striking their cover. Somewhere one of his men was crying in pain, but he couldn't determine where exactly it came from.

They'd stopped the first attack, but he knew a tank platoon

was pushing up behind this first wave, with more infantry behind. With visibility so low, the AT-4s might just come in handy. Williams looked around for his sergeant, "Where—"

He got no further as a quartet of Soviet aircraft passed low overhead as the F-16s had done, dumping their ordnance on the Americans.

On instinct, Williams curled into a ball, rifle forgotten, orders forgotten, thinking only of saving his own life. He nestled as deep as he could into the grass on the roadside. The sound was deafening, a dozen tons of high explosive detonating all around him. Concussive blast waves washed over Williams forcibly rolling him into another man who lay beside him. Williams' mouth and nose were full of grit and he hacked and coughed, wiping at his face and trying to get his bearings. He was alive, but he couldn't hear anything, only a sharp ringing.

The village was also mostly intact, a miracle—Williams thought—given how many bombs must have hit it, until he saw the wooded ridge with the first lieutenant's tanks.

Nothing remained. Pines were snapped and burned like matchsticks. The vehicles that sheltered among them were blackened and smoking, those that were not split open or in flames anyway. It gave Williams small satisfaction to see the Soviet attack group being harried by American fighter craft as they withdrew, a pair of them spiraling down in flames over the horizon.

One of Williams' sergeants grabbed his shoulder, startling him. The sergeant was shouting— screaming something at Williams, his words unheard.

The lieutenant pointed at his ears and screamed back. "I can't hear you!"

This time he read the sergeant's lips. "Withdraw!"

"Get the squad back to the LAV!" Williams shouted back, feeling his words instead of hearing them. "We're going!"

**

11

Testing a sound system was always tedious work. Checking the mics, the speaker placement, levels, making sure there was no interference—it really ate away at the day. It was a new venue, an old warehouse on the westside of Jacksonville. It was A good place for a show, but it also meant that it was virgin, untested and untried.

Vance slowly boosted the levels of the right remote speaker, feeling the bass thud of the dance beat in his chest. The speaker still sounded a little tinny, so he might have to check to make sure the bass didn't blow at some point.

With a sigh, Vance killed the music and looked up from the DJ booth across the empty cement pad that was the dance floor. Tonight this floor would be packed, mostly with college kids from Jacksonville University, but also any local dance music aficionados and party animals. It would be a place of revelry and joy, a place to lose your mind in the music. It brought Vance some small sense of satisfaction to know that he'd be part of that, yet as soon as he stopped the music, reality hit him in the form of a portable radio tuned to the local news station.

"The military hasn't released casualty lists yet, but they're anticipated to be in the thousands already," reported a stoic female voice . "Current reports put the Soviet army twenty miles inside the former Yugoslav border within twenty-four hours, with little sign of slowing."

Even as Vance prepared for a party, a war raged in Europe. It was amazing what people could get used to. East and West were at long last meeting on the field of battle without the plausible deniability of intermediate nations and people still wanted to party. Vance wasn't sure if this was the worst or best time for it.

Leaving the booth, Vance crossed the dance floor and followed the fat, black cable that ran to the remote speakers, checking that it was well taped-down and out of the way for the dancers. At the far end he reached the stack of sound equipment and began inspecting each speaker cup for tears or damage. As he worked, the radio was distant enough that he couldn't make out details, but he heard the broadcaster pronouncing unfamiliar city names one after another.

Officially, the Reserves weren't going to get involved in what was being called "a conflict" rather than a war. Congress didn't want to escalate things further and it was always an expensive and unpopular move.

Even so, he'd heard a rumor from his first lieutenant that a big week-long exercise was coming. It wouldn't be the usual catch up work at the shooting range either. Rather it was going to be a joint exercise in Georgia with troops from the Alabama, Florida, and Georgia National Guards, as well as some regular Army and Reserves. It wasn't every day that Uncle Sam ponied up the cash for such a big deployment.

Vance had also been asked to come in three days this week to help with administrative paperwork. It was all the precursor to a big call up. They'd qualified as many tanks and crews as they could and even had a number of soldiers on loan to Fort Stewart, where they were getting hands on with the new M1 Abrams and Bradley. No matter how you cut it, it was bad news.

"Don, you good man?" one of the other sound techs asked.

Vance nodded at him, "Yeah, just ..."

Both men looked at the radio.

"Dude, don't sweat it," the tech said. "This shit'll wrap up quick like the Aden Gulf did."

Vance was not so sure. Ethiopia's invasion of Djibouti was just two kids throwing down in the sandbox before Uncle Sam rolled up his sleeves and broke it up. This was the two biggest kids on the block squaring off. "Yeah," he said.

"Don!" one of the other roadies called from the small office at the front of the warehouse, "Phone's for you!"

Laying down his cable, Vance made his way over, taking the yellowing plastic receiver from the tech's hand. "Hello?"

"Don, is this a bad time?" Molly asked.

Vance looked back at the other techs who seemed to be moving along fine. "No, how did you know I was here?"

"I had to call the venue and ask around. Are you going into the base today?"

"Base? Yeah, I have to sign off some readiness reports. Why? Something wrong?"

Her tone indicated anything but problems. She sounded excited, urgent. "No, no. I need you to grab some forms. I have the numbers here." Molly rattled off the form codes which were unfamiliar to him.

"What are those for?"

"I was talking to Susannah today and she told me that the Army is looking for qualified communication techs for relay stations in Germany. You're *definitely* qualified for it with what you do. Just gotta fill it out and get it to your CO. She told me Derreck is transferring to a communication battalion."

Vance was at a loss, his mind working to catch up. He almost asked Molly why he would bother transferring until he realized what it was. "Is this about Yugoslavia?"

Now it was her turn to hesitate on the phone. "I think you'd like the work more than being a tanker." She sounded hurt.

"Molly," Vance rubbed his forehead and searched for words, "I can't."

"Why not?" Molly's tone was edged with defensiveness. "Susannah says Derreck did it."

"I'm a company commander, Molly. I can't … I can't just bail out."

"You're *not* bailing out. You'll be way better at this than command anyway. This will look better on a resume."

"Molly—"

"Don't '*Molly*' me! Why are you being so stubborn about this? We talked about you getting out last year anyway!"

Vance didn't remind her that the reason he had not let his

term expire was because the money was too good. "Molly, listen. I know, you're scared but...comms battalion isn't much safer. They get targeted in war too."

"Is that supposed to make me feel better?"

"No. I just ... listen, Molly, I made a commitment and I'm gonna uphold it. If I bail out now, these guys will get saddled with a new CO, one that doesn't know them. I've got to see things through."

"So you *are* going." It wasn't a question.

"You know I don't know that, babe."

The silence on the line grew to an uncomfortable length. "I don't like this, Don. I don't like this at all."

"I know. I'm sorry. The guys here were just saying that this might turn out to be another false alarm."

"Do you believe them?"

Vance's silence answered her question.

"Hurry home when you're done, okay?"

"Okay."

"Love you."

Vance prayed that this all would end before the training session of next week. He prayed that a ceasefire would go into place, talks would be held, and East and West could go back to mutual apathy. He prayed for all of these things even as he felt his stomach dropping out at the prospect of war. "I love you too."

***

Night settled over the former Yugoslavia, with both forces exhausted. The Soviet Army had been driving hard for twenty-four hours, though they had yet to secure a breakthrough. They'd shoved the West back with more aggression than outside observers had thought possible. They'd bent and mangled their lines, but NATO remained unbroken. Their fighting strength had been saved by brave delaying action and a rapid withdrawal to avoid being cut off.

NATO's advanced night and thermal optics allowed them to

rule the dark. It made any attempt to continue forward suicidal for the Soviets. On the other side of the line, the forces of the West were too badly disorganized to mount anything more than local counterattacks. Scattered skirmishing continued well into the night as the cavalry and recon forces of each side probed for weakness and gaps to exploit. Rocket and machine gun fire echoed over the countryside. The soldiers of both armies settled into fitful rest, cooking and eating pre-packaged rations in the dark and resting weary limbs. Some slept while they could, encamped inside or around their vehicles, lulled to sleep by exhaustion. Overhead, the air war also wound down.

That is, until thirty F-117 Nighthawk stealth bombers took to the skies.

The kite-shaped, angular bombers were close to undetectable on radar or thermal sensors as they stayed low to the ground and flew out, seeking out Soviet logistics and supplies. After infiltrating the enemy radar and SAM net unseen, they fanned out, each working in a pair, to close on pre-assigned targets: Bridges, fuel and ammo dumps, and command posts, all elements of the logistical machine that kept the Soviet army rolling forward.

With one fighter acting as a laser designator, the other would strike. Laser-guided precision bombs smashed cement bridge pylons or burrowed into even the most hardened command bunkers before detonating. Their deadly work done, the fighters streaked back for the safety of friendly air cover. Though most arrived, nearly one-fifth had been lost to anti-aircraft ground fire or patrolling fighters lucky enough to catch the blip of radar signature when the Nighthawk opened its bomb-bay doors.

Each strike was a stinging blow to the Russian armored columns, but not quite a decisive one. If the Soviets were to smash the Western forces here, Asgard Air Base would need to be dealt with and soon.

***

Sergeant Pinback was on a hair trigger. Ever since hostilities had opened the morning previous, things had been hectic at Asgard. The Croatian Army had gratefully opened the top of the line facility to Western use once fighting broke out, and soon specialists, crew, and planes were flown in from across NATO. Here atop Mount Pljeskavica, if the Sergeant were to poke his head from the half-buried metal shack that held all the monitoring equipment for this particular search radar, he would have a splendid view of the nighttime countryside here. An idyllic valley, it was lush and green in the day and cool and vibrant at night. Of course, he would also have himself busted back to private or court martialed out of the service for leaving his post, since he was on combat alert.

Pinback suppressed a yawn and sipped his coffee. His eyes were glued to a monochromatic green display, a visual interpretation of the radar waves sweeping from the dish installed a few dozen meters away. This radar was interfaced with the air defense net put up around the base. SAM launchers and AA guns interspaced at regular intervals ringed the mountain, and a constant pair of alert fighters were kept on standby, ready to leap into the sky at a moment's notice.

The base hadn't slept since the early morning hours of the previous day. Fighters were constantly launching and landing, needing refueling, rearming, and in some cases repairing. This war was just as hard on machinery as it was on people. It was a ravenous thing, it consumed both without end.

On a brief duty break earlier in the day, before Pinback had relieved the afternoon shift, he'd seen the jets coming in with flaps torn away, stabilizers and fins riddled with shrapnel and bullet holes. The nature of modern jet aircraft meant that in most cases any damage more severe than that was a hard kill. Even so, the A-10 pilots in particular had taken beatings that Pinback didn't think were possible, landing planes with damage to them that would have destroyed any lesser vehicle. They'd still suffered fearsome losses. NATO ground forces were screaming for more strafing runs by the famed Warthogs who were living up to their legend, but there were only so many pilots and so many craft to go around. Now, at least half of them were out of action from mechanical problems, pilot fatigue, or simple combat losses.

The last sortie of the night—the Nighthawk raid—had come home just a few hours earlier, not long before daybreak. Once it started to get light again, the air war would begin again in earnest.

Asgard wasn't the only air base NATO was operating from, but it was the best. All their other airfields had been hit with short-range missile bombardment from Soviet ballistic missile launchers. The enemy missile attacks had obliterated aircraft, repair facilities, and in some cases rendered runways into useless, cratered strips.

Asgard was wholly underground save for its runways. It meant that such long range bombardment techniques could never hope to damage the base's vulnerable fuel storage facilities or aircraft hangars. Without serious, heavily concentrated firepower, the base's facilities would remain fully operational. Despite the obstacles, the Soviets could not leave Asgard unchallenged.

Something blipped on the radar and Pinback choked on his coffee. He set the mug down too quickly and it sloshed a small puddle onto the side of his desk. With practiced speed, Pinback took notes on the craft coming into range. The target ascended from where it had previously been too low to be detected against the background clutter of the radar. The computer tentatively identified it as a Bear, a Russian heavy-lifter.

Pinback flicked on his radio console. "Asgard Six, this is Alpha Hotel. New contact, designate Raid-1 spotted north, fifty miles out an—." He broke off as his radar display dissolved into static a moment later.

"Say again, Alpha Hotel, Raid One spotted. Size and composition?"

"Asgard Six, Raid One was one heavy-lifter, probably a Bear or a group of fighters flying in close proximity, but be advised that I have lost contact due to heavy jamming."

"Copy, Alpha Hotel, keep us informed."

Pinback looked back to his washed out monitor. The radar dish was overwhelmed with bursts of incoming radar waves so that it was unable to monitor its own returning signals. An attack was inbound, but how many were coming?

"Affirmative, Asgard Six."

The base's two alert fighters were a pair of Panavia Tornados marked with the red, white, and blue of RAF roundels on their tails. Their engines burned a hot yellow in the dark as they ignited before tearing down the runway and into the sky. Missile guidance computers were warmed up while turrets and launchers swiveled skyward and a pair of AWACS planes were diverted to better cover the base.

The Soviets were ready for this. Fifty miles east, a squadron of MiG-29s engaged afterburners. They accelerated from the safety of their own SAM umbrella to cross the NATO lines at low level. They closed rapidly to the re-deploying AWACS craft before climbing and firing anti-radiation missiles. These weapons were radar killers, designed to track and follow the AWACS' own radar beams back to the source.

With no choice but to disengage its airborne early-warning radar, the radar plane did so and dove, executing violent evasive maneuvers as its escorts chased after the Soviet raiders. A similar attack was executed on the second AWACS plane though this raid hit disaster as their approach led them straight over a waiting British SAM site which engaged, downing half the craft and forcing the rest back.

In the intervening chaos, the Soviet raid on Asgard began in earnest. Thirty-six fighters and attack craft screamed toward the base along two different attack vectors. Many of them were armed with runway-cratering bombs and bunker buster missiles. This attack intended to neutralize the air base once and for all.

As the lead aircraft crested the valley, they were painted with the search radars that littered the mountainside. Fire signals were sent to missile batteries and gun crews, and the sky lit up with anti-aircraft fire. Rainbow arcs of tracer rounds cut the air and the bright flares of missile launches shone in the woods.

Leading a mass of aircraft straight into the open jaws of a prepared anti-aircraft defense was a quick way to get a lot of aircraft destroyed in a short time. The Soviets almost certainly would have been massacred had their pilots not been prepared. Electronic countermeasures were engaged, flares and clouds of metallic chaff launched, cluttering up the air with so much noise that the missiles had a hard time picking the correct targets. Many of the base defenders' missiles detonated harmlessly amidst clouds of metallic ribbon or against the bright thermal signature of a falling phosphorus flare. Some still made it through. One missile blew a MiG in half at the waist; another sheared a Sukhoi's wing away, causing the craft and its bombs to drop like a rock and trail a rolling fireball across the valley below.

The Soviet aircraft were not entirely defenseless. Ten of them were specially outfitted for SEAD—suppression of enemy air defenses—colloquially known in the US as "Wild Weasels." These craft carried special anti-radiation missiles designed to seek out the search and targeting radars of the SAM batteries on the ground. As their comrades juked and jinked, denying the missiles an easy lock, the SEAD fighters came in close behind them. Onboard computers picked out radar systems like Sergeant Pinback's, locking on before firing. Once released, the missiles rode the invisible radar waves back into their transmitters.

Many American crews, Pinback included, shut their radars down to avoid destruction by the enemy, but it was too late. The missiles locked on to their last known positions and exploded across the mountainside. Pinback's quick action spared his own radar dish, the missile going slightly off track to instead crash into the prefabricated building he was sheltering in. Sergeant Pinback was dead before he had time to be afraid.

With the air defenses mostly neutralized, the Soviets began

their attack run. Attack craft dove in to unleash conventional bombs across the mouth of the underground airbase. AA guns around the runway spewed shells skyward in a vain attempt to ward off the raiders. Unlike their more advanced, missile-firing cousins, AA guns were easier to avoid through evasive maneuvers and posed a lesser threat.

Bombs burst across the tarmac, raining chunks of asphalt and leaving huge cratered holes that prevented any aircraft from taking off or landing. One of the Russian pilots lost his tail fin to a rapid-firing Vulcan cannon. He ejected moments before his plane smashed into the mountainside, the explosion lighting up the night and igniting the neighboring trees.

The two alert Tornados spiraled overhead, locked in a death struggle with the Soviet fighters. They were forced to dodge allied ground fire that targeted them by mistake as they attempted to eliminate or drive off as many fighters as they could. One of the Tornados went down quickly, taking a missile hit almost right away, while the other was able to execute a scissor turn to get in behind its opponent and down them instead with a burst of gunfire.

With the battle turning to chaos, the final coup de grace came swooping in. A quartet of Mig-23 Floggers packing bunker buster missiles closed the distance, lining up with the mountainside. They used the runway mouth as their aiming point. The runway was clearly visible, framed by the plethora of downed aircraft and destroyed AA batteries burning around it. Target lined up, they fired their deadly payload—six missiles each—and pulled away.

Twenty-four anti-bunker missiles struck the earth at speed and burrowed in, smashing through meters of rock before detonating. Debris fountained down the side of the mountain and uprooted dozens of trees. Haphazard miniature landslides rolled down the wooded slope, caving in parts of the mountainside.

The Soviets withdrew as fresh NATO interceptors closed with them. They left millions of dollars in downed jet aircraft scattered across the once placid valley. Asgard's air defense network had been savaged with all but two targeting radars out of action and four of her five runways left heavily cratered. It was enough damage to put an airbase out of operation indefinitely. A normal airbase anyway.

No sooner had the Soviet raid pulled back than the air base's maintenance personnel emerged from the still-intact bunker complex, shoveling gravel and runway debris back into the craters to fill them in before covering them over with metal plates. The damage to the runways would be resolved in a matter of hours and they would be usable just in time for day break.

One of the engineers, looking back over his shoulder, had the impression that the whole mountainside was burning, turning the night into a fiery twilight. The bunker busters had left huge gravel-strewn craters on the mountainside, but still couldn't hope to penetrate dozens of meters of earth and rock down to the hardened bunker walls.

Asgard still stood.

***

The sky was beginning to lighten as the sun neared the horizon in the east, twilight dawned to the countryside. The concert of nocturnal insects and animal life was dying down, yielding the air to their diurnal cousins. Most of these were not yet awake, and just a handful of birds had begun to chirp and sing, heralding the coming dawn.

It reminded General Strelnikov of the ongoing conflict as the night forces turned over the field to the main combat arms. It was too early for the Red Army's howitzers to begin their deadly concert. The men of his division slept fitfully, wrapped in tarps and blankets nestled around the perimeter of their armored vehicles.

Strelnikov himself couldn't sleep. He had been up most of the night reviewing maps of the area and going over the latest recon photos. They'd been extracted with a high loss of life among the brave pilots of the Air Force. The photos showed him what he already knew to be true: the Americans were bending but hadn't broken yet. The entirety of the 105th Division had been expended in the last twenty four hours, the survivors were now withdrawing piecemeal to be overtaken by Dmitriyev's tanks and tracks of the 111th Division.

The ground was soft with morning dew and squelched under his boots as he walked the rows of parked APCs and vehicles. The machines—like their crew—were idle. Hoods and maintenance hatches sat open as the vehicles were gassed up and checked for proper performance. Only the maintenance and supply crews were active this early, as they went from vehicle to vehicle distributing ammo and fuel.

The aroma of cooking food drew the general toward the mess tent. The tent was a canvas lean-to built off the side of a kitchen truck. It sat parked in the shade of a large poplar tree close beside the main highway. The cooks were only just beginning to cook up a hot meal, something that would have to be consumed quickly in the predawn darkness before the advance could begin again. Exercising the benefit of his rank, Strelnikov secured an early meal of sausage, fried eggs, and a thick slice of rye bread which he ate in peace. He rested his back against the massive tire of a BTR while he looked out over his restlessly dreaming troops.

A UAZ 4x4 coasted off the highway. It's primary headlights were switched off. The truck drove only with the guidance of slit-apertured blackout lights which were intended to keep them less visible to protect against roving attack aircraft. The truck was unmarked and sported the same natural camouflage that all the vehicles in the army did. A heavy machine gun was also mounted on the back, manned by a nervous-looking private who had a shoulder-launched SAM tube propped beside him as well. Clearly this was a VIP.

As Strelnikov stood, Lieutenant General Gurov emerged from the truck. Like Strelnikov, he wore the uniform of a common soldier.

"Comrade general," Strelnikov said, stopping himself from

saluting his superior. No sense drawing attention to a man clearly trying to keep a low profile. "I wasn't expecting you."

"Good," Gurov said, "then it is as it should be." He came to stand beside Strelnikov while two of his men stood nearby with weapons at hand. "Radio communication at this level is unsafe. I've lost two decoy transmitters and NATO is getting better at finding the real ones. I don't intend to make myself an easy target."

Strelnikov nodded.

"Your division is prepared to continue the attack?"

"Yes, comrade general. My mobile artillery has had a long drive but we are all together again. How is the operation proceeding?"

Gurov's face was tight, the face of a man not enthusiastic about the future. "The French mongrels of their Foreign Legion are making hell in Bosnia, it's tied up most of the southern front. The operation seems to hinge on our ability to take Zagreb and quickly."

"What is the status of the 105th?" Strelnikov had seen enough evidence to know the answer, but wanted to hear it said.

"Spent," Gurov replied as if discussing a rifle cartridge. "The division is in shambles, its commander dead." He saw the shock on Strelnikov's face. "He died shortly after crossing the border. An airstrike."

Strelnikov felt only numbness. "I see."

"A good man. Good men, all of them," Gurov said. "It falls to you and that flamboyant parasite Dmitriyev. You know who I am relying on."

Strelnikov understood the distaste Gurov felt for Dmitriyev, but despite his airs the man was proving to be a competent commander. His forces made good progress yesterday evening. They'd acquitted themselves well.

"Once the columns begin to move," Gurov said, "I expect you will find me my breakthrough. I have held Mamedov's 88th tank division in close standby. If we can break through we can end this thing."

"Yes, comrade general."

"We attack NATO soon. Dmitriyev's men will lead off. I aim to push the enemies into the hills and drive your division on Zagreb. You *must* keep them moving, Do not sacrifice our momentum for anything."

Strelnikov nodded.

"Questions?"

"No, comrade general."

"Then make Mother Russia proud."

The phrasing surprised Strelnikov. Nationalistic reference to Russia was usually frowned upon in favor of more inclusive terminology . It seemed Gurov was falling back heavily on his experience in the Great Patriotic War. He watched Gurov return to his truck and speed back up the road, weaving around parked vehicles where he could.

"General, what are you doing up?" Colonel Mishkin asked, walking over to join his commanding officer. The hoarseness of his voice told Strelnikov that Mishkin had only just woken up.

"Planning."

"Was that General Gurov?"

"Yes. We're no longer the third in the column. We're second."

"Second?" Mishkin asked. "Dmitriyev?"

"Yes. He is to clear a path for us in the morning."

Distant howitzers rumbled like a petulant thunderstorm, the first elements of Dmitriyev's division beginning their attack.

"You sound troubled, comrade," Mishkin said, stepping closer. Even in the face of war his cautious optimism couldn't be quashed it seemed.

"I hope that our comrades in the air force have done well enough silencing the enemy air power, or this will be another bloodbath."

Mishkin made a sound and then hesitated, deciding his words.

"You know something, comrade colonel?"

"I have ... heard a rumor already this morning." Despite Mishkin's prestigious rank, he could not shake his peasant-like devotion to gossip and rumor. He always seemed to have an ear to the ground for such things.

"I would like to hear it."

"I have heard that our air force comrades have launched a large attack on NATO's primary air base in the region, a beast of a fortress that the Yugoslavs built, a place they call Asgard."

"Asgard?" Strelnikov asked.

Mishkin nodded and sipped his coffee, wincing at its bitterness. "I have heard it did not go well."

"This rumor," Strelnikov said, looking to the lightening sky as if he could observe the state of the enemy air forces, "let us hope it's unfounded. If it is true, high command has not seen fit to change our plans."

Mishkin joined his commander looking to the sky.

"Assemble the regimental and battalion officers," Strelnikov said. "I want to determine our marching orders.

"Yes, comrade general."

As Mishkin marched off to gather the general's senior officers, Strelnikov looked south. It was going to be another long, bloody day.

***

12

Beneath the waves of the Adriatic, the crew's elation at having sunk an enemy vessel had worn off as the rest of the day passed uneventfully. Yessov suspected their victim may simply have been caught by bad luck as they had found no other easy targets. Periodically the sub had risen to periscope depth to sweep for fresh prey on the surface.

The lack of surface ships had Yessov paranoid about enemy submarine activity. His Kilo-class boat may have been a wolf among lambs, but if there were Western attack submarines in the Adriatic he might rapidly find himself the hunted rather than the hunter.

"Sonar contact, comrade captain."

Yessov brought his head up, looking away from the depth chart he had been studying. The sonar station was two paces away from him and he crossed the distance quickly. "Report."

"Bearing is 090, distance uncertain."

"Identification?"

The operator and his subordinate consulted the computerized waterfall display, trying to match the faint sound signature to known vessels without luck. "There is too much interference to be sure."

"A guess?" Yessov said, fighting to keep his voice even and to hide his irritation.

"Surface vessel, large enough and quiet enough to be a warship."

A warship. Now that was a fitting prize, but warships—unlike oilers—had teeth of their own and the sensors to put their weapons where they needed to be. "Heading?"

The operator listened again, studying his equipment readout

and furrowing his brow in frustration. "My guess is 300. Southeast to northwest."

Yessov weighed his options. They were currently headed to the northern end of the Adriatic at two-thirds speed, following the strengthening radar signals of the carrier group. It was slow enough that he hoped any nearby ships or submarines would not pick them up on passive, but still fast enough that they were not crawling. It didn't account for the possibility that they may drive directly beneath a waiting sonobuoy and trigger a Western response.

They could ignore this rogue contact and continue north in hopes of reaching the carrier group undetected, or they could engage as a target of opportunity.

"Take us to periscope depth," Yessov said, inwardly cursing the weakness of their own passive sonar equipment. As it stood, visual confirmation was still the best way—short of active signaling—to identify targets at range. Commands were relayed and B-218 angled up, motoring silently for the surface. Leaving the Layer behind they came within a dozen meters of the surface.

With a command, Yessov raised the periscope, bypassing the usual first step of a passive radar sweep. He had a specific target in mind this time. Leaning into the sight, Yessov rotated the periscope to come in line with the ship they'd detected. It took him a moment to spot it since it was coming straight at him and was much closer than expected.

"Captain, the target is accelerating. Identified as *Spruance*-class!" Sonar called.

His words were unnecessary; Yessov had full visual identification. The fact that the destroyer was accelerating toward them didn't bode well, but it wasn't as bad as the helicopter he spotted racing in their direction.

"Emergency dive!" Yessov said, stepping away from the periscope that the helicopter had no doubt seen. "Helm, give me flank speed, hard rudder port!"

"Hard rudder port!" the helm parroted, obeying his command.

Yessov stepped back and seized a handrail with a sweat-slick palm and leaned against the hard dive.

The hull sang with the impact of a sonar wave, a noise no submariner ever wanted to hear.

"Target is actively pinging!"

"They have us," Yessov said to himself.

"Surface splash! Torpedo in the water!" sonar called.

Yessov squeezed his eyes closed, pushing aside his fear, pushing aside the heart-aching certainty that he'd been had. He only visualized the sub's course.

"Rudder hard to starboard! Deploy a noise maker!"

"Yes, comrade captain!"

The hard U-turn in the water would create a trapped eddy or "knuckle" that would reflect sonar waves and likely draw in any actively pinging torpedoes while the noise maker imitated a submarine's natural sounds and would draw in acoustic homing.

Yessov opened his eyes and looked at the navigational map.

"Confidence is high on those pings, captain!" one of his officers reported.

"Torpedo is going active, closing on us. Range is one kilometer."

"Helm, take us down to ninety meters."

"Captain, the charts only have the depth at one hundred meters!"

Yessov whirled on the man and snapped, "I know that! Do it!"

He was trying to get as low as he could to provide more reflective surfaces for the torpedo's active sonar to misread. Ten meters was not much room to play with though, an uncharted wreck or rock outcropping could end this trip here and now.

"Go to silent running," Yessov said. "Range to torpedo?"

"Fifty meters, forty—"

The sub shook with the concussion of an explosion and someone swore loudly before an officer scolded them to silence.

"Torpedo detonation," Sonar said, unnecessarily. "It struck the decoy, I think."

"Helm, take us to bearing..." he consulted the boat's map again to determine the American's relative position. "040. Line us up with the American's pings."

As his orders were carried out, the XO raced onto the bridge, buttoning his uniform jacket, clearly having been roused from sleep.

Yessov spared him a look, "Some bad luck for us."

"Surface splash!" Sonar said again.

"Another damn torpedo," Yessov said, suspecting this one was a rocket-launched weapon fired from the American destroyer.

"Torpedo in the water," Sonar confirmed, "Range one hundred and fifty meters off our starboard. Torpedo is pinging!"

"Depth?"

"Torpedo is in a search pattern at thirty meters, comrade captain!"

A searching torpedo would endlessly circle and ping until it found a target or it ran out of fuel and detonated. Yessov didn't intend to give it a target, but he was going to use it to his advantage.

"Take us down five more meters," he said, needing every inch of space. "And set heading for that torpedo."

"Captain?" the XO asked, his eyes panicked.

Yessov avoided looking at him, "Helm, take us forward right under it."

"Captain, that's—"

"An order," Yessov interrupted his XO.

"*Captain*," the XO whispered, his voice hissing. "You don't think we can get under it do you?"

"I do."

The order was carried out and a hush fell over the bridge as if there was a chance the torpedo may hear them even through the acoustically dampened hull. It was quiet enough, and the torpedo close enough, that they could hear it in the water. The torpedo's active sonar banged away into the sea, its motor whirred loudly on its circular course.

As they closed, Yessov's navigation officer read the distances to the torpedo's position which drew closer meter by meter until, as Yessov hoped, they passed under it.

Yessov sighed in relief, "All stop."

"All stop, captain."

Now, with even the propeller stopped, the submarine was utterly silent. With no nuclear reactor coolant pumps to whirr and hum, B-218 was a ghost in the night. Despite the boat and crew being silent, it was anything but quiet as the angel of death circled overhead in the form of an American homing torpedo. It continually fired its sonar uselessly in a circle hoping to catch the submarine they had known was here.

It was a remarkably advantageous position. Sitting under an active torpedo masked them nearly completely from the helicopter's dipping sonar and the destroyer's own passive arrays. With all the noise this weapon was putting off, any incidental sound B-218 made would be obscured. Not only that, but the Americans would not fire again where they had already fired. All that might spot them here now was the destroyer's active sonar, which would have to be brought in close to see them this near the bottom, and there was no chance the Americans would risk coming close to a torpedo that would attack anything that reflected sound. Even so, if the ploy didn't work, they were frozen in place until the American torpedo eventually ran out of fuel and detonated. If the Americans knew they were here, they would just have to lie in wait for B-218 to make a move. *No,* Yessov thought, *let them think we're dead. Perhaps their first shot killed us.*

The seconds blurred to minutes until after nearly twenty, the torpedo exploded overhead sending another minor shock into the hull.

"Anything?" Yessov asked his sonar operator.

The crewman screwed his eyes shut and listened. "Active sonar pinging to the south," he said. "No chance they've acquired us."

"South?" The XO asked, consulting a chart.

"They're trying to drive us back to the straits," Yessov

explained. "It is easier to keep the barn door closed than to patrol the whole pasture. Take us up to sixty meters," Yessov said, "ahead one-third."

"Yes, captain."

"Are we not going back for them?" The XO asked.

"The carrier is our prize. I won't risk detection again on a mere escort." Yessov did not add that he was too rattled to try that again. He'd gotten lucky. If that torpedo had run deeper he never would have slipped underneath it. Luck was not a resource he expected to hold out. "Once we get out of earshot of them we will continue at two-thirds."

The XO did not object but eyed Yessov uncertainly. No doubt wondering if his ever pretentious captain would get them killed.

Fine, Yessov thought, *let him wonder.*

***

The raging battle was just the ever-present rumble of guns and whine of rockets at this range. To Jean, It sounded every bit like some sort of demented thunderstorm. When she'd been closer to the front, the pops of cannon and rattle of machine guns echoed from all directions, never letting her forget that this was a warzone. Still, it was all background noise and she put it out of mind to focus on the target of her interview: a young, freckle-faced private who squinted in the sunlight and scratched at the day-old stubble on his chin.

Pete kept the young man in center frame through the lens of his camera, face set in a grimace of concentration while Jean held her microphone close enough that he could be picked up by the tape deck she carried.

"They got us running water and ammo up to the guys on the front right now," he was explaining from the open door of the two-and-a-half-ton truck he sat in.

"And have you seen any action?"

There was a boyish smirk, like he was embarrassed or excited. "I seen a lot of messed up tanks and stuff coming back." The smile faltered. "And uh ... you know ambulance tracks and stuff. Some Russian planes got chased off by the air force. Crazy shi— uh, stuff, ma'am."

Jean could cut the tape later to be a little more broadcast appropriate. "People back home say we're losing, what do you have to say to that?" A little controversy could always be counted on to get a good sound bite.

"I'd say those folks back home don't know nothing about what we're doing out here," he said, face hardening. "It's pretty easy to say that stuff when you're sitting safe and sound."

"Are we going to win?"

"Hell yeah we are!" the private replied.

"Yo man, we gotta go!" the soldier in his passenger seat said, propping his rifle between his legs.

Jean motioned for Pete to stop recording. "Thanks for your time, private!"

"Any time, ma'am!" he said, slamming the truck door closed and turning the engine with a belch of exhaust and a roar.

While the news team moved back from the truck it rolled forward and onto the cracked freeway and accelerated into the steadily moving loose chain of traffic.

"Great stuff, Jean," Pete said, lowering his camera and surveying the scene. Here, at the edge of a village that didn't appear on their maps, they'd been snagging interviews from passing military personnel when they could and getting lots of B-roll of military equipment coming and going. Some of the best had been the wrecked vehicles and packed ambulances that the private had described. War machines smashed to bits, tanks with fist-sized holes in their flanks and trucks with all the glass blown out, not to mention the sickening human toll.

"It's a shame we can't get closer," Jean said wistfully.

"Closer I think," Dario said, "is not good. Safer to be back here."

Since they were mostly dealing with Americans now, Dario had little to do, but dutifully remained with them to help interface with the locals. It was funny how many of them seemed to forget this whole affair was on their account, acting as if the Americans were part of the problem. They'd gotten a lot of dirty looks and hurried retreats when the news crew had tried for interviews.

Jean shielded her eyes from the sun and looked back at the village. All the windows lacked glass panes and stared back like eyeless sockets. Nothing stirred but a pair of US soldiers poking through one of the empty houses. In the middle of them all was the blackened, shattered form of some kind of jet craft. Jean wasn't versed enough in plane identification to recognize it as Eastern or Western, but it lay, burned and crumpled like a giant dead gull among the houses. Its nose was driven into one of the collapsed structures.

Maybe, Jean reasoned, this wasn't the sort of help the Croatians had expected.

The highway acted like a vital artery, fresh supplies and equipment went in and shattered wrecks and wounded men came out. The vehicles maintained good spacing but there was usually activity every minute or so.

"The hell is that?" Pete asked.

Jean followed his gaze and spotted a gaggle of armored vehicles rumbling across a cornfield, headed their way.

"Russians?" Dario asked, standing up.

"No," Pete said, "Americans. Looks like mobile artillery to me, judging by those big guns."

Tanks were all the same to Jean, but these did have large, boxy superstructures and long gun barrels coming off them.

As they watched, the self-propelled guns stopped and turned in unison, guns elevating.

"Pete," Jean said, but his camera was already coming up.

On instinct, Jean pressed her hands over her ears even though the guns were a good hundred yards away.

The guns fired in unison a minute later, blasting long plumes of smoke into the sky before adjusting elevation and firing again. Each round rocked them back on their tracks with the recoil. Jean felt each shot like a slap to her chest and winced every time, though Pete managed to hold the camera steady until the barrage finished.

"Wow!" Jean said, "That's gonna be good stuff."

The armored vehicles reversed dramatically and turned back the way they came without warning. Shooting and scooting.

She didn't hear the first incoming shell until it burst in the ruined village, throwing masonry chips around and sending the two scavenging soldiers scrabbling for shelter.

Dario hit the dirt at once, covering the back of his neck protectively where he lay in the grass by the roadside.

Jean staggered, dumbfounded as more rounds of counter battery fire whistled in, bursting in the air and on the ground where the American guns had fired from and steadily walking closer to the road.

Pete pulled her down and the two of them fell on the camera, holding tight to themselves and one another as the world was washed out with the deafening boom of explosions. A shower of earth scattered over both of them and something fiery-hot trailed across Jean's leg making her cry out in pain.

After the main bombardment tailed off, a series of softer bangs sounded in the air overhead and Jean heard the sound of fist-sized objects landing in the grass and the road around them.

After just a moment the barrage was over and they poked their heads up.

The highway was marred by an overturned Humvee and a respectable crater in its surface. The two men in the village lay still, dead, while someone trapped in the overturned Humvee started sobbing and wailing.

She and Pete looked at one another, ears ringing, eyes wide. Thinking quickly, Jean reached for Dario, grabbing his leg and making him jump. Alive. Their translator sat up and looked around them, spotting one of the objects they'd heard falling. It was a metallic sphere about the size of a tennis ball carrying small, red Cyrillic lettering.

Dario puzzled over it as he walked closer, stooping to pick it up.

Neither Jean nor Pete knew to stop him.

The artillery-deployed mine exploded in his hand the moment it was moved, shredding his arm up to the elbow and blowing him flat onto his back in an instant.

Jean couldn't hear herself scream over her intensely ringing ears. She covered her mouth in horror as Dario tried to sit up again, the ruin of his arm wheeling uselessly. He sputtered mutely, opening and closing his mouth like a fish. His eyes rolled wildly around before coming to rest onto his shredded stump. When his gaze came back to hers, it was blank, shocked. Dario stammered something in Croatian before passing out from blood loss, falling back to the earth.

"Medic!" Pete cried, turning to run for the nearby flipped Humvee. "Medic!"

Jean fell to her knees in the grass and wrapped her arms around herself, trying to fight the shivers coming over her. Her world felt as if it was unraveling. She could see the blue of Dario's windbreaker from the corner of her eye, coated with a thick layer of blood. Jean squeezed her eyes shut and threw up.

***

Major General Strelnikov would have traded the world to be closer to the front. He was a general, yes, but he was a soldier as well and his heart longed for the battlefield. On a battlefield like this, however, such a wish was tantamount with suicide. Gone were the days of leading a charge from horseback, saber held high, or standing atop a hill with binoculars to observe the effects of an attack. Modern war was characterized by a precision and lethality that made "sticking your nose out" fatal. He only needed to listen to the scattered radio reports coming back to confirm that.

Battalions were being chewed up whole by the war, companies and platoons annihilated in seconds. He'd seen a company of T-80s moving toward the front get nearly obliterated by a series of NATO air strikes. Strelnikov's SAM nets had been unable to beat the NATO air attacks back effectively.

Dmitriyev's men had done good work clearing back the enemy. It was bloody work, difficult, but necessary. While Dmitriyev's men weren't annihilated in the same way the 105th Division had been, they were used up all the same—spread out on the front, too broad to penetrate the enemy effectively. The man was a fop, but he wasn't useless. The road to Zagreb was clear—almost clear. All that stood between him and the open road was a few companies of stubborn Marines. That, and the incessant NATO air attacks from the base they called Asgard. It fell now to Strelnikov's men to forge ahead and smash a hole through the enemy lines.

A crater in the road greater than the BTR's wheels and suspension could handle sent Strelnikov lurching in the cramped cabin of the HQ vehicle, his head nearly striking a stowed radio transmitter. He didn't—he couldn't—let it break his concentration.

"We *are* giving you all the fire support assets we have, Colonel," Strelnikov explained to one of his regimental commanders. "I have a standing order with our air forces to kill anything moving on that road south of your position."

"Comrade general, it is not enough! I can't move my men forward without more reserves! A tank battalion is all I need. Something to drive the Yankees off those damned hills!"

Strelnikov released the push-to-talk switch and sighed, holding desperately to the wall of the armored personnel carrier as they bounced along backroads at close to top speed. He knew that two self-propelled anti-aircraft guns—ZSUs—were sandwiching his command vehicle as they raced around behind the warzone. Mobility and infrequency of transmit was the only way Strelnikov had found to keep alive in a world of NATO SIGINT air strikes targeting any radio that broadcast too often or for too long.

He knew that even if he supplied the colonel with the tank battalion he requested—pulling it from his carefully marshaled reserve regiment—that half of them would be smoking ruins on the road before they even reached the front, and the rest would follow soon after. Deploying a unit for combat in this environment was tantamount to expending a round of ammunition. It was a resource that would not return. The Soviet army had found that pushing a defended position with tanks turned out to be an exercise in suffering. So far they had only made progress when utilizing combined arms tactics. Suppressive artillery bombardment coupled with precision air strikes on enemy hardpoints had enabled their forces to advance.

With NATO's air forces operating round the clock, it upset the equation. The farther they drew from their air bases in Hungary and the closer the enemy fell back on Asgard, the weaker the Soviet air arm became. No air superiority meant that their rear areas were compromised, and massive artillery bombardments would be broken up before the guns were collected.

"Colonel, I have no tanks to spare. Our tank regiment is to be held in reserve only for a breakthrough. I will not commit it piecemeal."

"Comrade general, if you give me that regiment I will get you your breakthrough!" the colonel said, the banging of artillery faintly distant through the radio. "I can feel them breaking, general. Let us not miss this chance."

Looking away from the radio, Strelnikov consulted the map of the area. It was a poor place for an armored engagement, characterized by narrow roads and wooded, rolling hills, but it was as good as any in this valley. If he could punch through here, he would open the road to Zagreb. Even so, if he was wrong and committed his reserves early, then he may not get a second chance to try again.

"How soon can the tank regiment move?" Strelnikov asked Mishkin.

"Fifteen minutes' notice, comrade general," Mishkin said, voice brimming with the confidence of a well-prepared staff officer.

With a careful deployment of anti-air assets and signal

jamming, he had marshaled virtually the entire tank regiment intact into his rear areas. It would only take a few of those damn American attack aircraft to punch them full of holes and turn his precious tanks into slag. Not trusting his own radios, Strelnikov had dispersed them over a wooded area, refusing to form them into neat, orderly, and recognizable columns in a field like a May Day parade formation. They were being governed by a series of signal flares and couriers who passed messages between units. It was a slower way of doing business, but it also avoided problems with SIGINT.

The general depressed the button on his radio's handset. "Fifteen minutes, Colonel. I don't care what it costs you. Get the enemy off those hills. The tanks are on the way and I want a gap opened for them when they arrive. Commit whatever reserves you have, is that clear?"

"All or nothing! Yes, comrade general!"

Strelnikov let off the transmit button moments before the ZSUs fore and aft of his carrier opened fire. They sounded for all the world like gigantic metallic zippers being undone at top speed.

The crew of the APC braced themselves on the walls and averted their eyes from one another out of respect. It was unbecoming to look a man facing death in the eyes. No one wanted to see their comrades afraid for their lives, least of all the general.

After a moment the gunfire trailed off, their target either retreating or destroyed.

"Send word to the tank regiment," Strelnikov said. "Proceed down the E65 highway south. They are to commit to a breakthrough action there with maximum force." The radioman acknowledged and relayed the command.

Nearly thirty minutes later Strelnikov's command BTR was parked in the smoldering ruins of a village, the structures mostly reduced to ashes and charred cinders by a thermobaric rocket barrage. What would ordinarily be a sobering sight was made slightly more palatable to the general by the presence of a burnt-out American APC here.

In the intervening minutes during the final push on the American lines, Strelnikov had heard one of his officers die in real time. It came as the colonel marshaled his men and pressed the attack against the immense firepower NATO leveled against him. As the gallant colonel drove his men on in the attack, his radio transmitter was silenced by an airstrike. As the signal fell dead, so did he. His audio transmission had erupted in a squeal of melted plastic and fried wiring at the moment of death.

Painful minutes of impotent confusion passed where Strelnikov had no control over the attack and no clear understanding of what was going on before a major named Sidorov took up command.

"I estimate we have suffered nearly forty percent losses, comrade general," Sidorov said, his voice winded, pained. "The hillside is littered with our men."

Strelnikov grimaced at the officer's impertinence. Facts, he needed facts, not artistic depictions! "The tank regiment?"

"Going forward now, comrade!" Major Sidorov was partially drowned out by volleys of artillery fire.

Strelnikov scowled to Mishkin, "They were supposed to be through already, dammit!"

"Maybe this time, comrade general."

Strelnikov risked another transmission, "Whatever is left, press them! Give the tank regiment all the support you can. This *must* be decisive."

Sidorov took the instructions without complaint. All Soviet soldiers knew their duty, and all officers were well aware of what was expected of them.

The minutes stretched and the distant sounds of battle faded away gradually, the boom and pop of cannons becoming more irregularly spaced.

"Comrade General Strelnikov," came the triumphant voice of his tank regiment commander. "We are through them!"

"Drive!" Strelnikov responded. "Stop for nothing. We must reach the city before nightfall." As he spoke, he glanced at the dipping sun, there was precious little time to work with and he had to turn the screws to get high command to provide his division with an aerial corridor at all costs.

Zagreb was nearly in reach sight.

***

13

The setting sun had set the Adriatic aflame, painting its blue waves in gold, crimson, and amber. The warm air of the day was just starting to be replaced by a chilly breeze from the north when the call for emergency sorties came in to the USS *Gettysburg*.

The pilots of the carrier's air wing were exhausted, having spent all morning and afternoon flying to and fro conducting air attacks on the advancing Soviet forces. Thousands of pounds and millions of dollars of ordnance had been expended, brewing up tanks, trucks, and APCs alike as the enemy crept steadily nearer to the vital crossroads of Zagreb.

Further to the southeast, the 82nd Airborne had stalled out a Soviet attack near Daruvar, but a loss at Zagreb would leave the whole line untenable. Even now, American forces were pulling back to the Sava River, the last natural boundary before the foothills of the coastline. In the hills of Bosnia, the British Royal Marines and French Foreign Legion had savaged their Soviet adversaries, keeping the Reds well away from Sarajevo, though if the northern part of the line fell it would likely require the entire expeditionary army retreat to the coast—a move tantamount to defeat.

That couldn't be allowed to happen.

When the alert tone sounded in the pilot ready room, it was like the braying of the hounds of hell to the assembled pilots. They'd already lost close to a quarter of their number and had managed to get precious little sleep between the constant sorties and alert status. Their nerves were frayed near the breaking point and exhaustion had become their reality.

Machines were feeling the strain as well. When a steam

catapult or aircraft would experience a breakdown, it was almost a relief to the men who were slated to launch. It meant a short respite from work, but the knowledge that their rest came at the price of suffering from their brothers in arms inland soured that relief.

But now, time was critical. The alert fighters, a pair of Tomcats sitting on the ready catapults, had already leaped from the deck and into the twilight sky.

While the other pilots readied their craft as they were locked into the guidelines on the steam catapults, the Marines inland were being driven back; a single armored breakthrough in their lines threatened to cut off the entire division from its line of retreat if not properly countered.

With the demands on Asgard and the other bases at critical levels, this task fell to *Gettysburg*'s air wing. The captain of the vessel turned it into the breeze and ordered engines brought to flank speed. A dozen planes were launched in all, primarily ground-attack equipped F-18 Hornets being escorted in by a flight of Tomcats. With afterburners engaged they were mere minutes from their target operation area along the E65 freeway.

The pilots flew by instrument as the darkening sky and their low altitude made visual identification difficult to impossible. Minute-by-minute updated positioning on the Soviet tank regiment was brought in and—more crucially—the plotting of the Soviet air forces as they scrambled to try to protect this spearhead.

The pilots didn't speak while fiery ocean waves were left behind for rolling purple hills, save to exchange navigational information. Periodically, one of the four Tomcats would rise above the others, high enough to be clear of ground clutter, and activate his targeting radar, sweeping for enemy fighters that may be closing low on them.

"Six bandits at angels two," the lookout Tomcat reported suddenly, breaking the tense silence on the flight's radio network. "Twelve o'clock."

"Affirmative Razor 103," Razor Leader said, "Razor team, ready up for action. I want everyone fangs out."

The other Tomcat drivers responded in the affirmative. Their weapons operators warmed up the assortment of anti-air weapons they'd brought along. They carried missiles that zeroed in on both radar and heat signatures depending on what they faced. The Tomcat was a true predator of the skies, an aerial combat platform par excellence. There was virtually nothing in the Soviet arsenal which could outperform this venerable old war horse.

As the team signaled readiness, Razor Leader turned his head to the left so his RIO could hear him. The radar intercept officer was responsible for handling the Tomcat's myriad of electronics and weapons systems so the pilot could focus his efforts on flying.

"We good Slim?" Razor Leader asked.

"Hot to trot, Bugeye."

A disparaging callsign was a mark of respect in the naval air force, even Razor Leader wasn't exempt.

"That's what I like to hear." Razor Leader had run many of these sorties by now, but this would be his first headon shootout with the Russian pilots who certainly knew he was coming. He toggled back to the team channel. "Razor 103, what's our range?"

"We'll be on them in five minutes."

"Affirmative, we'll keep on the deck until then. Paladins," Razor Leader addressed the ground attack Hornets they escorted, "when we engage, break starboard and stay on, we'll try to rush you guys through."

The Hornet Paladin team confirmed. With their hardpoints loaded up with anti-tank missiles and cluster bombs they would be hard-pressed to participate effectively in this dog fight, either to attack or evade.

The time to engagement ticked closer to zero. With one minute left, Razor Lead checked in with Razor 103. "Are you on them?"

"Got 'em padlocked."

Razor Leader exhaled and tapped his stick backward, lifting

his fighter's nose. "Tally-ho!"

The traditional cry was echoed by his other fighters as they rose up above the ground clutter and their targeting radars lit up, pinning the Soviets ahead of them. Six to four was not good odds, but it was what they had.

"Fox Three! Fox Three!"

The channel was full of missile launches as Razor team lined up targets and fired. The Phoenix missile was an excellent weapon, but it was primarily intended to be used in defending against long range threats at sea, not close-in fights in cluttered terrain.

The missiles streaked from their fighters and toward the enemy craft, barely visible in the fading daylight as blips on the sky.

The Tomcat's radar lit up with return fire.

"Break, break!" Razor Leader accelerated and dove for the ground, the world revolving around him before putting himself perpendicular to the oncoming missiles. With luck their tracking computers would mistake him for stationary ground clutter and lose the lock. A second later a pair of missiles flashed by him, close enough that he passed through an exhaust trail. They'd lost him in the background noise and were now aimlessly cruising southwest.

Razor 102 wasn't so lucky; a missile struck him dead-on, shearing the nose from his craft and detonating the onboard fuel, turning his fighter into a tumbling funeral pyre for pilot and weapons operator. One of the other Razors was hit with shrapnel from a detonating missile, losing some maneuverability but sparing his life. The Soviets fared little better, two craft were snuffed out in an instant and a third started a lazy death-spiral toward the ground that ended a moment later with a rolling fireball that climbed back to the sky.

Then the fighters flashed past one another. They barely managed to weave between each other with alerts warbling and blaring in their ears. Somehow they all avoided a midair collision or unplanned rendezvous with the ground.

Razor Leader strained his neck, looking back over his shoulder to make out the twin-engined Soviet fighter craft that passed by them. The Soviets hesitated and then changed course to pursue the running Hornets. They saw the real prize.

"Razor Team, break and engage! Keep them off Paladin. Guns, guns, guns!"

The surviving three Tomcats came about and kicked on their afterburners in an attempt to close distance with the Soviets that were racing after the Hornets.

The RIO of Razor Leader's plane unleashed a Phoenix after getting a solid lock. It was a snapshot, but one that paid off as the warhead burst and shattered the MiG's back, rolling the plane over to break apart midair. Another Phoenix was lost to electronic counter measures and ended up locking onto the dying MiG, delivering a second, unnecessary blow to the falling craft.

Then they were too close for radar or missiles; all that mattered was performance and reaction time. Razor Leader triggered his onboard Vulcan cannons and tried to keep his crosshairs fixed on the juking Soviet craft before him. G-forces crushed him into his seat as he executed a tight turn to keep an evading MiG in his sights.

Tracer rounds flashed out around the enemy jet, tasting only air and exhaust.

Everything was occurring too fast, the Soviets evading and scrambling, trying to get behind the pursuing Tomcats while the Americans did their best to lure off the enemy. All Razor Leader had was the target before him. The rest of his team was on their own; trying to make sense of this dogfight was impossible.

The opposing MiG executed a series of sharp, banking turns, trying to lose speed and cause him to overshoot. As Razor Leader mirrored the scissor turn and tried to bring his speed down, he struggled against the shifting G-forces, desperately willing his gunsights to come back onto the MiG.

One of Paladin's Hornets exploded from a missile strike shortly before another had its wing snapped off by gunfire and was thrown into a flat spin.

As the Soviet pilot came out of the scissor turn, expecting to be behind his Tomcat opponent, he was startled to discover the American finishing a barrel roll and dropping into a perfect firing position *behind* him.

Razor Leader triggered his guns again and was rewarded as the engines on the MiG flared and went out. Twenty millimeter shells ripped through the aircraft's powerplant and turned it into a multi-million dollar gliding brick. While Razor Lead banked off and searched for more targets he saw that the initial MiG group he'd faced was fleeing, breaking off their attack on Paladin team.

"Razor Team, cease," Razor Leader said, seeing that the team now only consisted of him and Razor 103.

"I've got more bandits inbound," Razor Three said. "Six more contacts at four o'clock and closing fast."

A glance at his own radar was enough info for Razor Leader. They'd be in the thick of things in mere minutes. He looked up through the Tomcat's bubble canopy at what was left of Paladin Team. They wouldn't be able to escape on afterburners alone. They needed cover. "Form on me, Razor 103. We've got work to do."

"Copy, lead."

Razor Leader thought about his wife. He hoped she could forgive him if he didn't come home. Maybe he'd save some other potential widows from being created. He just regretted that it would likely come at the cost of his own life and the lives of his teammates, but there was no time for second thoughts. "Tally-ho!"

**

Lieutenant Williams could only distantly hear the rumble of bombs to the north. After the flight of Hornets he'd seen streaking overhead, he could only assume it was the result of air strikes on the advancing Soviet tank regiment. A desperate effort to buy more time. The deep breakthrough had sent the entire division into panic. They didn't have the heavy weapons to stop them, not dead cold on open ground, and so they withdrew.

Recon and AT platoons were left behind in a thin skirmish line to buy time. Men in concealed positions with anti-tank weapons intended to sow confusion in the advancing Russians and force them to move with caution.

Cohesion among the Marines was breaking down. Williams was a junior officer, but that fact was still plain as day to him. Companies were shadows of their former strength and platoons were largely intermixed to form ad hoc combat units as the need for them arose. The makeshift platoon he'd found himself in charge of had—like his original command—disintegrated in sustained combat operations and now he was again alone and retreating. A general evacuation had been called once the line was breached and Williams was no exception.

The lieutenant stared down at the bare spots on his collar where his rank patches had been before he'd cut them away during a quiet moment. With no visible rank, Williams was now no different than anyone else around him. He was just another tired, mud-smeared Marine in ragged battle dress. The others in the two-and-a-half-ton truck he rode in paid him no mind and were evidently unaware of who he was. For now, the truth haunted him alone. It was a knot in his gut and ice in his veins that refused to be forgotten. This was all his fault. All of it. A navigational error, a single missed turn, and now thousands were dead, many thousands more wounded and maimed. Lives were irreparably torn apart for his mistake. Inevitably when this ended he would have to report to someone who would make sense of who he was.

Williams buried his face in his hands, propping his elbow on his knees, and tried to forget. He let the cool evening air rush over him and listened to the bass rumble of the truck's engine as it rolled toward Zagreb.

This particular road was flanked on both sides by wooded

hills and ridges. It was a long, winding valley that pointed like a dagger at the exposed artery of Croatia—a vast open plain that surrounded the city of Zagreb. Once the Soviets reached that, they could break out and have their way with the rest of the country.

Williams had learned all about the Russian way of war in Officer Candidate School. The Soviets longed for a war of maneuver. They prosecuted the attack with overwhelming firepower to pin enemy assets in place and then attacked any weak points in force to break the line in as many places as possible. A sort of modern-day blitzkrieg.

Williams looked out the rear of the truck, down the dark highway and along the thin ribbon of headlights and vehicles tailing along. He knew that not far behind them was an entire regiment of Soviet tanks, eagerly closing in to overrun the withdrawing Americans. Uncle Sam was throwing everything he had at that column but, if the screaming dogfights that could be seen overhead from time to time were anything to go on, then it was no guarantee they could be stopped with aircraft alone.

Movement on foot caught his eye as the truck slowed. A pair of dirt-caked Marines stood by the road side watching the convoy pass. One carried the ubiquitous M16 rifle, but the other had a bulky tube on a sling over his shoulder. It was a Dragon, a shoulder-launched anti-tank weapon.

The men met Williams' eyes and he saw … nothing. They were blank, unreadable, the gaze of the damned. Williams looked away from the faces of the men he'd condemned.

Volunteer tank hunter teams like this were being dotted across the road like the artillery-deployed mines being sowed behind the retreating Marines. It would not stop a concerted attack, but it would slow it down, eat away at it enough to buy the main body time to withdraw before being overrun.

The two men were left behind, fading into the twilight as they trudged away from the road and out of the headlights of the passing vehicles.

Williams had seen maps of the area and knew that if the

Marines could entrench on the other side of the Sava river and around Zagreb they could stop any Soviet attack thrown at them. They just had to get there.

The truck slowed suddenly again, throwing swearing men into each other in the back. Before anyone could ask or complain, the truck veered sharply off the road and stopped, tires throwing dirt. Williams stood up with the others and peered forward into the traffic jam of military vehicles to the source of the stoppage. He saw armored bulldozers and floodlights ahead.

Silver, fist-sized balls were scattered over the road. Artillery mines, likely dropped by the Soviets to slow them down.

"Christ," someone said.

"Be faster to walk."

Williams looked back toward the north, wondering exactly how far behind the Russians were.

"When the armor gets here we'll throw them back," one Marine told another.

"Fat fucking chance! you think the brass are gonna send more tanks here?"

"Well, why the hell not?" the first asked, bewildered.

"They'll need them for the real show," a sergeant interjected, drawing looks from the others. "Germany."

"You think this thing'll blow up?" the first soldier asked

"Why wouldn't it? Shit's already tits up," the sergeant said.

Williams felt sick all over again. He wasn't sure how to handle starting this war but ... a Third World War?

After a moment the truck began to inch forward again, rolling back onto the highway and then along a narrow corridor that had already been cleared by the engineers. A man with a .50 caliber gun on the roof of a Humvee was shooting the bomblets that lay strewn in the opposite lane to detonate them. The lane through the loose mines was a narrow path that had been cleared quickly by the engineering team, and it meant the trucks moving through passed slowly and single file.

A gaggle of men on the side of the road drew Williams' attention. He saw some engineers standing in a loose circle around a Navy corpsman who knelt beside a wounded Marine. The man who lay on the ground was shivering and moaning, flat on his back with his arms held up above him—what was left of them anyway. Both limbs had been cut away above the elbow and the corpsman was dutifully wrapping them in gauze.Williams caught the corpsman's eye as they passed. He saw the same look of hopeless determination that he'd seen on the faces of the tank hunters. The corpsman looked away first, returning to his work of dressing the engineer's wounds. It was an image that the lieutenant couldn't shake from his head, even after they'd cleared the makeshift minefield and returned to speed. He thought about the armless engineer, the corpsman, and that tank hunter team up until the trucks reached an assembly point. The assembly point was just a small village crossroads with some MPs directing traffic and a pair of tanks standing overwatch from concealed positions within hollowed out buildings.

While they awaited "marching" orders, Williams and the others debarked from the truck, some relieving themselves on the roadside, others lighting cigarettes or just milling aimlessly. Zagreb and the promise of a better defensive position wasn't far now.

Just outside the main crossroads, Williams saw a number of men checking Dragon AT rockets and stacking them carefully. He went to them and found a sergeant directing the operation. "Are these for the tank hunters?"

The sergeant looked at Williams like he stepped in shit, sparing only a moment to glance at his nametag. "Are you volunteering, Williams?"

Williams wasn't used to being talked down to that way by enlisted men but was well beyond caring. "Yes, sergeant."

The sergeant blinked in surprise then looked over at the dragons. "You qualified for these, private?"

"I am." It was the truth. Williams had spent some time familiarizing himself with anti-tank weapons in peacetime and was confident he could operate one and operate it well.

"Right," the sergeant waved another man over. "This is Corporal Steiner. You and he will be a team then."

Corporal Steiner was young and fresh-faced. Any trepidation he felt about volunteering for this assignment had evidently been buried.

"In twenty minutes we're ghosting this place," the sergeant explained. "Corporal Steiner, you and Private Williams will remain here and delay the Soviet armor however you can. Understand?"

"Yes, sergeant," Williams said.

Steiner hefted one of the Dragons and handed it to Williams who slung the heavy missile tube on his back.

"Good luck," the sergeant said, turning to leave.

"Sergeant," Williams stopped him with a hand on his shoulder, "wait." Reaching up, Willams unhooked the toe tag from his dog tags.

"Private you ca—"

Williams handed the tag to the sergeant. "Keep it. It's important. Please."

The sergeant puzzled at the tag and then at Williams, that hardfaced scowl softening somewhat. "Just … keep the other one on you, okay?"

"Yes, sergeant."

The sergeant pocketed the tag and looked at Williams differently. It wasn't respect, it wasn't pity. It was something that was both and neither. "Good hunting."

Williams looked to Corporal Steiner, his ostensible superior. "Ready?"

"Ready," the corporal gestured up to the edge of the woods on the valley's side. "Good ground up there, I think."

Williams adjusted the sling of his rifle. "Let's go."

***

It amazed President Simpson how the wheels of government continued to turn no matter what got in the way. The war in

Yugoslavia was all over the headlines, yet it didn't occupy his entire schedule—it couldn't. A reception lunch for delegations from a number of West African nations was planned and was occuring on time. Another round of applause swept the room after an uplifting and heartfelt speech about increased economic growth in the region.

Simpson clapped and smiled with the others, but his eyes kept going to the door that led out of the hotel's function hall. This time he was grateful to see Walt Harrison coming back inside, pausing in the entryway for a switch in speakers, before coming to the president's table.

"They got the division out," Harrison said, his voice low as he sat on the opposite side of Simpson from his wife. "The marines have fallen back on Zagreb and the Sava."

"Thank the Lord," Simpson breathed, "How bad is it, Walt?"

"Worse than the media knows. The 82nd is holding their own so far, but it's better ground there. The Marines are getting the brunt of it. We're talking upwards of three thousand casualties."

Simpson winced. That was a tough pill to swallow for a relatively inconsequential piece of ground. He took a moment to remind himself that this war wasn't about Croatia, it was about standing up to the Soviets and not letting them upset a finely maintained balance of power. "But they did get out?"

"Yes, sir. It was touch and go, but I just confirmed with the Joint Chiefs that the division got out. We pulled them out of the fire this time, but only just barely."

The master of ceremonies took the podium next and followed up the last speaker's points before announcing the next to speak and yielded the stage.

"We can have the 101st fly in in twenty-four hours, land them at Ljubljana and move to help the Marines."

"Hell no," Simpson hissed, glancing at his chief of staff like he'd gone crazy. "Wanna start shipping in reserves? Why not drop the whole goddam Army on them then? If we scratch this thing like it itches then we're gonna be up to our eyeballs in it."

Harrison hesitated, "Rick," he said, low enough that no one

could hear him but the president, "if we *don't* scratch ..."

"Are we gonna stop them, Walt?" Simpson asked.

"I've got high confidence from the Joint Chiefs that we can stall them out at the Sava. Bleed 'em dry, but without some heavy reinforcement ..."

Simpson shook his head, "Don't give me that. You know we can't ramp this up. We gotta make do with what we got."

Harrison didn't reply, but his silence spoke for him.

Simpson sighed, "If we can't stop 'em for good then we'll have to play smarter, not harder. Then tell 'em if they don't meet us at the conference table things are gonna get worse."

"What about the walk point?"

"They ain't got to Zagreb yet," Simpson said. "Maybe we got Ivan at his walk point already. Float—uh —" Simpson glanced around to make sure his lack of attention on events hadn't been noticed by the others at the conference. "—float the idea of a negotiated drawback. Hell, I'm willing to sweeten the pot a little, but try to find out what they want. Tell Wanda I want this *off* official channels. No red phone bullshit."

"Yes, sir."

Simpson snagged Harrison's sleeve when he went to stand, "How close was it, Walt?"

"The Soviets got through us, sir," Harrison replied. "Took airstrikes from Asgard and *Gettysburg* to slow 'em down enough for us to get out."

The president snorted, the derisive sound of someone who narrowly avoided a disaster, "Thank God for them then."

***

14

The mood in Moscow was decidedly darker than it had been only a few weeks prior. Activity on the city's streets had decreased even by its usually low standard. Military rationing was in effect, limiting the amount of drivers on the road, and strict curfews were in place. Each street corner was watched by a pair of tense-looking reservists, men called into activity duty with the commencement of hostilities. The guards were Tarasov's suggestion, but one Gradenko suspected had been forwarded to him by Karamazov.

Gradenko watched them from the rear windows of his car as he passed. These were men just out of their normal terms of service, pressed into action to free up the younger, more recently trained recruits for the front—or the potential front. The Politburo—or more accurately, the Troika—did not believe in half measures. To Gradenko, the buildup was ridiculous, an unnecessarily aggressive action in a delicate diplomatic environment. The foreign minister knew full well that Western spy satellites were able to detect such changes in readiness state, not to mention the likelihood of spies, despite Karamazov's insistence that his agency had swept the city clear.

The massive callup of reserves hadn't yet begun, nor the movement of forces to the European front. That would have certainly escalated things farther than Gradenko and the Troika were prepared to go. So long as the Americans didn't begin any massive call up, they would follow suit. Yugoslavia would remain an isolated conflict.

Gradenko looked at his driver—his *new* driver. Only the back of the man's head was visible to him and he did not give any sidelong glances to Gradenko in the rearview mirror, nor did he flaunt ill-gotten wealth with expensive watches or jewelry. He'd come highly recommended from one of the candidate members of the Politburo. With no real power to speak of, Gradenko felt the non-voting candidates were the only ones he could trust.

It wasn't a long trip from the Foreign Ministry downtown to the apartment block where Gradenko lived, the stylish Patriarch's Ponds neighborhood which housed many of the Soviet Union's ruling elite. The pond for which the neighborhood received its name was artificially square and inky black in the moonlight. Come winter it would freeze over and become home to recreational ice skaters.

Gradenko's driver skillfully parked the car in an empty spot. "Will there be anything further, comrade minister?"

"Nothing tonight, Petrov," Gradenko said, gathering his things and climbing out. "Goodnight."

"Goodnight."

Gradenko watched the car leave while he stood on the curb. His briefcase felt unnaturally heavy in his hand despite only holding a few documents. They were documents he wasn't meant to have—casualty figures from Yugoslavia. The numbers on the paper were statistical and unfeeling, but they told a bleak story. The attack was proceeding, but it was well behind where it was expected to be by now. The promised breakthrough on the second day had been backhanded by Western air power.

Damn Asgard! Tarasov's short war would not come to fruition should these frustrations keep up.

The minister savored one last breath of cool autumn air and entered the apartment, ascending the stairs with creaking knees to the fifth level—his.

The door was unlocked and opened easily at his touch. The cold, sterile hall gave way to the quiet warmth of his home.

"Home," Gradenko called, closing the door behind himself. He noted curiously that the lights were on and he could hear the sounds of conversation. He found, to his surprise, company in his kitchen. Seated across the table from his wife, Katya, was his son.

"Papa," his son Vladimir said, grinning at his father. "A late night in the ministry, I see."

Gradenko was not feeling in the mood for levity, but partook in the ceremony anyway. "For some of us, we have real work to do." Placement within the Soviet leadership for many came through nepotism—*who* they knew and not *what* they knew. Gradenko was no stranger to this tradition and ensured his son worked under him in the Foreign Ministry.

Vladimir laughed, harder than he should have. The explanation to that discrepancy came from the open bottle of vodka that sat between mother and son.

"Vladimir has made a trip to see us, dear," Katya said. "Sit, Andrei, have a drink."

Gradenko did as he was told and held his glass while his son poured. "What's the occasion?" There must be a reason to drink, but in the Soviet Union there was always a reason.

"The agreement with the Italians has been signed," Vladimir said, voice welling with pride. "At the cost of ten thousand tons of natural gas, we will have medical diagnostic equipment of the highest caliber from the West."

"That is good news," Gradenko said, downing the burning liquid in one go, refusing to wince or cough.

"It will be better once the equipment is in our hands," Vladimir said, the hint of uncertainty impossible to miss.

So this is why he's come, Gradenko thought. It would take some more teasing out. "Have you heard from Ivana?"

"Ivana?" Vladimir asked, pretending for a moment to forget his younger sister. "She hasn't called in some time. Mama?"

"She is still on the steppe," Katya said, "Agriculture school."

"Trying to get water from the stone, no doubt," Vladimir said, referencing the Soviet Union's eternal failure to make Central Asia a truly productive agricultural region.

Gradenko hid the dismay he felt at his son's flippancy. The man was old enough to be a father in his own right but still often seemed the same restless youth he had been in primary school. To criticize the government, even in such a sidelong fashion was dangerous in any climate, but especially this one. The wild days of the Socialist Spring were well behind them. "We all do what we can," Gradenko said, trying to be diplomatic.

"And what are we doing about Yugoslavia, papa?" Vladimir asked, downing another tumbler of vodka without hesitation.

Gradenko this time could not hide his wince.

"Vladimir!" his mother chided, shocked at her son's openness.

"Ah, that badly then? We sweep it under the rug like the rest of our mistakes?" Vladimir asked, the vodka edging his voice with bitterness

"Nothing is under the rug. The war is contained."

"For now, yes?" Vladimir asked. "The people in my department say that the East European branch is afraid of things spilling out of control. I have heard that one of our bombers crashed inside Italian airspace."

It was a rumor that Gradenko had not heard, which meant it could be true or false. "Everything there will be over soon, Vladimir," Gradenko said, choosing his words carefully. He did not like to have such conversations in his apartment. He didn't believe it was bugged, but he wouldn't put anything past those weasels in the KGB.

"Soon," Vladimir said with a sigh. "Always soon."

"Come," Gradenko said, standing up stiffly. "I will call you a car, I think you ought to get home."

Vladimir opened his mouth to argue but closed it after a moment. "Papa—"

Gradenko shook his head, "You worry about our trade deals with the West," he said, "let me worry about the war."

A tense silence settled over the supper table. Vladimir's face darkened and he turned away from his father, making no reply.

A short phone call later, and the two men stood outside waiting on their driver.

"Vladimir," Gradenko said, not looking at his son, "we are all afraid, but we face challenges that no one man can overcome. We support the party and we support our country."

"You are part of the Politburo," Vladimir objected, "Surely you can do *something*. What good is that power if it cannot be used?"

Gradenko had no answer.

"You must speak to them, papa. You must stop this insanity."

The words remained with Gradenko well after his son had departed. When he returned upstairs to the apartment, feeling winded, his wife stood by the window, nervously looking out over the city before drawing the blinds closed. With the same causal grace that first brought her to his eye on the very frozen pond outside their apartment, Katya made her way to a small shelf that held a tape cassette player. The device had been imported from West Germany at no small expense, and was one of the few imported luxuries that Gradenko allowed himself. "Would you like some music, dear?" Katya asked.

Gradenko didn't smile, "Yes, that sounds wonderful. Tchaikovsky?"

Katya depressed the "play" button with an audible click and the cassette's reels began to spin. The first strains of Tchaikovsky's moody, string-driven score began to emerge from the speakers attached to the player. She came close to her husband as the music filled their house, hopefully drowning out their conversation for any listening bugs. "We should go to the dacha," she said.

Gradenko knew her meaning; he thought about Finland, Sweden, Switzerland, Paris. "No. It is too delicate a time. I have too much work."

"But ..."

Gradenko caught her eyes, imparting as much of his fear and resolve into the look as he could. "There is no where we can go—" he said, "—that they will not follow."

"Is it really that bad?"

The two of them sat on the nearby couch and Gradenko stared unblinking at the cassette player. "Karamazov and Tarasov," he said, "the three of us are running things now."

"Then you can stop this madness," she said, the hope in her voice was heartbreaking. "If you are with them."

Gradenko shook his head, "It is outside of my area of control."

For a moment Katya said nothing, her hands going to his to hold them tight. She was trembling. "Vladimir is afraid."

"We all are," Gradenko said. "I can promise you that this war will end and things will return to normal."

The phone rang and Gradenko jumped. A phone call at this hour of night was never good, let alone when conversations had turned conspiratorial. Gradenko paused the waltz and picked up the phone. "Yes?"

"Comrade minister," the voice was familiar but unwelcome.

"Chairman Karamazov, working late?"

"Something like that," the chairman said. "I have news about the war. Are you free to discuss this?"

Gradenko realized the foolishness of telling the Soviet Union's spymaster of the possibility that this line was bugged. "Yes, of course."

"Earlier today President Simpson made unofficial contact with us through some of our operatives. He's put out a diplomatic feeler, but one that avoids the regular channels. I thought it should be brought to your attention."

Gradenko relaxed. This was good news. Peace talk was a welcome subject, so much so that he decided not to take offense at the KGB meddling in diplomacy. "Yes, thank you. What does he have for us?"

"The terms are quite fluid, but he is suggesting we halt our advance at the Sava and then discuss a staged withdrawal."

Gradenko considered it. A staged withdrawal might look like defeat in the eyes of the world, especially after the Soviets tried to dictate policy on Yugoslavia to the West. "A viable start," Gradenko said. "I can draft peace terms by the morning." Gradenko hesitated before continuing, pained that he even had to be thinking in terms of geopolitical standing when he'd rather simply end the fighting. "We can only accept these terms if they lead to a unified Yugoslavia. The Americans will want free elections and we'll want to make sure they don't steer the vote their way."

"That sounds agreeable," Karamazov said, "however, might I

suggest that you wait twenty-four hours before presenting any terms."

"Twenty-four hours?"

"Yes. Our offensive on the Sava river will begin then and Comrade Tarasov has promised us a swift victory. I have an operation of my own that will help us on that front."

Gradenko steeled himself, thinking of his son's words. "Comrade chairman, I respect your suggestion, however I have to insist that we take peace negotiation seriously. I can't see the benefit of prolonging combat, even if it means a victory." If he was a part of this Troika, he might as well act like it. What good was his power if he couldn't use it?

Karamazov was silent for a minute before speaking. "I appreciate that, comrade minister, however I will remind you that military operations are outside of your area of oversight. Even so, assuming you get your peace, would you prefer that we risk our gains on the battlefield in a boardroom? If we take the American offer of a ceasefire, we will not again regain the element of surprise. The sacrifices of our brave soldiers may all be lost at the stroke of a pen."

Gradenko gritted his teeth. Was a futile peace really better than a victory forged in blood? "What operation do you have planned?"

"One that will even the playing field, that is all I can say," Karamazov said.

Gradenko hesitated, refusing to meet his wife's eye. "Twenty-four hours, comrade chairman," he said, "then I will speak with the Americans about peace."

"This is acceptable to me. Until then." The chairman hung up and Gradenko followed suit.

Gradenko thought about Finland again as he turned away from his wife. "I will do what I can." He didn't wait for her to respond before he left.

***

The convoy of trucks and army vehicles rumbled along the dusty service road toward the cavernous entrance of Zeljava airbase, the one the Americans called Asgard. To the left of the convoy, the nearby mountain range was visible only as a rising darkness against the starry sky. Beneath those mountains the airbase itself was buried, deeper than any bomb or missile could reach. The land surrounding the base had once been verdant woodland but, after a series of failed air attacks on this place, now it was mostly a crater-pocked ashy wasteland. Here and there splintered tree trunks stood up like burnt matchsticks, the ground around them sooty and gray. The charred fuselage of a delta-winged Soviet fighter peeked out from the burnt undergrowth.

Major Petrovski sat in the passenger seat of what had once been a Yugoslav Army 4x4, watching American air crews readying fighters on the runway or shuttling supplies into the base—things like water, food, and ammunition, essential products to keep the base's human component functioning. Petrovski's truck was the head of a column of heavy vehicles hauling loads of gravel.

The crew of the base didn't pay Petrovski's column any mind. After all, the Croatians were their allies in this fight. The locals had offered the use of construction equipment and delivered gravel and rubble for filling in the cratered runways the Soviets left in the wake of their futile air attacks. The Croatians were friends.

Only Petrovski and his men weren't Croatians. His team of Spetsnaz commandos had left the Croatians who were intended to deliver this rock dead in a roadside ditch not far from here.

A lone Humvee with an exhausted crew led the convoy of trucks toward the small loading dock set into the mountainside a hundred meters away from the hangar entrances. They couldn't tell a Russian from a Croatian so there was no problem there. All the same, Petrovski had made sure that each truck had at least one Serbian militiaman onboard in case they needed to maintain appearances longer. The Serbians intermixed with his team were simply a small contingent from the much larger band of militia he knew to be assembling at the outskirts of the base now.

His carbine—a compact AK-74U—was nestled in the dark between his legs but he picked it up now and pulled the charging handle to chamber a shell. The AK-74U was much like its larger brother—the venerable Kalashnikov rifle—but only half the size. It was a favorite of paratroopers, armored crewmen, and special forces across the communist bloc.

"Thirty seconds," Petrovski's driver, a Serb, said in thickly accented Russian.

The major confirmed this with a glance at his own watch before he nodded. The seconds to zero ticked by while the other commandos readied their weapons, unseen by the men they drove past.

The first mortar shells screamed in seconds early, bursting harmlessly on the northernmost runway. Even as the soldiers and airmen scattered across the base scrambled for cover, more shells were coming in. The shells did next to no practical damage, but wreaked havoc with the base's personnel. The NATO air crews had come to expect aerial attack but this mortar strike arrived with no advanced warning. An alert siren split the night and base security trucks raced to the perimeter. The Serbs outside pressed their attack, assaulting the base's main gate and peppering it with rifle fire. The hail of bullets was interspaced with rocket propelled grenades that detonated on the hardened cement structure.

Petrovski could hear and imagine the attack, though he couldn't see it. He had no illusions that these well-motivated but poorly trained irregulars would succeed in breaching the base perimeter, but they were creating just the sort of chaos he needed.

"Go!"

The Serb driver floored the truck's accelerator and yanked the wheel, taking the heavy truck off the gravel road to the loading area and onto the paved tarmac of the runway. The other trucks in the convoy followed suit, turning as one and accelerating toward the hangar entrances. As the speedometer's needle crept higher, the truck closed on their target site.

It took only a moment for the lead Humvee to realize something had gone wrong with their convoy and turn to race after them. The vehicle's passenger was shouting something into a PA system mounted on the outside of the Humvee.

Petrovski shouldered his carbine, leaned out of his window and fired a long burst through the Humvee's windshield. The driver jerked and slumped. The entire vehicle slewed to the side and skidded to a halt. Petrovski pumped the rest of his magazine into the decidedly-not bulletproof vehicle, hoping to ensure the Humvee's occupants were all dead or incapacitated. Petrovski dumped the empty magazine to the floor and slapped a fresh one home before priming his weapon again.

With no more base security forces to delay them, the two trucks assigned to this particular hangar skidded to a stop within the mouth of the entrance to the base. Ahead of them was a taxiing American jet fighter and a gaggle of bewildered ground crew.

Petrovski debarked the truck while firing from the hip, mirroring the men from the other vehicle as they sent the ground crew fleeing for cover.

The Serb driver in Petrovski's truck put a burst of fire through the fighter's cockpit windscreen, painting the interior of the glass red with blood before return fire from base personnel dropped him with a grunt.The major didn't wait to see how the rest of his men fared; instead, he circled to the back of the truck and clambered into the bed, digging in the gravel with the metal folding stock of his rifle.

It didn't take long to find the high explosive compound hidden beneath the rock. He carefully primed the charges as bullets snapped and ricocheted off the rock ceiling above his head. The bombs were ready. He set the timer—thirty seconds —and jumped back to the ground. He landed hard enough to momentarily buckle his legs before he restored his stance and ran. His breath came and went in regular bursts as he made for the bunker exit as fast as he could. What had taken the truck seconds took a lifetime to cross on foot.

The major didn't have to run the entire distance, though. The second truck, having dumped its gravel, pulled alongside him. A Spetsnaz trooper offered Petrovski a hand and pulled him into the metal bed. The getaway vehicle's engine protested as it was pushed to its limits. The guide lights of the cavern mouth flashed by as the truck accelerated before bursting out into the open air.

"The charges?" the commando asked Petrovski.

The bombs spoke for themselves. Each exploded with sufficient force to buffet the dump truck's rear, making it swerve slightly. A spreading smoke and dust cloud emanated from the bunker mouth, blocking the view of the bomb's effects. A trio of identical blasts came from each of the other hangars.

A bullet panged off the side of the dump truck as it raced down the runway, headed for the safety of the perimeter. Even so, Petrovski stayed standing at the rear, one hand on his carbine, the other gripping the lip of the dump bed, squinting into the dark to see some sign of his work. He glimpsed a rock tumble through the dust. They'd succeed in collapsing the hangar mouths. It wasn't insurmountable damage, but it wasn't something that could be cleared away in a day.

Petrovski sneered triumphantly. "Finished."

***

The night wasn't at all unpleasant, which somehow made it worse. Lieutenant Williams would have preferred that his last night on earth be miserable, cold, and wet, anything that might make him welcome death at least on some level. Instead he got a warm, star-filled night, serenaded with the sound of chirping insects and the sporadic hoot of an owl.

He and Corporal Steiner didn't sleep, but instead waited.

The Dragon sat perched on the lip of the simple blind they'd constructed of fallen pine branches in front of them. With luck it would hide them from observation until after they'd fired.

The corporal didn't say much, working mostly in silence with only the occasional instruction to Williams. Once the work was done, all they had to do was wait. The two men laid side by side, facing the road that lay down the hillside beneath them. Here they listened to the insects and the detonation of bombs, far enough away that one might be forgiven for thinking it was thunder.

Williams had no wife, no children. He was mostly worried about his mother. When the truth about him came out it would devastate his father—a man who served before his son, coming home from Vietnam with a bum leg and a medal. His father would recover, though his mother... she might not understand why he'd done this.

Williams looked to Steiner. The other man's eyes were just visible beneath the brim of his helmet. They reflected the small television display of the Dragon's infrared sight as he stared intently up the road, toward the enemy. "Corporal," Williams said, "are you ... do you have anyone back home?"

"Nah," Steiner said. He was young, young enough that he had no business getting married and even less having children. "Just a couple cats I guess."

"Parents?"

Steiner shrugged. "Forget 'em. You?"

Williams hesitated, "Yeah. Parents."

Neither man asked the other if they would miss their folks.

"Steiner, what are you doing out here?"

The corporal looked at Williams confused, "What do you mean?"

"I mean ... why didn't you go with the others."

The corporal looked baffled, tried to formulate an answer, stopped, and started fresh, "Someone had to stay, right?"

The simplicity of the answer surprised Williams.

"Why? Why did you stay?"

Williams considered feeding him a lie but didn't see the point. "This is how I'd rather be remembered."

Steiner had no reply.

It wasn't much later before they heard the approach of a heavy engine rumbling in the night.

Steiner scooted aside to let Williams man the Dragoon. The lieutenant sat up, legs in front of him, feet against the Dragon's bipod to hold it steady. He rested the launcher itself on his right shoulder, feeling the weight of the fiberglass tube's deadly payload. Then he pressed his face to the sight and peered into the dark.

The source of the noise was approaching. It was a four-wheeled Soviet armored car, a scout vehicle of some kind, racing up the highway. Its machine gun turret swiveled side to side, the crew nervously on alert for ambush.

Steiner looked over his shoulder to ensure the Dragon's backblast area was clear, and then he slapped Williams on the back of his helmet, "Let 'er rip!"

"No," Williams said. "This is a scout."

"What?"

"We let this one pass," Williams said, "I want a shot at the main body."

"We take out this one and maybe ..."

Williams took his face from the sight and looked back to Steiner, "Maybe what?"

"Shit, I don't know."

Any bravado the men felt was long gone by this moment. It was show time.

"We wait," Williams repeated, keeping his sights fixed on the armored car as it passed between trees and out of sight continuing down the road.

With the rumble of the scout's engine fading away, a new sound became clear, the clank and squeak of tank treads and roar of engines. The sound—like the heralding of doom—grew in intensity and made Williams' stomach tie itself in a knot. His hands were shaking and it took all his concentration to keep the

Dragon still. He had to keep his sights firmly on his target or the rocket would miss.

"They're coming," Steiner whispered, crouching lower behind their blind.

"We want the leader. A tank with antennas."

"Second one looks like," Steiner said.

"Second one," Williams repeated, adjusting his grip on the weapon, feeling his hands sweating. This was it.

The tanks came into his sights, dome-turreted and covered in foliage and equipment. They moved in a single file line, two dozen meters between each tank with a second platoon coming up behind them. The crews were exhausted and afraid, just like the men they fought. Williams hated to kill them, but it was war. He flipped off the weapon's safeties and drew his sights on the second tank.

"Clear," Steiner said, tapping his helmet again.

Williams tightened his grip and steadied the targeting indicator. He only had one shot. He wished he could say something to Steiner but there was no time. In that moment he felt nothing but pain and regret. Regret for the life that he wouldn't get to lead now. All that was left was to atone the only way he could. Williams would rather die a hero than live with his mistake. He snapped the trigger.

The Dragon spat fire and a missile leapt from the tube, streaking on a trail of fire toward the tank column, riding an infrared beam straight toward its hapless target.

The tank exploded, the turret leaping into the air as its ammunition cooked off.

Williams and Steiner didn't survive the return fire.

**

15

Wakefulness came painfully to Strelnikov. The early morning chill seeped through his poncho and made his bones ache. The cold somehow seemed to exacerbate the crick in his neck. He hadn't remembered falling asleep and only recalled the day before as a blur. The air smelled of damp earth and smoke. It wasn't the sweet smell of woodsmoke, but the pungent, sinus-scorching sting of burning plastic—the remnants of yesterday's pitched battle.

The general sat up and shifted the dew-wet poncho from his body. Strelnikov was by no means an old man; just entering his forties, he was something of a rising star in the Soviet Army. All the same, he felt twice his age right now. Sleep was a precious commodity on the modern, high-tech battlefield, one that could ill-afford to be squandered. Planes could be refueled mid air, worn out vehicles could be swapped for spares, but men needed rest and four hours of fitful sleep on the ground was simply not enough. Reaction times would decrease, fatigue would increase, and mistakes would be made.

"General."

Strelnikov startled at Mishkin's voice and looked up at his chief of staff with surprise, blinking to clear his dry eyes. "Time?" he croaked.

"Yes, General. The meeting will begin soon."

"Time," Strelnikov insisted.

"It's 0445," Mishkin said.

Strelnikov was too tired to complain. He'd wanted to oversee the recon battalion's probing attack earlier in the morning. Instead, he stood and wiped at his face as if the exhaustion he was feeling could be swept away. All around him were the huddled lumps of sleeping men scattered around their vehicles —an army at rest. Delaying no further, Strelnikov followed Mishkin through the camp to a waiting jeep with a pair of guards in it, including one in the back armed with a shoulder-mounted surface-to-air missile launcher. A flimsy but important defense against low-flying NATO aircraft.

The drive was a short one, just a few miles away from the front to the meeting area. On the cusp of the 21st Century, all the advanced communications technology of the Soviet military counted for nothing. Command decisions would be made at meetings in the woods. Here, a loose perimeter of soldiers stood guard on foot, a single platoon spread through the woods. Many carried anti-air rockets on their backs or had them propped on nearby trees.

Strelnikov saw Gurov and Dmitriyev talking at the base of a tree alongside a colonel that he didn't recognize. No one saluted at his arrival, it wasn't a good idea even in an area where they thought no one was watching.

Dmitriyev noticed Strelnikov's arrival first.

"Comrade Strelnikov, I'm glad to see you well." His tired eyes undermined the warm smile he gave Strelnikov.

"As well as can be wished for," Strelnikov replied. He'd never considered himself close to Dmitriyev, but with the hell they'd both put their men through, it was hard not to feel a sense of true camaraderie.

Before either of them could delve into it, Gurov spoke. "Comrades, I am authorized to tell you that the American air asset codenamed Asgard has been neutralized."

The weight lifted from Strelnikov's shoulders was tremendous. Air attacks in the night had reduced his tank regiment to a wreck; only a single battalion remained relatively intact, with the others having been utterly savaged.

"Tomorrow we move on Zagreb," Gurov said. "Comrade Strelnikov's bold armored thrust has brought us within striking distance of the city. It is a vital transit hub for this entire region and should provide us with open ground for our armored reserve, the 88th Tank Division, to strike south."

"What defenses do we expect, comrade general?" Dmitriyev asked. His flippancy had been reduced, Strelnikov saw, and that ever present smirk was gone. It seemed even the jester of the 10th Army had a heart.

"The remnants of the American Marine division we have been fighting, as well as reinforcements from the Croatian army. They do not amount to much, but we have seen they are tenacious fighters and are holding good ground." Gurov motioned to a nearby aide who produced a folding table and map for the generals to study. "Zagreb sits north of the river Sava, just behind a large forested ridgeline. It means our attack will have to come from the east, around the ridge and toward the bridges east of the city."

"The Americans will have already wired these to blow," the colonel said. It appeared he replaced the ill-fated commander of the decimated 105th Division.

"To that effect," Gurov said, scowling at this uppity subordinate, "engineering battalions have been provided from the front. The most appropriate crossing point is here—" Gurov indicated a small northward salient in the river. "—where the E65 highway crosses the river. Any other crossing point won't allow our heavy equipment close enough to the river."

"There is no alternate point?" Strelnikov asked, astonished. A singular focus for the attack would not only make it difficult to conceal their intentions, but drawing up reserves would be even harder.

Gurov studied Strelnikov for a moment before speaking, "The only other suitable bridges lie within the city limits themselves. If we are forced to attack the city directly, our plans will not come to fruition."

Strelnikov of course knew that the Red Army had built a reputation for itself with heavy city fighting, crushing the fascist armies in Stalingrad and in the heart of Berlin. He was not keen to have to prove that prowess again.

"It would be better," Gurvo said, "to bridge the river further downstream, but it means more distance from the highway and more difficulty with the killing thrust."

"We should aim for both approaches then," Dmitriyev said.

"Most of our bridging equipment has been destroyed by NATO airstrikes," Gurov said. "I am informed by my engineers that we have enough pontoons and spares only to cross the river at one point."

Strelnikov studied the map in detail. The E65 highway crossing really was the best, closest position, which meant that the Americans would be watching it with everything they had. Just beyond it lay Zagreb's airport, a prime position for a forward airbase. It was useless to the Americans at present since it lay within range of the Soviets' long range gun batteries, but if it could be captured it could be used for re-supply operations and air strikes. Still, the obviousness of the target meant it would be a difficult proposition. Whatever division was tasked this time with taking the lead would surely meet the same fate as the 105th.

"Comrade General Strelnikov, the 121st Motor Rifle Division will secure the bridgehead."

Strelnikov's blood ran cold. Taking the lead again?

"The 105th and 111th will support your attack. I have also secured as much of the fire support assets our front can provide, as well as a number of air attack wings," Gurov said, as if he had not just handed Strelnikov a disaster waiting to happen.

"Comrade general," Strelnikov said, trying to be diplomatic, "my men are tired, we have pushed hard in the last day, and my tank regiment is depleted."

"The remaining tank battalions from the 105th Division will be placed under your control," Gurov said.

"Comrade general, perhaps another division—" Strelnikov was not allowed to finish.

"There is no other division," Gurov said with finality, eyes hard. "The only reserves we have now are Mamedov's 88th Tank Division. If we throw them away then we have nothing left to exploit our breakthrough."

Strelnikov felt hope slip away. Somehow his division was in the best condition despite their losses. "I understand."

"Don't worry, comrade general," the colonel said, "the 105th will be there beside you."

It may have been a veiled barb at Strelnikov for fretting over his comparatively light losses. The absence of the 105th's original commander was reminder enough of the price they had paid for their own river crossing.

"When does the attack begin?" Strelnikov asked, burying any apprehension.

"The attack will begin at dawn," Gurov said. "The rising sun will be in the face of the enemy and will play havoc with their infrared-guided weapons."

Strelnikov wasn't sure how true that was, but would take any advantage he could get.

"The attack will open with a full bombardment of identified enemy strongpoints, then the 111th will attack further south, toward Ivanic-Grad, followed by the 105th attacking Zagreb's outskirts. Ideally, they will draw off as many reserves as possible. Then the 121st will go forward under the cover of our bombardment."

It was a good plan on paper. In practice ... they would see.

Strelnikov had time to consider his options during the drive back to his division HQ. THe HQ itself was nothing more than a wheeled APC parked in a clearing with a nearby radio transmitter and SAM launcher. "Have Colonel Rastayev meet with the new battalion commanders from the 105th," Strelinkov told Mishkin, referring to the tank regiment's commanding officer, as they walked from the jeep toward the APC. "I don't want any miscommunications or foul ups. The tanks will once again be critical to success."

"Yes, comrade general." Mishkin's memory was impeccable and he refrained from writing orders down.

"We'll be splitting the division into two wings."

"Wings?"

Strelnikov didn't explain himself. "The left wing will be led by our mechanized infantry and the right wing will—" Strelnikov stopped and Mishkin had to circle around to face him again. "Send a courier," Strelnikov said. "I want to assemble all our broken companies into ad hoc battalions. We'll form them into one mixed regiment."

Mishkin gave him a sidelong glance. "They've been through a lot, general. I'm not sure how much more fight they have in them."

Strelnikov ignored him. "They'll lead the advance on the bridge, with the tank regiment in reserve." Strelnikov knew he was putting his weakest, most vulnerable forces before his most important objective. It was a risk, but it was the only way he would be able to get close. "I'll want constant radio contact with them and a continual artillery barrage along the riverfront, a mix of smoke and HE shells."

Smoke hadn't seemed to have much of an effect on American fire with their infrared sights able to pick out heat sources through the relatively cool smoke. Even so, it might help and was worth the effort.

"Yes, comrade general."

***

Simpson stood alone outside the Oval Office. It was warm enough that the suit jacket he wore felt entirely too hot. The night was peaceful, and the sounds of DC traffic were just a quiet murmur. Here, his only company was the lone Marine sentry by his office door and a patrolling Secret Service agent who stood a good dozen yards away.

The door to the office opened—not for the first time that night —and let his chief of staff out.

"Wanda says the Russians are giving her the cold shoulder, sir," Harrison said.

Simpson swore and turned away, gripping the tasteful white railing that ran the length of the porch. He'd heard that President Slater would stand out here and smoke when he was feeling the stress. Simpson had quit before coming into office, a bad habit he'd picked up in his teenage years. He'd never wanted a cigarette more than he did at this moment. "Back channels?" Simpson asked.

Harrison shook his head sadly. "Nothing from the Soviet foreign ministry or from our government contacts."

"Bastards are holding out on us after they bushwhacked Asgard," Simpson said.

"I suspect you're right, sir." Harrison came to stand beside the president. "Reconnaissance imagery shows the Soviets are gearing up for another big push."

Simpson made a non-committal noise. "Any sign they've reinforced?"

There was reluctance in Harrison's voice, "No, sir. No large scale unit movement over the border."

"Sounds like the Reds want to keep this thing contained."

"Why shouldn't they? With Asgard down and every other airfield in range bombed to hell we don't have much left to stop them with."

"Italy?"

"They've dug their heels in, sir."

"Greeks?"

"The Greeks know where they are. If they stick their noses into this too far—"

"—They're liable to lose them, right," Simpson said sourly. He sensed more from Harrison. "What else?"

"Mr. President, I spoke with the Joint Chiefs again. They're not confident about their ability to stop another push with just *Gettysburg*'s air compliment. They're hustling *San Juan Hill* up through the Suez now but with the whole Soviet Mediterranean squadron camped outside of the straits we don't know how that'll go."

Simpson waited for more, "And?"

"And I'll remind you that the 101st is on rapid response standby at Ramstein AFB. I can get the first brigade on the ground in twelve hours, the whole division in twenty-four. We can fly them right into Zagreb, beef them up with some armor and turn the whole offensive back."

Simpson looked away from his chief of staff and out over what he could see of DC's buildings. He was tired, but he didn't want to sleep, not when America and Europe were holding their breath over the biggest showdown since Korea. NATO and the Soviets were facing one another down and whoever blinked was going to come out the worse for wear. Even so, sending in more troops meant escalating. The Soviets had played by their—admittedly skewed—rules and kept the attack to in-situ forces only. If he upped the ante now, who knew how they might react?

"Naw," Simpson said , grinding his teeth. "We're gonna hold 'em with what we got. I let this thing brew up into what it is; I'm not gonna let the whole damn pot boil over."

Harrison was silent for a moment, his way of making it very clear to his boss that he felt he was making a grave mistake. "Yes, sir."

"Walt, get some sleep."

"You too, sir."

"I'll sleep when this thing is over," Simpson said, longing for that cigarette. "Soon I hope."

***

"Have they spotted us?" Yessov asked, leaning over the shoulder of his sonar operator. His voice was low as if the British warship pinging their hull might hear him.

"No change in activity, comrade captain," the operator said, listening to his phones. "They continue southward."

The frigate they'd spotted was passing within a few kilometers of them, pounding the sea ahead of it with bursts of noise from its active sonar, seeking out any Soviet submarines lurking about. Yessov was unsure if any others in his squadron had made it through the straits intact, but it was possible that NATO was searching only for him.

Yessov straightened up and paced to the navigational station, checking the course his boat was weaving northward. It was a zig-zagging bolt steadily creeping up the Adriatic toward high levels of radar activity—believed to be the carrier *Gettysburg*'s current location. The water here was too shallow to make use of the thermal layer, and so Yessov was forced to scoot along on one-third power, making a trip of a few hours into one lasting days.

Another electronic ping echoed across the sub's hull and Yessov fought his desire to flinch.

"We have a clear fire solution," Yessov's XO said from the weapons station. "The enemy vessel is within range of our torpedoes, comrade captain."

Yessov consulted the chart again. The warship was going to pass far to starboard, presenting a flank shot, a near perfect opportunity to strike. Even so, they were close now to the carrier's expected position. Very close. If they were to reveal themselves now to sink an escort it might ruin the game. "We will hold fire and continue on our present course," Yessov said. The XO said nothing.

"What is the time?"

"0530, comrade captain," his XO replied.

Just before dawn. Yessov carried on his present course long enough to let the frigate slide peacefully by him and then brought the ship up to periscope depth. It was time to check for their quarry.

The radar mast went up first, poking just a couple meters from the water's surface but at once being inundated by signals. "I have high confidence," the radar operator said, indicating the source of the signals, "that this is the enemy carrier group."

The radar signals came from dead ahead and were strong, strong enough that there was a fleeting possibility B-218's radar mast might itself be detected. Yessov had it lowered and silently hoped that it would be overlooked in the chaos or perhaps mistaken for a small fishing boat or one of the Adriatic's many small islands. "Sonar?"

"Faint engine signatures north. It is not enough for

identification. Multiple ships some distance away."

Yessov weighed his options. That was almost certainly the fleet, but he needed confirmation. "Up scope."

His face went to the leather-padded scope and he rotated it to peer north.

There they were. A gaggle of gray warships, small and faintly visible on the horizon. The distance between the individual ships was great, but from a distance they were clearly a cluster. The close conditions of the narrow Adriatic prevented truly broad distribution. They formed a large ring around a central behemoth, the flat-topped aircraft carrier *Gettysburg*. The scope was coming back down before Yessov realized he'd given the order. He turned to the small black and white monitor beside the periscope and reviewed the footage again, over and over. The fleet was there alright, headed south obliquely, possibly re-positioning for more attack sorties. The carrier was like a bloated bovine ripe for the slaughter; it was the many escorts and their accompanying aircraft that Yessov feared. He'd experienced firsthand how quickly the seemingly sluggish anti-submarine warfare ships could strike.

The carrier was ringed with protection, a double layer of escorts probing the waves with active sonar and ASW aircraft dropping sonobuoys and dipping sonar arrays into the water, listening for any Soviet sub threat. Here the water was only sixty meters deep, far too shallow to try the trick of hiding beneath a pinging torpedo again.

There was only one chance as Yessov saw it.

"Helm, take us to 080 and proceed at silent running." Yessov gave the order and double checked his thinking with a glance at the navigational charts.

"You're taking us ahead of them?" the XO asked.

"Make them—" Yessov said, tracing his finger in a line from the carrier group to a spot over his intended position, "—come to us."

They would get in front of the group and lay silently on the seafloor, going active only once the enemy escort ring had passed beyond them. It was risky but it was their best chance.

Yessov smiled confidently as his orders were carried out and tried not to think about what he would do when he had to escape this ring again.

***

The men of Strelnikov's ad hoc regiment stood poised and ready, concealed from the waiting Americans by a small rise of earth. These were the men who'd seen the brunt of the fighting the past few days and bore the mental scars to prove it. There was no room for idle chatter even if a voice could be heard. The air was full of the sound of hundreds of idling diesel motors, purring heavily while they waited to be unleashed. Above that was the constant thump and boom of the barrage. Having started just before daybreak, the shelling continued fitfully as the other divisions launched their own attacks nearby.

If Strelnikov were to join the scout platoons lurking at the edge of the woods ahead, he would see the American line shrouded in a thin blanket of smoke. Gouts of earth were thrown into the air here and there, where artillery shells buried themselves into the ground before exploding.

As Strelnikov looked up at the distant scouts, one of their recon BDRMs rolled forward. Fallen tree branches crackled beneath its wide tractor tires. Once it crept close enough to the lip of the hill that its roof-mounted turret was able to peek over it, it loosed a single anti-tank missile to speed out of sight, toward whatever target it had spotted. After only a few seconds it rolled back quickly, just fast enough to avoid a TOW missile that flashed by and exploded uselessly in the treetops.

This particular recon vehicle had been lucky more than once. A half-dozen silvery guidewires from anti-tank weapons lay draped over it like tinsel, evidence of more near misses.

Strelnikov sheltered in a hastily scraped out earth dugout behind the main assemblage but risked a look around in the open air. The scale of modern warfare meant a general could no longer oversee his entire army at once, so he chose to watch these men in particular. He could see a battalion's worth of armored personnel carriers, mostly old BTR-60s, and a handful of BMP-1s salvaged from a savaged tank battalion. These were spaced out, twenty meters between each idling vehicle. Behind them, the second echelon of the attack waited. Hundreds of T-72 main battle tanks sat ready to exploit any breakthrough these troops might find.

The troopers here were antsy; they'd been subjected to heavy artillery bombardment all morning as well as repeated NATO airstrikes. A dozen armored vehicles burned where they sat. Their fat rubber tires blazed like the sun while the ammunition inside popped off like fireworks.

Every moment they hesitated here allowed more American firepower to come to bear on them.

Strelnikov turned away from this scene of lambs led to the slaughter and went deeper into his bunker. The sounds of battle were muffled here, but not by much. A large folding table sat in the middle with a map of their area of operation spread over it.

At present, American units from along the Sava river front were concentrating before his forces, deploying in treelines and villages. They gathered not only behind the river, but in front of it as well. An armored detachment in a small industrial park before the bridge was wreaking havoc on his forward elements. No matter how many cluster bombs the Soviets dropped on the warehouses and storage tanks there, the enemy fought on. Twisted metal ruins provided just as much cover as orderly square buildings.

A handful of radio stations were here as well, their operators receiving and parsing information from across the battlefront. Picking up a free transmitter for this purpose, Strelnikov patched into his battalion commander's network.

"Comrades," Strelnikov said, "the enemy is before us. This river, the River Sava, is the last obstacle between us and the Adriatic. Today we will make our fathers and grandfathers proud. Today we will show the Americans how Soviet men fight!" Strelnikov did not feel the bravado he put into the speech, but he knew such things were important to the men. "Commence the attack."

There were no dramatic cries for the motherland, no unanimous "Ura!" going forward, but the throaty roar of a thousand diesel engines accelerating at once had close to the same effect. The lead elements, anti-tank units, fired snap shots down at the American armored units they could spot.

No sooner had they fired their salvos than the steady bombardment increased tempo from a rhythmic pounding to a near constant curtain of noise. The ground the men of the Soviet Union advanced on now looked more like the surface of the moon than Southern Europe.

The lead elements of the attack suffered horrifically. A dozen armored vehicles blew up at once as waiting American tanks took their shots near simultaneously. The new American M1 tank was proving to be well worth its price tag as it decimated the lead elements of the attack. American loaders slammed fresh shells into place in time to begin picking off the aging Soviet tanks that cleared the hill.

The Soviets were firing blindly into the smoky morass ahead of them, engines struggling to advance as quickly as they could. Unlike the Americans, their crews did not have the electronic miracle of thermal gun sights allowing them a peek through the smoke and haze. Attack helicopters from both sides lifted above hills and treelines, firing wire-guided missiles to nail enemy tanks or sometimes one another. Rotary autocannons spewed shell casings that rained down on the advancing armored forces beneath them. Whole platoons were wiped out in seconds, others—losing all cohesion in the face of this deadly onslaught —broke and ran for the rear. Tanks reversed, APCs came about in tight circles. Some collided and became hopelessly entangled, forcing their crews to bail out and flee this deadly morass on foot.

Aircraft from both sides sought advantage in the air, dueling overhead and streaking by low enough to clip tree tops. A rocket barrage tore apart the north end of the industrial park the

Americans sheltered in, collapsing a large metal building with little other obvious effect.

The losses the Soviets suffered crossing in the open were truly nightmarish, but they made progress despite the challenges. The lead elements of the attack were disgorging infantry platoons to advance on foot and sweep American infantry clear of the villages and woods before the bridge. Soviet and American troops quickly became locked in a series of brutal, close-range firefights.

Reports that came back to Strelnikov were confused and disheartening as unit commanders were swiftly picked off leaving their men directionless. The attack was stalling, bogging down in the open. The Red Army's huge volume of fire support lacked the precision to adequately clear out the opposition they faced.

Strelnikov hated to be locked in a bunker so close but so far from the fighting; it was torturous to listen to his men dying in droves with nothing more he could do. Operational necessity had dictated the direction and object of his approach. He could do little more than send it forward.

Still, his regiment surged on. Infantry on foot hacked a path with machine gun and RPG fire to the river's edge. Once there they took murderously precise return fire from the Marine riflemen on the opposite bank, mortar rounds dropping among both sides. The E65 bridge was already blown. Huge concrete slabs lay toppled into the river like a giant's playing blocks. It was clear that the Marines on the north side of the river were ordered to hold at all costs, and most fought and died where they were.

Despite their progress, Strelnikov knew his men had no real chance, even if he had sent the bridging equipment forward with them. The defensive position opposite them was too perfect and the problem was compounded tenfold by Strelnikov's insistent focus on this position. His ongoing artillery barrage had merely telegraphed his intent to the Americans and his heavy use of radio traffic made it clear to them that this was his axis of approach.

The Marines had anticipated this textbook plan and stationed defense in depth, drawing reserves to this focal point and forming up two armored companies just behind the river itself, stationed in villages inside the curve of its salient. While they were suffering immensely, they knew that as the Soviet main advance, this attack had no hope of working. They knew they would stop him cold here.

They had not yet realized they were wrong.

Reports from his ad hoc regiment were increasingly pessimistic as more units broke for the rear. Others became bogged down in place, content to blindly put rounds toward the Americans and maintain position without advancing.

Strelnikov nodded, satisfied. "They've done well. Heroes, all of them." He turned to a lieutenant seated by a nearby radio console. "We'll send the main body. Order the mechanized regiment to begin their attack."

The lieutenant nodded and switched his network to broadcast to the division's mechanized regiment.

***

From the second story of the farmhouse, the view of the battle was dominated entirely by smoke. Jean saw the thin pillars of black smoke marking vehicle kills, the billowing gauzy veil of Russian concealment smoke from the bombardment, and the thick brown geysers of earth and dust that vomited up from the ground with Russian artillery strikes. The rattle and boom of fighting carried the few kilometers back to the house to be picked up by the built-in microphone on Pete's camera the same way his lens captured the smoke.

The only part of the actual combat Jean and Pete could see was the intricate dance of death in the sky. Fighters weaved across a blue sky overhead, playfully chasing one another with streaking missile launches and ripping bursts of gunfire. It seemed mostly for show but every now and then one would disintegrate in a fireball or go tumbling down to earth like a wet moth.

Neither Pete nor Jean spoke, even as they dutifully documented the unfolding battle. They were not merely spectators anymore, not after they left Dario's body with a casualty recovery unit during their ongoing retreat. They'd inevitably become a part of the story. While never truly impartial, they were hoping more than ever for the Soviet attack to falter and fail. They didn't know what was unfolding nearby. They thought they were safely away from the fighting.

They were wrong.

**

The commander of the 121st division's mechanized regiment, Colonel Lukin, was head and shoulders out of the commander's hatch on his BMP-2. Ordinarily it helped to get some fresh air rather than breathing the stale stink of other men's breath and sweat, but now the outside air reeked of burning rubber and cordite, the smells of war. He felt the concussive blasts of explosions and dull thumps in his gut, but he paid them no mind. He'd received the attack signal. Until now, the entire regiment had maintained strict radio silence. He broke that silence with a burst transmission. "Regiment forward."

The command was simple but the reaction was dramatic as hundreds of vehicles surged forward on whirring tracks. This regimental advance would ordinarily face the same problems as the ad hoc attack except that this unit was already on the other side of the river. The Soviet Union's heavy investment into amphibious armored fighting vehicles was paying off for them as these troops raced forward.

With most American forces drawn off into the river salient around the E65 bridge or southward to face Dmitriyev's feint, they had been able to cross nearly unmolested further to the east, between the two attacks. They'd taken backroads that would not support an army-level advance. Ultimately, they dove into the cool waters of the Sava before fording them. Now, with water still beading off their metal hides, they came up behind the waiting American second defensive line.

Autocannons belted shells into peaceful villages as they advanced, setting buildings alight and blowing apart lightly armored trucks and APCs. The BMP's turret mounted anti-tank rockets dealt killing blows to the American M60 and M1 tanks they encountered. Many of their shots struck these tanks in their relatively unprotected rears.

Colonel Lukin was careful to maintain the impetus of his attack. He spread his battalions across the axis of his advance and seized control of choke points as he encountered them. The 303rd mechanized rifle regiment drew a noose around the neck of the Sava River's defenders.

With the trap sprung, any pretense of secrecy was gone. The Soviet movements were now plain and in the open. The Americans reacted as best they could, marshaling up reserves and mobile forces to try to stem this deadly tide.

Isolated, this regiment wouldn't hold on its own; Strelnikov had to get across the river quickly now. He relayed his orders to Mishkin, "Bring up Colonel Sidorov's regiment. They'll screen the advance of the engineers."

Mishkin wasted no time passing the commands on to the subordinate regimental and battalion commanders as the 111th's relatively fresh motorized infantry regiment rolled up the same hill from which the ad hoc regiment had staged . They would be passing by the flaming wrecks of their predecessors as they began their attack. Strelnikov only hoped it would not rattle their nerves.

***

The Marine colonel frowned at the map harder as if that might change things. It was all he could do; screaming wouldn't help. The attack on the bridge was a feint after all. The Russians had slipped a whole regiment over the river and now had pinned most of his combat forces against the river.

"We have a pair of Croatian battalions," one of his

subordinates explained, "just to the south for rear area security. We can send them to try to break through."

It wouldn't be enough. The colonel knew that the Croatians didn't have the heavy firepower needed to dent those Soviet mechanized forces. They would need substantial fire support and all his assets were tapped. He only had one more trump card. "Send them in, and get *Gettysburg* on the radio. We need everything they have to spare and we need it *now*."

***

16

B-218 sat virtually on the bottom of the Adriatic as the *Gettysburg* task force's escorts passed overhead. Their sonar pulses bounced off the ocean floor around them and returned nothing out of the ordinary. Here, they were relatively safe from active detection, but there was the ongoing threat of passive sonar. B-218 was as silent as the dead while sitting motionless on the bottom.

It just meant that Yessov was going to have to take things slowly.

The submariner wiped a thin sheen of sweat from his forehead and tried to keep the situation clear in his head.

"Sonar, any further contacts?"

"No, comrade captain, the pinging sonar contacts are at 150 and proceeding away. We should be out of detection range."

So the only worry was passive sonar.

"Helm, take us up to 50 meters, ahead slow."

"Yes, comrade captain."

The submarine rose silently from the sea bed and set her screw turning slowly enough not to make any undue sound.

"Weapons, arm tubes one and three with torpedoes and two and four with missiles," Yessov said. He wanted maximum chaos and he knew that firing torpedoes alone would likely give him away. Those missiles might help buy him enough panic to escape. It was times like this that he wished he had a hundred weapons tubes to use at once instead of just four.

Yessov paced the bridge and came to stand behind the weapons officer. His XO hovered over his shoulder. "Confidence on our target?"

"One hundred percent, comrade captain."

Yessov nodded and looked up, toward the bow of his boat as if he might see the behemoth Antietam-Class carrier through the hull and ocean. "Distance to target?"

"Three kilometers, comrade captain."

It was point blank as far as naval combat was concerned. It didn't get much closer than this.

"Flood all tubes, open outer doors and prepare to fire. Set active pinging at two kilometers."

B-218's forward torpedo tubes were flooded and opened, the sound detected by a dozen separate escort ships at once.

"Fire tube one."

"Firing!"

Yessov counted to three, "Fire tube three."

"Firing!"

"Torpedos away, captain," the XO confirmed, reading displays over the sailor's shoulder.

"Cut the wires and bring us hard to port, helm, flank speed."

Though he felt nothing, Yessov could imagine the submarine's batteries feeding yet more power into the screw, accelerating the Kilo up to her full twenty knots. His only hope now was that being this close to the carrier meant that the enemy would not feel safe using homing torpedoes. If so, then he was in a weapons blind spot.

"Surface splashes!" Sonar called.

"Rocket deployed torpedoes probably," his XO said.

Yessov was't particularly worried about it given the distance between his submarine and the splashes. The Americans were groping in the dark for him. They were panicking and it showed.

"Set both our missiles for active homing," Yessov said, ignoring the depth charge warning. He had no defense but to run now. "Fire two and four."

"Firing!"

The submarine shuddered as both tubes were discharged. The missiles rose rapidly to the surface and burst free in a column of smoke to race into the sky. Their onboard radar guidance systems locked onto the nearest targets—which in this case were

Gettysburg's escort ships.

"Torpedos closing on target, range to target one kilometer," the weapons officer said.

"*Gettysburg* is accelerating, going to flank, making a hard turn," Sonar said.

"They're too late," the XO said, sounding more defiant than confident.

He was correct.

"Torpedo one hit! Torpedo two!"

"A kill?" Yessov asked but was interrupted before he could get an answer.

"Missile one—both missiles have hit targets!"

With missiles, a hard kill was unlikely; damage above the water line was unlikely to sink it, but with luck one or both ships were aflame and full of toxic smoke with multiple critical systems dead. The end result would be a disabled ship, but not one Yessov would be able to verify without surfacing and confirming visually.

Torpedoes which failed to find a target detonated nearby, sending a shudder through the submarine. Yessov could only imagine what a hit might feel like. All around him the crew held tightly to their stations, faces sheened with sweat, eyes wide.

"Are those tubes reloaded!?" Strelnikov demanded, his fear letting his temper through.

"Nearly, comrade captain!"

"Captain, transients from the *Gettysburg*, she's taking on water and has disengaged her engines."

If the carrier had gone full stop it meant the damage was likely severe enough that they didn't want to risk the forward movement of the ship causing them to take on more water. All the same, it was nearly impossible to truly sink a ship of that size, not without much more fire power.

"Go to silent running," Yessov said. "Bring us down to fifty meters and come hard to port."

The submarine deck plating tilted as the boat banked, turning hard to go north, away from the ships they'd struck with missiles. With some luck, the American escorts and aircraft would be racing toward that gap in the ring and would miss him quietly sneaking out.

"More surface splashes," sonar said, "They're to the south."

"Steady on," Yessov said, more for his benefit than anyone else's.

A few moments later those charges also exploded, further away than the first salvo. The water was full of the sound of beating sonar, thrumming propellers, and of course the noises of a crippled vessel taking on water. It was next to impossible for a single submarine to be heard through this commotion. At least that was Yessov's hope.

"Tubes one through four report loaded and ready with torpedoes, comrade captain."

"Set aim point for 180," Strelnikov said, "Range two kilometers. Fire all torpedoes and cut the wires."

"Yes, comrade captain."

The ship shuddered with the launch of a new spread of torpedoes. Firing so many from such a depth was rapidly depleting their reserve of compressed air, but Strelnikov needed to ensure he allowed for maximum chaos.

The plan worked. The Americans floundered in panic as they frantically searched for the wolf in the cow pen, hammering the ocean floor with active sonar and dropping homing torpedoes —in the wrong area. Strelnikov slipped north, right under their noses even as they scrambled to react to the fresh spread of torpedoes that blew a hapless frigate in half and sent others scurrying away at flank speed. Every kilometer Strelnikov put between himself and the sinking carrier was another degree of safety added until he no longer heard the sounds of anti-submarine operations above him.

The gripping fear of combat slipped away. Gradually, Yessov's nerves calmed, terror fell away incrementally. He dared to look around at his men, dared to see their faces. Their tension was replaced by degrees with the rush of victory. He cracked a smile, an expression his XO mirrored. They had done it. He had done it.

Gettysburg was no longer a factor.

***

The sound of engines heralded the approach of the Soviet mechanized battalion. The sound arrived only a few moments before the vehicles came into sight.

"Pete!" Jean turned her cameraman so he faced the new arrivals.

Tracked APCs were cresting a nearby hill in twos and threes, fanning out across a cornfield to flatten the crop and chew the ground with their treads.

"Those look Russian," Jean said.

"Can't be, they'd have to cross the river first."

Their allegiance became clear enough once they opened fire. Their auto-cannons belted out shells that shredded a parked Humvee not far away. Shards of its metal skin tumbled through the air as its gas tank cooked off, engulfing the truck in flames. The rear ramps on the BMP-2s dropped and soldiers spilled out, firing long bursts from the hip as they moved forward. The Marines in the area ran for cover and fought back as well as they could.

Pete tracked the APCs as they drove forward, firing on the move. The sound of their guns was deafening at close range. One drove right by the farmhouse they were in, vibrating the wooden structure.

As they passed. Jean saw straight down on top of the vehicle. A Soviet crewman had his head poked out of the hatch. His characteristic black leather padded helmet caught the sun as he relayed orders into a microphone. Jean picked up her own still-shot camera and raced to the opposite side of the room looking out the other side of the house where she saw more Soviet forces including a tank moving up. This farm was directly in the middle of their line of advance. "Pete!"

"What?" He lowered his camera and looked back, coming back to the moment.

"We're surrounded."

Small arms fire tore through the far wall of the room, filling the air with plaster dust and sending Jean and Pete to the wooden floor for cover. Another burst followed the first one before it fell silent.

The two reporters traded looks and scrambled to their feet in unspoken agreement; they had to escape now. They flew down the rickety steps of the upper room and into the main floor of the abandoned farmhouse. They'd left the door ajar when they'd first come in and left through it now. There they found their rented 4x4 still parked on the gravel pad beside the house.

A pair of Soviet attack helicopters thundered low overhead in a looping, erratic course as they closed on whatever target they'd sighted.

Jean yanked open the driver's side door and slammed it behind her as Pete pulled his own door closed. She didn't buckle up before starting the vehicle and whipping it around, throwing a spray of gravel as the truck's off-road tires spun out. In a flash they were past the thick hedge tangle that surrounded the house and racing toward the freeway.

One moment they were in among the advancing Soviets, a confused tangle of Russian soldiers and tracked vehicles crashing through hedgerows and farm fences, the next they were free, going south away from the coming encirclement. They were left unmolested, perhaps—Jean thought—the result of their press identification.

A few miles down the road a new force materialized: the Croatian army. It was the same type of ragtag force they'd encountered in the early days of this war, before the superpowers became inexorably entangled in it. The Croatians were mostly equipped with liberated Yugoslav army gear and modified civilian vehicles like pickup trucks. The vehicles were all emblazoned with a white, hollow triangle on their roofs, an aerial identification mark to seperate them from the Serbian militias that were still scattered around the country operating in guerilla fashion.

The Croatians were fanning out into combat deployment, riding trucks and tracks forward, weapons at the ready. They let Jean pass without issue as they closed on the Russians.

***

A flaming American fighter fell from the sky and plunged into the Sava River in a great gout of white water. River water showered down over the Soviet assault engineers struggling across the river in rafts and amphibious armored vehicles. American machine gun fire stitched across the rolling surface of the water, occasionally catching an exposed engineer to pitch him into the cool, rushing river water.

Frantic radio calls to the rear brought more mortar fire down on the river bank, blanketing the area with smoke in a futile attempt to stave off the most murderous fire.

The latest American air attack had been brutal, leaving one of the pontoon trucks in flames and a dozen engineers dead and wounded, but it wasn't enough. There were too few planes and too many anti-air emplacements. Even now, gun crews hurriedly deployed a fresh AA gun to look over the pontoon bridge which was taking shape. The bridging engineers were paying heavily for their work, but they progressed all the same. They expertly maneuvered the pontoons together as they had a hundred times before in simulated runs, steadily forming a clear crossing point. This time the defensive fire they were taking was very real. Teams of assault pioneers had done their best to secure the opposite bank but faced stubborn, close-range resistance from the Marines who had chosen to fight and die where they stood rather than break or surrender.

"We ought not be here, comrade general," Colonel Mishkin said, holding tight to the Kalashnikov rifle he'd been provided. Mishkin and Strelnikov had moved forward to observe the crossing personally, the two of them sheltering in a shallow rifle pit just over the crest of the wooded ridge. It was less likely to be targeted with a guided bomb than a tank or command APC, but was exposed enough that a stray shell splinter was just as likely to claim them.

Strelnikov paid Mishkin no mind. His eyes were glued to the sights of a pair of binoculars. He swept them over the battlefield with morbid fascination. Though he was certain many hundreds or thousands of men were dying at this moment, the scale of the conflict drowned out their suffering. Men who bled and cried were blotted out by burning tanks and streaking missiles. It was so easy to forget that they existed—to forget that each one of these dozens of smoldering wrecks along the highway and riverbank represented a funeral pyre for the crew or squad that sheltered in it.

"They can't stop us with that," Strelnikov said, watching a trio of bomber aircraft driven off with concentrated SAM fire. The missile contrails crisscrossed in the sky over the bridge. "Do they not realize we're almost across?"

Mishkin had no answer and only muttered to himself, curses or prayers, his general couldn't tell.

A trooper came running up the hill toward them, his camo smock spattered with dark mud, the metallic folding stock of his carbine flashing in the sun. He dropped to the earth beside them breathlessly, "The first bridge will be complete in another twenty minutes, the second one in thirty."

"Good," Strelnikov said, "and the old causeway?"

The engineer looked over his shoulder toward the toppled cement blocks in the river. "Once we get heavy equipment across we can start building a metal girder bridge to cross that."

Strelnikov nodded, and turned to Mishkin, "Get back to the APC and radio General Gurov, inform him that I am about to make our final push. Tell him we will need *all* of the 10th Army's remaining bridging equipment moved here on the double and have the 88th Tank Division ready to move."

Mishkin hesitated, he wanted to argue about having to run back and forth across this hellscape. However, when he saw the engineer who'd addressed Strelnikov clap a hand over his helmet, struggle to his feet and sprint back for the river, past flaming tank hulls, he knew he had no room to complain. "Yes, General."

With both men scattering back to relay these commands, Strelnikov looked forward again, trying to make out the distant battle on the far side of the river. A number of Croatian army battalions had attacked and were in the process of being torn apart by his mechanized regiment—the best in his division, carefully marshaled for this moment. Without air superiority, the Americans had no hope here. He lowered the binoculars and felt positively giddy. This was it. *This* was the breakthrough.

True to the engineer's word, the river was spanned by a pair of pontoon bridges on either side of the old causeway within half an hour. Mere minutes after that, both were host to a seemingly unending stream of Soviet main battle tanks pouring across the Sava river to bypass Zagreb and drive like a dagger for the Adriatic coast. With nowhere left to run, the Americans would have to talk terms or be defeated in detail. His next order would be to send word to high command in Moscow.

***

Gradenko watched Minister Tarasov's face like a hawk as the defense minister listened to the report on the phone. The call had come early into a Politburo meeting and all proceedings had been stopped so it could be taken.

The old soldier ended the call and handed the receiver back to the aide that brought it before grinning at the table. "Checkmate."

***

The darkened situation room mirrored the colors that the TV screen wall displayed. Currently they were taken up with aerial photographs of the *Gettysburg*, aflame and listing badly. The deep blue of the Adriatic around her appeared immune to the carnage on her surface. A flock of helicopters hovered around the stricken ship, occasionally braving the black smoke rolling out of the carrier to land on her flight deck to shuttle wounded off or bring in more medical personnel.

Last Simpson had seen, the death toll was up to over a hundred sailors and airmen as they battled with the catastrophic damage done to the ship's belly.

The image flickered and changed to one of a digital map of Yugoslavia, Russian progress marked in orange with NATO's in blue. A finger of orange shot out from Zagreb toward the coast, the Soviet breakthrough that minute by minute was nearing the Adriatic.

"Zagreb is gone then?" Simpson asked, looking at the chairman of the Joint Chiefs.

The old Marine's face was unreadable as a blank tombstone, his eyes cold and hard. The defeat at Zagreb had no doubt hit him on a personal level, as many of the officers leading the Marines out there were personal acquaintances of his. "The city is still being held by elements of the 8th Regiment but they are largely cut off now, Mr. President."

"Any hope of getting them out? Keeping them supplied?"

The chairman looked at the other military and Department of Defense personnel gathered around the conference table, as if seeking a challenge to the facts as he understood them. When none came, he looked back to the president."No, sir. Plans have been made to break out of the city, but with each hour the Soviets are tightening their grip around it. Aerial supply was considered, but with Asgard out of operation we don't have a safe airfield to fly them in from."

"Their SAM network is being strengthened as well, sir," the chief of staff of the Air Force said sourly. "Breaking through it will be costly."

"What about our stealth fighters?" Harrison asked, "We had a wing of them out of Asgard."

"A lot of them are stranded inside the facility," the chief of the Air Force admitted reluctantly. "The ones we have available aren't going to be enough to break the hold."

"What about drawing back to a second line?" Simpson asked.

"There is rough terrain along the coast of the country, but we'd need to drop back the whole expeditionary force. We've already had to surrender Sarajevo to avoid getting cut off," the chairman of the Joint Chiefs said. "There is also the matter of the breakthrough."

An aide tapped a key on a hidden panel and the map enlarged to show the breakthrough in more detail.

"Intel suggests that this is the 88th Tank Division, Class A, equipped with the latest gear and best officers. They're driving hard for Rijeka and true to Soviet doctrine they're not stopping for anything. They're likely to capture the city before we can draw back. If they do that, we lose one of the main ports in the region for getting heavy supplies in or out."

"They'll strand the whole force," Harrison said, reducing it to its effect and sinking back into his chair.

"Unless it's reinforced, that's correct. As it stands, if we fight in place we'll be cut off and if we run we'll be at the coast before we're ready to fight again."

"Mr. President," Harrison looked to his boss, "The 101st is still on standby in Germany. We can have them on the coast before the Russians get there, form a defensive cordon and start looking about pushing back."

Simpson kept his face impassable but in the pit of his stomach he felt sick to the point of nausea. All those men dead, all for nothing. Sure, he'd stood up to the Soviets, but what had he shown them aside from their ability to beat the Americans in a standup fight. "We send in the 101st," Simpson said speculatively, "What's the likelihood that the Ruskies call in their own reserves? They've got 'em don't they?"

"Yes, sir," the chairman said. "A few divisions in Hungary at last count."

"We attack from Greece and they'll have to counterattack, maybe land troops in Turkey, then we're off to the goddam races." Simpson stood in disgust and forced himself to look at the map again. Yugoslavia ran red. "No." He sighed, "No, they got us on this one. This little patch of nothing ain't worth starting a real war about now is it?"

"Are we just going to walk?" Harrison asked, horrified. "Pat them on the shoulder and say 'good game'?"

"What the hell else do you want me to do?" Simpson demanded, "Drop an H-bomb on the Kremlin? They got us, Walt. Fair and square. We gave it our best, but I'll be damned if I go down in history as a butcher. We'll call it even."

The mood in the room fell even lower. No one vocalized it, but it was clear this was going to become remembered as a military debacle, a defeat worse than the Vietnam War.

"We lost the battlefield," Simpson said, "but we aren't gonna lose the war on this."

"Sir?" Harrison asked.

Simpson ignored him for the moment, "I want a ceasefire, we'll finish this thing up in a boardroom like we should have done all along. We're not gonna come to the Russians hat-in-hand. We're going to be the bigger side here." An idea was already starting to formulate for a way to salvage this defeat. "Walt, get Wanda and Bill on the line. We're spinning this as 'peace' and not 'defeat'."

"How do you aim to manage that?" Harrison asked, incredulous.

"Hell, I'll go to Sarajevo myself if I have to. This won't be a Saigon City all over again. This'll be cooler heads prevailing. The Reds'll love it to settle their people down, and we can avoid a total PR blowout on this. I walk up, shake hands with Kavinski and we play nice at a big conference, get some kind of concessions and we'll come out as close on top as we can. Let's bring the Russians up to speed on this, too." Simpson tried not to notice the cool gazes of the Joint Chiefs but he knew there was more to winning wars than just coming out with the highest kill count or the most land. He'd settle for the perception of victory, and if anyone
could swing that, it would be Rick Simpson on the ground in Yugoslavia in front of a camera.

***

Molly hugged Vance harder than he'd ever experienced in his entire life when he got home from the show. Her arms were like a vice around him, a more substantive force than gravity itself, like her love for him made manifest. She buried her face in his neck and cried, her tears hot on his skin.

"What?" Vance asked, bewildered, "What happened!?"

"It's over," she sobbed, "the war's over. It's all on the news."

The words hit Vance like a baseball bat to the temple and he was left feeling dizzy. He'd locked off his emotions and buried his fear. He had half-accepted his fate. To be told now that it was over, it was like seeing the sky for the first time. He hugged Molly back, one hand stroked her shoulder as he comforted her. She'd never been good with this sort of thing.

"First chance you get," she said, voice muffled by his shirt, "you are *not* re-upping."

"I'm done after this," Vance said, "I promise."

***

"Peace," Gradenko said, dramatically holding the printed document up over his head, holding the attention of all dozen other members of the Politburo. "This is a transcript of my conversation with the American secretary of state." Gradenko laid the rolled document down on the table and looked between his fellow members. "She has been authorized by the president to secure terms for a ceasefire and end this war." He ended by looking to Karamazov. "It's not often that we get a second chance for peace. Their suggested terms are quite reasonable. An immediate ceasefire and drawdown of forces. We will retain control of Zagreb and Sarajevo while they hold the ports and start to withdraw troops."

Karamazov's face remained unchanged as Gradenko spoke.

"The Adriatic will be made a safe zone again with free navigation to all forces," Gradenko finished.

"This is the result," Karamazov said, "of the splendid performance by our comrades in the military." He did not directly address the ceasefire and instead gave a tight smile to Tarasov.

"Thank you, Comrade Karamazov," Tarasov said without jubilation. "It was hard fought. Our opponents are masterful soldiers, but they underestimated us."

"A fatal mistake," Karamazov agreed. "How secure is our position in the country if we were to stop our advance?"

"Our ultimate victory depends on capturing the Dalmation ports," Tarasov said, voice guarded. "If we don't press our advantage we might find ourselves fatally outmaneuvered. Wars are not won by showing mercy."

"Wars are won by signing documents," Gradenko countered fiercely, meeting the old soldier's gaze. "We have a victory now, a total one. We only have to reach out and take it." He looked back to Karamazov. "Refusing this American offer might lead to an escalated war. We've been lucky."

The KGB chairman's lip turned subtly, the hint of a scowl. He saw that Gradenko was hoping to sway the main body of the Politburo again. "It seems to be a generous offer, but when have the capitalists ever been trustworthy?"

Gradenko was shocked that the chairman was leaning on old party rhetoric to try to back his argument, but didn't let it deter him. If he was to be a true member of this Troika then he had to exert his influence and not allow himself to become a pawn of the other two. "I spoke directly with Mrs. Shilling," he said, referring to his American counterpart. "I have spoken to her many times before and I can read her well. She is sincere—the president is sincere—in their desire for peace." Gradenko again addressed the other members of the Politburo, "We have proven our superiority on the battlefield, now let us show our superiority at the meeting table. The world will see the Americans submitting to our wishes and will know that the next century will belong to the Soviet Union!"

At that moment, Gradenko knew he'd won. He could see it

in the grudging smirk on Tarasov's face and the cold ire in Karamazov's.

All the same, the KGB's chairman fought on. "It might be prudent to finish off our foe before we show him mercy."

"Comrade Minister Tarasov," Gradenko said, "should hostilities continue, what sort of reserves does NATO have to draw upon?"

The old general was eternally unfazed. "A few airborne divisions in West Germany could be re-deployed in time to turn the battle. Italy may yet decide to uphold her NATO commitments. It is a substantial force."

"On paper," Karamazov added.

"On paper," Tarasov agreed.

"It sounds to me that we ought not risk escalation. The Americans have fought this war with one hand tied behind their back, just as we have. Do we risk them untying it rather than allowing them to yield? Might things have turned out differently if they had not decided to abide by the rules we established?"

"Comrade Karamazov," Tarasov said, "I believe the matter is ready to be called to vote."

"There is no need," Karamazov said, failing to hide his bitterness. "I believe we are all in agreement here." Karamazov's yielding of the point made the decision unanimous, in true Soviet fashion.

Gradenko hid his smile the rest of the meeting as they detailed the exact nature of the draw down. Karamazov and Tarasov had gotten their short, victorious war, and Gradenko had gotten his peace. He even managed to talk them into supplying a Soviet frigate to assist with returning *Gettysburg* to port in Taranto. Socialism—of a breed agreeable to the Soviet Union—would be restored to Yugoslavia and their bloc protected. It was, as he said, a Soviet triumph.

**

17

For the first time in his life, Major General Pyotr Strelnikov, commander of the 121st Motor Rifle Division, looked out over a field of battle that he had decisively won.

The sight was beyond appalling.

The fires of burning tanks had long since guttered out. Anything combustible in them had been consumed in the days after the battle, leaving only the twisted blackened wrecks of war machines which now served as the graves of men who'd died in the service of their mother country.

The grass—what hadn't been churned to mud by tires and tracks—was dewy under his boots and squeaked with each step.

Battlefield cleanup crews scoured the field. Men in body details marked the locations where soldiers had fallen for retrieval and later burial, while engineering detachments detonated unexploded ordnance and mines. The pop and bang of their work interrupted the stillness of the morning.

"It's awful, isn't it Mishkin?" Strelnikov said, allowing himself a moment of weakness alone with his chief of staff.

Mishkin had said nothing as they walked the battlefield to this point. "It is. 'There nothing except a battle lost that is half so melancholy as a battle won.'"

"Wellington," Strelnikov remarked, smiling wryly. "I dare say that I hope this was my Waterloo."

"How do you mean, general?"

Strelnikov glanced back at the sound of an approaching motor and saw a UAZ 4x4 struggling through the muddy field, coming toward him from the highway where a steady stream of logistics trucks passed. "Waterloo was the last," he said.

The vehicle stopped a short distance away and allowed

General Gurov and a handful of aides to emerge, crossing the remaining distance on foot. "Comrade Strelnikov," Gurov called.

Strelnikov—free of wartime restrictions—saluted his superior. "Comrade general, to what do I owe the pleasure?"

Gurov produced a small, velvet jewelry case and Strelnikov's heart sank. "The eve of your success of course. The eve of the victory you've delivered to us." The case came open and the silver and gold face of the award flashed tantalizingly at Strelnikov. "The Order of Bogdan Khmelnitsky, Second Class," Gurov pronounced, presenting the medal to his subordinate. "There will be a formal ceremony of course. I wanted to take the moment to present it before then."

Strelnkiov took it gratefully and marveled at its surprising weight. "An honor, comrade general." He looked to the ruins of his division. "I would like my men to be credited with the work though. They braved hell for this."

"And they will be," Gurov said. "They're minting enough Orders of Lenin to forge a main battle tank out of them. Your division fought hard, Strelnikov." The lieutenant general turned to survey the carnage for a moment. "War is never easy. There is a price for everything. We should be glad that your decisions lessened the cost."

"Yes, comrade general."

Gurov saluted and Strelnikov returned it. "Tomorrow morning your division is slated to be withdrawn. You'll proceed to the rail yard at Zagreb and entrain for Pilsen in Czechoslovakia. It will be an easy deployment; your losses will be replenished there. And your men given rest."

Desperately needed rest, Strelnikov reminded himself. "Very good, general."

"Until later," Gurov turned on his heel and made back for his jeep, aides in tow.

Strelnikov looked down at the medal in his hands and felt a distant welling of pride. It had come at a terrible price, but it was true he'd saved the army from even greater bloodletting. He closed his fist around the box, clapping it closed. "Come,

Mishkin. We have work to do."

***

The mood in the port-side bar was contradictory and bizarre. People drank and strange European copies of American pop songs played over the radio, but the many of the people here were muted, almost somber. The war had not touched Rijeka directly, but it had come damn close. Reminders of the fighting were all around them, from the large transport craft in the harbor onboarding US Marines to the pair of Soviet submarines tied up in port.

It was almost unfathomable to Jean that both militaries could peacefully coexist just a week after such an intense struggle, but it was clear to her that despite political rhetoric from both sides there was little personal animosity. All the same, the population of the city was tense as it was forced to play host to both sides. The powers that be had decided to keep the two forces as separate from one another as they could, with different bars and port facilities being designated for one side or another. This particular bar had been designated for Russian use and a pair of Soviet sentries stood at the doorway, conspicuously armed.

They'd given Jean and Pete no problems, but inside the crews of the two submarines drank and celebrated uproariously in stark contrast to the more sober civilians.

Jean felt little reason to celebrate.

"To Dario," Pete said, hoisting his mug of beer.

"To Dario," Jean echoed weakly, tapping her glass to his before drinking.

"It was quick for him," Pete said, softer.

"I know," Jean said. "Hell, I've had people I know die just ... not like that."

Pete didn't have an answer but drank deeply. "It's funny," he said, "the balloon went up and came right back down. Cooler heads prevailed. Who'd have thought East vs. West would end on pretty good terms?"

Jean found it strange too. The fact that the two superpowers had faced one another on the battlefield and the planet had lived to tell the tale felt almost like a relief. Like nature was telling them humanity loved nothing more than to quarrel with its own kind, but still had enough sense not to burn the planet. Jean wasn't sure if that was a positive attribute or not.

"Two World Wars is enough for one century," Jean said.

"Century's not over yet," Pete said with a morbid grin.

This time it was Jean who was left without an answer.

"Have you heard from Tony yet? Are we headed north?"

"It's a mess right now," she said, "but that sounds like the plan." Jean paused to take another swig of beer and wait for the sailors to quiet their cheering a bit more before continuing, "With the Yugoslav government coming back into power, it sounds like the situation with our visas is getting more complex."

"Ah hell, Jean, they're not gonna turn us down."

'I wouldn't be so sure," she said, "The country is still a mess and the comrades in charge don't usually like that sort of publicity."

The ceasefire was hardly a day old now and there were still reports of sporadic skirmishing on the old frontlines, mostly in Bosnia between the Bosniaks and Serbs. Guerrilla bands were still operating in the rural areas. Slovenians and Croatians still fighting for independence, there were even Serbians who hadn't gotten the memo about the peace taking potshots at Western forces. It was a mess.

"Still, we got a hell of a lot of good footage, we got a lot closer than we bargained. We *broke* the story, Jean."

That fact wasn't lost on her. She wondered how much of that had played directly into the war getting sparked in the first place. Another long drink pushed the thought from her mind. She was only reporting the truth, nothing more.

"Maybe a nice layover in the States would be good for a bit," Pete said.

"Nah." The last thing Jean wanted was to be alone with her

thoughts, the memory of Dario's death. "I think we'd do better to head back into Zagreb. The story isn't over and you know there's going to be trouble. Croatia's going to be in flux for a while now, a battleground of ideas and that's where the scoop'll be."

"I wonder how long till they can convince everyone out there to take the peace seriously," Pete mused.

Not soon enough was the answer as far as Jean was concerned.

Near the bar itself, the Russians clapped and jeered events out of her understanding.

Jean watched them curiously. They didn't seem much different than any other sailors she'd encountered before. Lots of bravado and lots of alcohol. Still, it was strange to see their officers drinking among them; normally the enlisted and officers went separately for such things. Maybe war had bonded them.

***

Yessov's mind was a little swimmy even though he hadn't touched a drop of alcohol despite the general inebriation of his crew. His taking out *Gettysburg* alone was worth celebrating, doubly so when he discovered his actions may have allowed the breakthrough at Zagreb that won the war. Couple that with his reception of the news that he was to be awarded the Order of the Red Star for his daring transit of the Adriatic and successful attack on *Gettysburg*. The final word was two frigates sunk, a destroyer stricken and left ablaze, and the *Gettysburg* left barely afloat. Five ships total since beginning the mission. That made him an ace of sorts.

Yessov closed his eyes and imagined it. His approach and conduct in the battle would be studied by officer cadets at Polyarny for generations to come. He'd successfully written himself into Soviet naval legend. Even so, that wasn't all that excited him.

"Comrade captain," a very drunk political officer said, sitting across from his captain heavily. "Allow me to congratulate you on your transfer again. The Northern Fleet is quite a prestigious posting! I am sure our comrades in the North could use your expertise and experience."

"Thank you, comrade," Yessov returned, belying the sheer elation he felt. He'd received the news via ULF broadcast. Not only was he to be decorated, but he was being redeployed to the Nuclear branch, captaining a brand new Akula-class attack submarine, K-461, a dream come true. "I am sure you're in good hands now," Yessov said, doubting his own words. His XO had been promoted to take his place, yet he knew that man had little to do with his success here.

"Yes! That is so, he has always been well-liked among the men. Still, we will miss you, comrade captain."

Yessov gave the man a tight smile and wished he could be left alone. Though he sat in Rijeka his mind was already in Polyarny.

***

It was dark out when *Air Force One* landed at Ramstein Air Force Base to be topped off with fuel before continuing on to Sarajevo, and most of the press and staff onboard were tired and antsy. Some took to pacing the halls or trying to place phone calls while they waited to take off again. This was a moment long in the making, days of negotiations, days of speculation. Now the time was almost at hand. The American military forces in the region were now totally evacuated, leaving the Yugoslavians largely to their own devices.

Long plane rides never bothered Simpson; he always found them kind of relaxing and a good way to detach. Despite that natural enjoyment, this particular ride was more stressful than most. At the end of the trip was not some foreign dignitary to be impressed or trade deal to secure, but a mortal ideological enemy to confront. Money wasn't at stake, it was hearts and minds. The perception over winner and loser was on the line and he was damned if he'd come out looking like a fool.

"We're already running a press release," Bill Laursen,

Simpson's press secretary said, "that makes it clear we turned down an option to escalate the war. We don't flat out say it, but we're implying the defeat came from divided Yugoslav opinion."

"We're going with Yugoslav?" Simpson asked.

Bill nodded, his glasses flashing in the light, "Yeah, it'll fit better with the narrative when the Soviets beef up the Yugoslav government again. We call them Serbs or Croats and we just remind people that those states didn't get their independence."

"Right, right," Simpson nodded, trying to commit the terminology to memory. Yugoslav. Yugoslav. The Yugoslavian people. "Still, I want it to be clear we're not abandoning these people. I don't want another Saigon." The image of all those people lined up and waiting for helicopters that would never come haunted him.

"I've talked with foreign minister Gradenko at length about this," the secretary of state, Wanda Shilling said. "We're going to establish some ground rules for the autonomy of the people of these regions. They'll be Yugoslavia in name but functionally it'll be a federation still. I've got his word on that and we can put that in writing."

"Gradenko?" The name was unfamiliar to Simpson, "What's Kavinski got to say about all this?"

"I've only dealt with Gradenko and Karamazov, the—"

"The KGB guy, right? Andropov's protege? Smells like a coup to me."

"It's possible, sir," Wanda said. "Gradenko is on the ground in Sarajevo and he'll be signing the treaty with us."

"Can we play that up?" Simpson asked, looking at Bill. "The angle that the Reds won't even send their leaders to finalize this thing?"

"It might come off too aggressive, make us look like we're rattling the saber," Bill said. "We *might* be able to swing it to look like you're going in—hands on—to try to fix this thing right."

"Work on that," Simpson said, looking up at a polite rap on the door.

"Sorry to interrupt, Mister President. Vice President Bayern is on line one for you, sir."

Simpson nodded to the aid, "Thank you!" He held up a single finger to his cabinet members and scooped up the phone, "Simpson."

"Rick, glad I caught you on the ground. What a mess, we're really throwing in the towel on this?"

Simpson winced a bit, knowing Jerry was probably smarting at not having been brought in on this call. Still, it had been Simpson's name in big letters at the top of the ticket and his call to make. "I don't want to but we don't have a lot of choice on this. Looks like you were right, better to have stayed out of it."

"We don't know that," Jerry said. "Maybe we sat out Yugoslavia and watched Austria go next."

"Maybe," Simpson said, glancing out the small window attached to his airborne office and watching the ground crew of the Air Force base running around in the harsh yellow light of the runway. "There aren't second chances in this stuff, Jerry. I'll leave the speculation to the eggheads."

Jerry chuckled at his boss's flippancy. "Ballsy to fly out there though. Trying to get a PR win?"

"That's the idea. I've heard the fighting is mostly done with. Still, we'll be going in low and round about with fighter escort, the whole nine yards. I'm more worried about this Gradenko fellow. If he's like the rest of them, he'll be an empty suit; maybe I can look halfway competent just standing beside him."

"I don't think that'll be a problem," Jerry said.

"Alright. When do you touch down in Washington?"

"We're about ..." there was a pause as Bayern checked the time, "three hours out."

"You'll be there after I touch down then," Rick said. "Safe flight, tell Dahlia 'hello' for me."

"Will do."

"Bye, Jerry." Simpson hung up the phone and looked back to his staff, wiping his eyes to ward off fatigue. "Alright, let's go back to the actual document signing and go over the phrasing."

As they worked out the particulars of what to say, how to

say it and when to say it, *Air Force One* finished refueling and took off, banking south toward Yugoslavia. After clearing the Austrian Alps it would begin descending and flying a hook pattern, coming at Sarajevo from an unanticipated direction and flying low. It was a simple trick that would ward off any potential air attack—a precaution, but one that was often taken, especially in dangerous times like these.

***

As uncomfortable as it was keeping a night watch, Lazar Jelic welcomed it. The free, cool air served to remind him about his captivity just a few short days ago at the hands of the so-called Croatian army. His black eye had mostly healed, but his ribs were still tender from being punched and kicked while tied up.

Much had changed during his captivity: the foreigners had mostly been driven out, the Soviet Union was now backing a unified Yugoslavia, and his old commanding officer had been killed. Lazar was lucky to find his old unit at all in the chaos enveloping the country.

He took a long drag on his cigarette and blew the smoke up toward the lightening sky. Soon it would be morning and he could return to sleep, replaced at watch by the day crew.

The war had been a boon to him in more ways than one. The Soviet invasion had firstly created enough chaos that he'd been able to slip away from his captors and return to the Serbian People's Army. Besides that it had also resulted in a victory over the Croats, Slovenes, and Bosniaks. The talk of Yugoslavia and Socialist brotherhood was just rhetoric to him, not a real dream but something his parents might have enjoyed. Lazar felt no such brotherhood; he felt only fear and disgust for those aliens around him who might try to force their way of life on him.

Out here in the woods there was peace, though. While his unit had been driven south, into Bosnia, they'd linked up with other Serbian fighters to continue their struggle. They were north of Sarajevo, in the wilderness near a small town called Cares, which was only notable for the nearby iron mines its population worked.

Now the mountain peaks around the mines provided an ideal position for their KUB surface-to-air missile battery.

Lazar paced between the radar unit and the launcher itself, studying the surrounding countryside as it became visible in the gaining daylight. The missile battery had been a gift from the Soviet government in the days leading up to the Yugoslav Civil War, and now served to fight the country's enemies.

"Sir!" The radar operator had thrown open the hatch to his armored vehicle to call out to Lazar. "Radar contact, sir!"

After his commanding officer had been killed, command had fallen to Lazar. As the only one who had a firm technical understanding of how these vehicles operated, he was the only one who could effectively command them.

Lazar threw his cigarette to the ground and approached at a run, ducking to scramble in through the hatch and sit at the second operator console, looking at the amber display showing the signal being pinged back to them.

"It's low and *big*," the other fighter said.

Lazar shook his head at the man's ignorance. "No, it is multiple targets. See?" he pointed out the discrepancies on the display. "A fighter escort probably." Lazar frowned.

"It's headed toward Sarajevo."

Lazar checked his bearing. The target wasn't coming in on the usual bearing for civilian traffic, though the characteristics matched a large civilian airliner. There was only one other possibility.

"A B-52 bomber," Lazar said "Or a C-141 transport. That is a heavy aircraft under escort." But why? With most of NATO's forces gone there should be no reason for a heavy American force. Unless it was a surprise attack. Some sort of clandestine operation, a precision bombing strike or a plan to deploy paratroopers and special forces. It was no secret that many of Serbia's enemies were carrying on their fight. This represented some kind of new escalation perhaps. Whatever the case, it wasn't his job to decide, this was an unidentified craft in his airspace. He only had one job in cases such as these.

He pulled on his tanker's helmet and plugged the microphone jack. "Heads up, unidentified aircraft coming for Sarajevo. Let's wish him 'good morning'."

"Affirmative," the missile operator replied, rotating the rack of three missiles to angle northward. "Solid lock."

"Fire when ready," Lazar said, grinning. At this range the craft stood no chance.

The SAMs screamed out of the launch rack, rocketing into the sky to follow the fat radar signature of the target.

Lazar watched his radar with keen interest as the missile closed rapidly on their target.

***

"SAM south! SAM south!" the lead escort pilot cried on seeing the flame of the missile exhaust as it climbed to meet them. "Countermeasures!"

The two fighters popped a spread of flares, an action mirrored by *Air Force One*, though the large aircraft also dumped payloads of metallic chaff to confuse radar-guided missiles.

The fighters dropped down below *Air Force One* hoping to lure in the missiles that were not at all interested in the flares.

The first SAM reached the chaff cloud and exploded harmlessly. The second turned to pursue the escort pilot's wingman who dove down in a tight corkscrew, hoping to lose the lock.

The third missile was smarter or luckier than its siblings. It ignored the flares that it couldn't see. It overlooked the rapidly dispersing chaff cloud and opted to pursue the larger radar target over the pilot's small fighter.

The escort pilot could only watch in mute horror as the missile exploded just beneath the 747, snapping a wing clean off and sending the whole plane flipping end over end as all semblance of control was lost. His stomach dropped out in a way no aerial maneuver could replicate and he was powerless as the president's plane spiraled down to its inevitable death in the Bosnian countryside, a few miles outside of Sarajevo.

"Ramstein!" the pilot cried, breaking radio silence to reach out to the air force base. "Ramstein! *Air Force One* is *down*! Repeat, *Air Force One* is *down*!"

***

"What do you mean 'gone'?" Gradenko asked the military liaison with him, feeling growing horror.

"Comrade minister, there is no other way I can put it. We have lost contact with the American president's plane," the officer said.

A grandfather clock in the grand hotel's reception hall ticked dutifully while Gradenko stared uncomprehendingly at the soldier. He was waiting for the president's arrival at the conference hall to finalize the peace treaty. *Air Force One* was set to land within the next twenty minutes, why should they lose contact now? "You're saying something has happened?" Gradenko asked, feeling numb.

"There was … a report of missile fire. A Serbian anti-air unit."

"Son of a whore," Gradenko swore unthinkingly. The liaison wasn't saying the president was missing, he was saying he'd been *shot down*. "Son of a *whore*." Gradenko jumped to his feet from the plush chair he'd been waiting in. "Get me a line to the Politburo! At once!" Gradenko was wringing his hands.

The President of the United States had been shot down en route to a peace conference.

"Bastards!" Gradenko cursed the Serbs as the liaison raced off to find a phone. "They won't stand for this," Gradenko said, pacing fretfully, "No." He knew his country had lost their minds when Brezhnev was killed, but that was at the hands of a Russian citizen, a lunatic, *not* the result of war. No, whatever happened next would be much, *much* worse. Gradenko swore again, loud enough for the soldier to flinch.

***

Vice President Jerry Bayern was hardly off the last step of *Air Force Two*'s debarking stairway before he was beset by questions from reporters. He wasn't a media hound like Simpson was, but he didn't shy away from it either. He knew that his good looks and quick wits made him the popular target of interviews and snap questions. The media liked to have a charismatic face delivering sound bites. "Alright everyone," he smiled at the crowd to quiet them, "I'm a little jet-lagged now so you'll have to forgive me if my answers are slow but I'll do my best." He picked someone at random.

"How do you think the news of a peace treaty with the Soviet Union will affect the internal markets in the United States? Some are saying investors will be nervous given the unstable climate."

Jerry gave the reporter his full attention as they spoke—or tried to—there was another press member in the crowd who was openly talking on a bulky cell phone, his tone hushed. The reporter was fully engaged with the phone call instead of the interview which alone was a distraction. "Put simply, it won't," Bayern said. "American investors are smart enough to differentiate a foreign war from problems at home. One of our strongest sectors right now is agriculture, and I've seen that first hand on my trip out to Washington state. Rain or shine, war or not, agricultural exports from us are going to be in high demand. It takes more than this to rattle us." He ended the statement with a smile.

"Do you feel that this treaty comes at an inopportune time? There is some fear that we're abandoning our Croatian allies to their fate."

Jerry remembered the talking points Simpson's office had forwarded to his office shortly after their phone call. "The Yugoslav people—" he stopped to glance at the reporter on his phone who was talking excitedly now, eyes wide, hand cupped over the receiver to try to keep the noise down, "—have always functioned under a federal system in recent years—one not dissimilar from ours. It's worked in the past, and will work in the future. The Croatians will have a say, as will the Serbs, the Bosniaks, the Slovenes, the Montenegrins—all of them. It's one of our primary goals in this peace treaty. We won't leave anyone behind."

The reporter with the cell phone shoved the phone back into his pocket and held up a hand for a question, his expression unreadably frantic.

Almost apprehensively, Jerry pointed him out.

"What about the disappearance of *Air Force One*?"

Jerry blinked, "Repeat the question?"

The reporter did, annunciating each word. "*Air Force One* has been lost on radar on its way to Sarajevo. Do you have a comment on that?"

The hush that fell over the assembled press was unnatural, as was the question. "I ... I'm sorry, I wouldn't know," Jerry said, "It's standard practice to fly under the radar in dangerous areas though. It's not inconceivable that—"

The Secret Service agent next to him suddenly held a hand up to his earpiece, listening to an unheard communication.

"—that it's just interference," Jerry finished.

"What about reports of a plane crash in that area?" the reporter pressed.

Jerry's skin felt cold suddenly.

The agent beside him took his arm and whispered in his ear, "We have to take off."

Jerry gave the agent a puzzled look even as he was being ushered back toward the plane.

Now the questions were coming fast and hard, shouted by the press who were desperate for an answer. "Mr. Vice President! Has *Air Force One* been shot down? Is the president safe? Have the Russians broken the ceasefire?"

Jerry had no answer for them.

The moment he was back on *Air Force Two* the stairs

were withdrawn and the plan throttled up without hesitation, conducting an emergency take off.

Minutes later, on course for the Throughwood bunker complex in West Virginia, Jerry Baryern was sworn in as President of the United States of America. The oath was a blur, but he was confident he said the right things at the right parts, unable to comprehend what was happening.

"It's true," the phone said. A phone was pressed into his hand and he had put it to his ear on instinct. "*Air Force One* went down north of Sarajevo. French Special Forces reached the crash site. No survivors." It was the secretary of defense on the line.

Their faces flashed before his eyes. Bill, Wanda, Rick, their staff, their security detail.

"Oh my God."

"Intelligence is still sketchy, but the Soviets are denying everything, calling them rogue actors. Speculation is this might be a decapitation strike prior to hitting us with everything they've got."

"A first strike?" Jerry asked.

"Maybe, Mister President."

The title was foreign to his ears.

The secretary of defense continued, "We're getting the nuclear codes together just in case, but we need to send a message to them that we're not so easy to catch unawares."

Jerry's bewilderment was steadily being replaced by fury. Fury for those lost and fury for those who'd seen them killed. "What kind of message?"

"A co-ordinated strike on Russian high-value assets. A non-nuclear strike. Something to show them that we're just as capable of well-planned operations with or without a president."

"Attack? Isn't that hasty?"

"Not if the Soviets are testing us, looking for panic, weakness."

"Do we have high confidence that's their plan?"

"We know a large number of Soviet attack plans hinge on a 'bolt from the blue'. Garrison forces in the Eastern Bloc will simultaneously march west, cross the border and drive for the

Atlantic. Sometimes preceded by a decapitation strike."

"You're talking about a full scale war," Jerry said, incredulous.

"Yes, sir. *If* they think they can get away with it. They might be trying to knock out our leadership, eliminate our ability to conduct a coordinated response."

Jerry closed his eyes. He'd been an officer in the Navy. He'd always been ready to make hard decisions, but he never expected to have to make these kinds of calls for the fate of the country. To order strikes on Soviet assets ran counter to every fiber of his body. But to wait was to risk a fate much worse. Deterrence only worked if the threat it posed was credible. If the Soviets hit them, then they had to hit back twice as hard. "Alright. Let's hit them back. I want a proportional response though. We're not going to go crazy with it. Nothing nuclear."

"Yes, sir."

Jerry hung the phone up once it went dead and slumped into his chair, staring fixedly at the wall. Even though it was possible he was about to see the US get hit with a massive attack, all he could think about was what he might say to Rick's wife when he next saw her.

***

AFTERWORD

Thanks so much for reading!
Please be sure to leave a review and let other
people know what you thought about it.

https://www.amazon.com/dp/B09QYXL65Y

Also consider following me on Twitter to be kept aware of
upcoming releases or feel free to drop me a line on email.

TKBlackwoodWrites@Gmail.com
https://twitter.com/TkBlackwood

Keep reading for a preview of Iron Crucible: Red Front

ABOUT THE AUTHOR

T.k. Blackwood

T.K. Blackwood is a full time IT professional and part time writer who lives in North Carolina with his wife, child, and too many reptiles.

RED FRONT

Prologue

September 1992

Major Ken "Voodoo" Morris kept his eyes glued to his instrument panel in the dim glow of his cockpit. His fighter, an F-15 Eagle, was flying just meters above the twilight surf of the Baltic sea. Each twitch of his flight stick threatened to plunge him nose-first into the churning surf. At the speed he traveled, dipping into the waves would be like swan diving into solid cement at a hundred miles an hour. Morris's heart was in his throat, though it wasn't the alarmingly low altitude of his flight that left him so nervous. He was no stranger to risky and intense flight patterns, this particular run was different from any other he had ever undertaken.

Flying this low was stressful at the best of times, but here it was amplified by the knowledge that he was on his way to attack a Soviet naval base. His was one of two air raids which were launched simultaneously nearly 5,000 miles apart from one another, separated via the earth's time zones by seven hours.

In Denmark it was just past sunset when Morris and the other NATO attack craft climbed noisily into the sky while Hokkaido, Japan was expecting the sun to come around the Earth shortly and herald a new day. The aircraft that took off were all manned by American airmen. Like Morris, they were all ostensibly combat pilots, though few of their number had seen anything like combat. The world had been relatively peaceful for them, save for the brief debacle in the Balkans. Despite this, they still approached their targets with nervous confidence. This was the moment they'd trained for for years, conducting countless virtual bombing runs. All their approaches were plotted, mapped, timed, and honed. They'd killed these enemies a thousand times before in mockups and simulations. All that was different now was that the casualties would be real this time.

The attack force that Morris flew with was a mirror of the one flying from Hokkaido targeted at the Soviet military port of Vladivostok. Both attack groups were built around a quartet of slender B-1 bombers alongside an escorting fighter squadron and electronic countermeasure aircraft.

The B-1 "Lancer" had been built originally to replace the aging but venerable B-52. Its original purpose was long-range delivery of nuclear payloads to strategic targets deep within the Soviet Union. Now these vast bomb bays were occupied with thousands of pounds of laser-guided glide bombs ready to be scattered over the Soviet port facilities.

Alongside the B-1s were a pair of EF-111As. The EF-111A or "Raven" was an electronic warfare specialist, built to house the latest and greatest in information warfare sensors, jammers, and spoofers. What had begun its life as a tactical bomber known as the "Aardvark" was affectionately called the "Spark-Vark" by those who operated them. These two Ravens flew just above and ahead of the B-1s. Their high-tech detection and jammer suites were engaged with monitoring and neutralizing the extensive air defense assets of the Soviet ports. The Soviets were masters of defensive air warfare, utilizing overlapping networks of detection and anti-air missile batteries to form a protective umbrella around the entirety of their nation. The Ravens had their work cut out for them, pinpointing dozens of individual sources of radio traffic and detecting and jamming radar transmitters.

The Americans weren't content to rely on their technological wonders alone. Escorting the core of the attack force was a squadron of missile-laden combat fighters like the one Major Morris flew. It would fall to him and his pilots to protect the B-1s and Ravens when things inevitably turned ugly.

Despite the impressive array of military technology deployed here, the raid was particularly vulnerable at present. To avoid detection by the Soviet search radars ringing Kaliningrad the American pilots had to fly as low as possible, almost low enough to surf. When combined with the radar spoofing and jamming of the Ravens, Morris hoped it would be enough to mask their approach until the last minute. With a little luck, the Soviets wouldn't know the Americans were here until they were right on top of them.

Despite the relative cover his low altitude afforded him, worry itched at the back of Morris's mind. For all its cutting-edge flash and glamor, modern air warfare was in many ways little different than even the most primitive forms of combat. From muskets to F-15s to bows and arrows, the same adage held true: he who holds the high ground wins. For air-to-air engagements height advantage was significant. Height granted both extended detection and observation capability but also longer range and greater speed for missile launches. With a thinner atmosphere to contend with, missiles launched from higher altitudes could go farther faster and sometimes struck without warning. After all, what was a missile but a modern day javelin?

There were also fewer tactical options available for low-flying craft. Once detected they could only rely on countermeasures or basic evasive techniques. With nowhere to dive and no way to climb quickly it left pilots hugging the ground sitting ducks if detected.

Morris tried not to think about it. Focussing his attention on his instrument panel, he worried only about keeping formation and altitude. Those problems were out of his hands right now.

"Five minutes to Point Charlie." The voice was just above a whisper in Morris's helmet but came through as clear as a shouted command. His senses were all on edge, it felt as though his skin were electrically charged and every slight change registered like an explosion in his mind. After all the training, all the waiting, it was finally here. This was the thrill of fighting, the fear of combat. Morris flexed his hands one at a time, working tense muscles and cracking his knuckles.

From Morris's vantage point in the cockpit, the Baltic Sea looked like a turbulent oil slick in the dark. Only the white caps of chopping waves broke the inky blackness, set starkly against the warm watercolors of the fading daylight in the sky. In another hour this faint twilight would be gone, a cool evening chased away by the dark of true night fall. If all went according to plan, they would be long gone by then.

With near total radio silence being enforced, Major Morris had no direct way to check in with the other pilots of his escort group, callsign Wyvern. By craning his head around he could just make out each of the fighters of his squadron arrayed around him, twelve in all, spread out in a thin line to screen the follow-on bombing team. Just behind them, almost impossible to make out in ther dark were the four F-16s of the laser designator group and distantly behind, invisible in the night, were the two Ravens and four B-1 bombers carrying the payload that was to be unleashed on the Soviet naval facility at Kaliningrad.

Kaliningrad—once the German city of Konigsburg—was a stark reminder of the cost of the Second World War. The city was signed over as the spoils of war to the victorious Red Army and what civilian population remained afterward was forcibly expelled, replaced by Russian nationals. The entire city was militarized, converted to act as a forward operating base and headquarters to the Red Banner Baltic Fleet. What was once a center of art, history, culture, and a home to thousands was reduced to an industrialized war center. Kaliningrad bristled with anti-air defenses, its coastal waters were relentlessly patrolled by naval craft and its perimeter guarded night and day by Soviet soldiers.

It was hard, Morris reflected, to feel anything like sympathy for the Nazis, but all the same the efficiency with which the

Soviets subjugated their old enemy was chilling. Kaliningrad had been reduced and subsumed and was now simply another cog in the Soviet war machine. Now, tonight, the city would have a new grim chapter written in its dark and bloody history. A fresh battle would be fought here as the American retaliatory raid closed in.

Truthfully, Morris didn't know the full reason for this attack. No clear justification had been given during the hurried briefing back on the ground in Denmark, and none was supplied once they were airborne. All he knew was this attack was in response to a 'first strike' executed against American leadership. It didn't take much to fill in the gaps and determine something bad had happened to President Simpson. Last Morris had heard, Simpson was en route to Sarajevo for the anticipated peace talks. If the Soviets had taken that chance to launch a decapitation strike ... But that was then, the past. All that mattered to Morris was the now and the rapidly diminishing time before action.

With each passing second, the attack team drew closer to the coastline, closer to the target, and deeper into possible detection range. The Ravens could only take them so far before their electronic charade would collapse under the blistering spotlights of a dozen Soviet targeting radars.

Morris glanced at his own early warning system and frowned behind his oxygen mask. With his F-15's targeting radar powered down he wouldn't spot a Soviet interceptor force until it was on top of them. He was wholly reliant on Ravens' ability to detect the enemy before they detected him. It wasn't a comfortable thing to rely on someone else for protection.

"Condor is climbing." Condor team—the F-16s—were the laser designators of the raid.

Morris didn't envy the Falcon drivers, theirs was arguably the most dangerous job of this mission. They needed to hold position high enough to mark the target with built-in laser targeting equipment until the B-1's glide bombs reached the specified targets. It required careful control to maintain a smooth flight, it required guts to fly above the relative safety of low altitude, and it took precision to designate the right targets. The job became infinitely more difficult if the enemy sallied to meet them.

The Enemy. It was almost frightening to Morris how naturally the thought came to him.

The Soviets had become "the Enemy" in an instant. It was like a switch had been flipped, a political idea committed to. It was clear to everyone involved what the careful planning and preparation of the last five decades had been about. The United States Strategic Air Command's motto "Peace is Our Profession" was a comical lie. No one believed that the military preparations both sides undertook were intended for anything other than an all-out war between East and West. Yet, somehow the West had managed to delude itself. No, this wasn't preparation to fight the Soviets specifically. It could be *any* hypothetical adversary, or it could be no one.

Now the taboo was broken, the Cold War made hot. East and West had come to blows in the Balkans. Both sides had discovered the truth in that short and deadly conflict: it was easy to spill blood, and just like the proverbial cat, it couldn't be put back in the bag.

Morris hovered a gloved finger by the toggle which activated the targeting radar nestled in the nose cone of his Eagle. When things got hot Morris would light it up. Either the moment they came within range for the glide bombs- about twenty kilometers- or as soon as the Soviets spotted them, whichever came first.

"Wyvern Leader, Shadow One. We have bandits ten o'clock turning hot. Confirmed weapons free." Shadow One, the man commanding the pair of Ravens, said the words with the same clinical detachment that a surgeon might use to describe an incision.

Morris knew that—just like a surgeon—Shadow One was sweating bullets behind that cool facade. It was time. With no more reason to delay, Morris flipped on his own radar and keyed up his squadron channel. "Fangs out, Wyverns.

Bandits incoming. Climb to angels thirty and prepare to engage. Weapons are free."

Unleashed from their obligation to be as unobtrusive as possible, the dozen radars of his squadron snapped on in unison. Hungry electronic eyes swept the sky and returned a clear picture of the opposition facing them but, conversely, revealed themselves to the enemy. A Soviet air patrol advanced at speed from Kaliningrad and entered the outer range of Morris's missile engagement envelope. The F-15s climbed thirty thousand feet in just under a minute, going from deck-level to a more comfortable fighting altitude in mere seconds.

With his targeting radar active Morris knew that he could now see the enemy just as well as they could see him. Morris's heads up display flashed with warning as the quartet of Soviet fighters fixed their electronic gaze on him.

"Wyvern Two, nails." The voice was Grinder, one of Morris's pilots. The single-word code phrase carried weight to it. It was a warning of an enemy radar lock, no surprise given the short range and head-on approach. Distance between the two approaching forces was falling fast, the enemy fighters were making straight for them. It seemed to Morris that they were eager to intercept the American raid well out of range of the base itself. Games of chicken were no rarity in the Cold War, each side had pressed its luck countless times, probing enemy defenses, measuring reaction, testing technology. The Soviets were merely playing the game they'd always played, they just didn't realize the rules had changed.

The open channel was soon hit with a thickly accented voice advising the American planes to turn back at once or be fired upon, a standard warning in peace time.

A warning that fell on deaf ears. The fate of these hapless Soviet pilots was already decided.

Morris beat them to the punch and secured a firm lock on the lead plane. "Spike," he said. The tone of a solid lock hummed in his ear. "Wyvern One, fox one!" Morris squeezed the trigger.

The AIM-7 Sparrow missile decoupled from his under-wing

pylon and engaged its rocket motor, streaking away from his craft. The missile homed in on the radar signature fed back to it by Morris's onboard radar targeting system. It was joined by just over a half dozen other missiles as his pilots voiced their own fox one launches.

Missiles outnumbered targets by nearly two to one and the Soviets were caught flat-footed, having not expected an American attack. The Soviet pilots broke formation late, scattering and diving for the deck. Diving to lower altitudes or "going defensive" was the easiest and best defense against hostile missile launches. It gave the evading pilot a boost of speed and "dragged" the attacking missile through denser air as it pursued. The end goal was to use this advantage to outrun or outfly the missile, or at least let it exhaust its fuel and detonate.

Ultimately, it was a numbers game and the Soviets were too slow.

Two American missiles found their marks perfectly, swatting down the jet fighter craft while the others missed, thrown off by electronic countermeasures and hard evasive action. Ordinarily anti-air missile bursts were anti-climactic; most of their energy was channeled to the task of hurling lethal shrapnel into their targets rather than dramatic fireballs. Here, in the dark Baltic skies, each explosion was a micro sun for an instant. They popped on the horizon like fireworks, a flashbulb illuminating a pilot's final moments.

With the Soviet pilots undertaking defensive maneuvers, none of them had an opportunity to fire back. A clean, one-sided fight.

"Wyverns, break by pairs and engage the remaining craft," Morris said, eyeing his instrument panel and checking for more hostiles on radar as he maintained course. "Primary concern is keeping bandits off Condor."

The squadron replied with affirmatives and a few more missile launches finished off the fleeing alert fighters. Just as in Yugoslavia, soldiers found slipping off the bonds of pacifism was frighteningly easy. There was no greater thrill, Morris found, than coming out on top in a fight to the death. He didn't have much time to dwell on it, though it did occur to him that the Soviet Union might find it similarly easy and thrilling to hit back.

Fresh targeting radars lit Morris's threat display. Ground-based arrays around Kaliningrad and its port were warming up, pinning the Americans and illuminating them for surface to air missile batteries.

"Sam launches! Sam launches!" Daisy, one of Morris's pilots, called on the radio. "Wyvern Six defending!" The Eagle turned away from the launch and dove for the deck, seeking to out turn and evade the missile.

Morris's thrill turned to stomach-clenching dread at the sight of inbound missile tracks from the city. The worry only lasted a moment before the missiles climbing for Wyvern Six broke their radar lock suddenly and sailed aimlessly into the sky or dove hard into the water.

Morris allowed himself a small, nervous smile behind his oxygen mask. It looked like the Spark-varks they'd brought along were good for more than just show. Their powerful onboard jamming gear had scrambled the missiles and sent them off course.

"All callsigns be advised, Greyhounds are loose and targets are marked."

A few kilometers behind Morris and his F-15s, the B-1 bombers opened their bomb bay doors and dumped their flock of glide bombs into the air. The bombs' wings snapped open like stiletto knives, converting a weapon almost a century old into a killing device fit for the modern era. Infrared sensors in the bombs' nosecones locked onto the laser pathways that Condor team's designators carved in the night, guiding the bombs in.

"Wyvern affirm," Morris said, fighting against pressing G-forces as he banked to the appropriate point before breaking away with his squadron to form a defensive circle around the F-16s holding overhead. The F-16s didn't have the luxury of maneuver and had to fly smooth and level in order to continue lasing the targets in nearby Kaliningrad.

As the sky darkened to a shade of purple, Morris could faintly see the hard cityscape crouched expectantly by the water. If there was any warning to be had for the men in the port facilities, it was vanishingly short. Death came for them on silent wings.

Morris kept an eye on his instrument displays, making sure he and Grinder were keeping formation. His radar lock early warning blared to life. "Wyvern One, nails!" Morris said. He banked the craft right, sweeping its radar over the distant city until he spotted the approaching contacts. "Two bandits at twelve O'clock."

"Copy confirm," Grinder said.

The enemy aircraft were closing head on, climbing from a lower altitude, likely having just taken off from Kaliningrad air base. They'd closed distance at low altitude to evade detection and were now close enough to burn through the EF-111's jamming

Morris's own radar lock buzzed to life, growling in his ear.

The Soviets fired first. His radar registered a pair of missiles accelerating toward them.

"Wyvern One defending! Break! Break!" Morris peeled away Grinder who was executing his own defensive maneuver, turning and diving for the ground.. The dark surface of the Baltic raced up at him. At the last moment, Morris hauled the stick back and he felt the cruel embrace of gravity. G-forces crushed Morris into his flight seat, his breath came in hard, gasping rasps as blood rushed to his legs.

He swooped up, skimming just above the ocean surface. In the dark it was impossible to see missile tracks, but at this range he'd almost certainly dodged the Soviet fire. He began climbing again, pulling his nose vertical to gain altitude.

"Wyvern Two, fox one!" Grinder said. Overhead Morris saw a flash of missile launch visible beneath Grinder's Eagle overhead.

This shot gave Morris the break he needed as the Soviet fighters broke formation.With most radar-guided missiles, the pilot had to keep the target nose-on in order to maintain radar lock for the missile itself could only passively follow the returns from it's parent-craft's radar. It was a modern day joust, with both sides charging on one another. To blink first meant giving up your chance to strike.

"Dodged it," Grinder said, disappointed that his shot hadn't connected.

Morris angled his own craft's nose at the defending Soviets. "Wyvern One, fox one!" Morris squeezed his trigger and unleashed a missile a moment before he'd realized he'd blundered. At this angle there was no chance of getting a kill, the Soviet fighters—older MiG-23s from their radar profile—were already defensive and going too fast.

"They're getting in close," Grinder said.

"They want to get to fox two range," Morris said. The Soviets likely wanted to close distance for their heat seekers to come into play, something the Spark-varks couldn't jam. "Wyvern Two, take the left one, I've got right."

"Affirm," Grinder broke into pursuit of one of the separating Soviet craft. So long as the glide bombs were still in the air, the spotting-craft of Condor team were vulnerable.

Morris and his target were closing range fast, each had a radar lock on the other, and the two electronic tones competed for Morris's attention. The angles were all wrong for a shot, Morris wasn't going to waste a missile on a snap shot.

His opponent wasn't quite as cold blooded.

Morris's radar warning blared again. "Shit. Wyvern One, defending again!" Morris rolled his fighter over and banked away, pulling hard until his radar warning fell silent, the enemy missile overshooting. The Soviet MiG followed a moment later and Morris merged with him, pulling tight on his stick and bringing his craft's nose up to kill speed and bank in a tight circle.

The Soviet pilot was doing the same, coming about in a circle to engage Morris.

All of Morris's situational awareness had been reduced to

exclude everything but his plane and the enemy's, he tuned out Grinder's similar duel with another pilot and the chatter of the rest of his pilots guarding against further SAM launches from the city defenses.

Morris and his opponent came around at the same time, headed nose-to-nose again in another joust. There was no time for either to think. The MiG spewed a trail of flares intended to sucker in a heatseeker.

"Fox two!" Morris fired at the same time as the Soviet pilot and triggered his own counter measures.

Morris tensed as the enemy missile shot just over his eagle, chasing the heat signature of a flare, his own shot went wide, passing by the MiG to pursue its own false read. "Shit!"

Both jets shot past one another, already banking around for another pass. They formed falling double helix as they circled one another, diving steadily toward the sea below as they jockeyed for ideal firing position. Morris kept his neck craned, looking up through his canopy and gauging the enemy's own plan from what he could make out in the dim light. The spiral flattened out at wave-top level and Morris pulled his stick back tight, lining up his shot. G-forces crushed him again but he grit through it. "Wyvern One, fox two!" Morris's last sidewinder screamed off and the Soviet pilot popped flares again. The dark water was lit by a string of them a moment before each fell into the surf and was extinguished. It wasn't enough.

The Sidewinder struck the MiG and exploded.

"Splash one!" Morris pulled up and swooped over the burning wreckage as it plunged into the Baltic. There was no chance the pilot survived that hit.

Angling up, Morris again gained altitude and checked his instruments for any additional threats and felt relief when there were none. Adrenaline from the dogfight was still surging through his body but he willed his hands not to tremble as he found his squadron and re-joined them. Grinder returned a moment later after splashing his own MiG.

A quick radio check confirmed Wyvern Squadron hadn't

suffered any losses, a perfect mission. "Wyvern shows scope is clear," Morris said on the raid channel.

The airborne raid was already pulling back as the bombs sailed the last few dozen meters above the choppy waters of the Baltic to pass over the shore. There they found their targets after following the laser designators of the F-16s and struck with explosive force.

Morris was just close enough to see fireballs rising from the port repair facilities and oil bunkers. Secondary explosions ripped through the evening air and sent another roaring fireball skyward.

"Targets prosecuted. All callsigns come about for point Delta." Point Delta was a little under four hundred kilometers back the way they'd come, south of the Danish island of Bornholm.

As the raiders ignited their afterburners and raced away from the blazing port facilities at Kaliningrad, Morris found himself hoping that Karup Air Base would still be there in Denmark when he returned. No matter how you cut it, blood had been drawn. The showdown of the century—maybe the climax of history—had begun. East versus West. The Third World War was here.

-AVAILABLE NOW-

https://www.amazon.com/dp/B09VZN12K4

Printed in Great Britain
by Amazon

83218315R00161